SUSPICIOUS MINDS

CHRISTY BARRITT

Kregel
Publications

Suspicious Minds: A Novel
© 2008 by Christy Barritt

Published by Kregel Publications, a division of Kregel, Inc., P.O. Box 2607, Grand Rapids, MI 49501.

Library of Congress Cataloging-in-Publication Data
Barritt, Christy.
    Suspicious minds : a novel / By Christy Barritt.
        p. cm.
    1. Crime scenes—Cleaning—Fiction.   2. Elvis Presley impersonators—Fiction.
    I. Title.
    PS3602.A77754S87 2008
    813'.6—dc22

                                                                    2008007974

ISBN 978-0-8254-2540-0

Printed in the United States of America
08 09 10 11 12 / 5 4 3 2 1

To anyone who's ever felt lonely

Acknowledgments

THANK YOU TO:

My husband, Scott, for being understanding whenever I get a crazy research idea. You knew I was weird before you married me. And yes, it is important to know if my heroine could drag someone approximately your size down a hallway.

My mom, Louise, for watching Eli when I needed to write. I'm surprised "Two Mom" weren't his first words.

Janet—without your prayers I'd go insane! Your friendship is a wonderful and sweet blessing.

Lori Morris-Hughes. Your giving spirit is such an inspiration. Thanks for listening and answering my endless questions about dead people. You rock.

Jenness Peak, Nancy Farrier, A. K. Arenz, Ginger Casebeer, Susan Sleeman, Jennifer Moore, Cara Putman, and Lynette Sowell. You all helped to make my book stronger. Thanks doesn't say enough.

And my nephews, Christopher, Nick, and Andrew, who always brighten my day with great suggestions on how to make my book better—including dragons, space travel, and three-headed monsters. Maybe one day . . .

CHAPTER 1

"THERE ARE two kinds of people in this world."

Riley Thomas did his famous eyebrow cock at me from across the smooth wooden table at the coffeehouse. "And that would be?"

I swirled the remainder of my hazelnut latte before meeting his gaze with a cocked eyebrow of my own. "Those who drink their coffee black and those who don't."

Riley leaned closer, a smirk forming in the corner of his mouth. "And what does the fact that I drink my coffee black mean, Gabby St. Claire?"

I stared at my neighbor—the lawyer—dressed in his pressed shirt and silk tie. His once shaggy dark hair was now cut in a respectable neat trim and lightly gelled. Type A, all the way. That was Riley.

"You're straight-laced, practical, and tough," I said.

Riley's head slowly bobbed as if considering my analysis. "I'll accept that. And what about people like you who drink their coffee with lots of sugar and fancy creams?"

"It means I'm way more interesting, of course." I flashed a grin and pushed the remainder of my drink away in sync with my chair scraping across the tile floor. "And now this extremely interesting gal has to go to work."

I grabbed my sequined purse, a present from my boyfriend, police detective Chip Parker. The bag really wasn't me. At all, for that matter. But bless the dear macho man's heart, he was trying . . . for something. I wasn't sure exactly what yet.

"What's the job order today?" Riley leaned into his chair in the laid-back manner that always made my heart melt. Well, not anymore. Not now that I was dating Parker. Of course. And not since my-neighbor-the-lawyer had broken my heart by going off and getting engaged . . . or should I say re-engaged? . . . and right when our relationship was on the threshold of something great. The whole situation was complicated, to say the least. But I was over that. Really. The fact that "Could Have Been So Beautiful" had become my theme song lately was completely irrelevant.

Riley—who'd since re-broken the engagement—waited for my answer, his blue eyes focused on me. My job order. Right. Focus, Gabby. "Mold."

"Mold? That's not exactly a crime scene."

"I know, but what can I say? The crime rate is down. While everyone else in the city rejoices, I still have bills to pay. This man called, wants to sell his old childhood home. Apparently there was a pipe leak, and he needs someone to clean up the crawl space before he sends an inspector out to estimate the home value."

Riley tapped his ceramic mug with his index finger. "Have you ever cleaned up a crawl space?"

I shrugged. "I have the equipment. I need the money. What more can I say?"

His finger paused from its incessant rhythm. "Gabby, I have some filing that needs to be done down at my office. You know if you ever need money . . ."

Riley was probably remembering the scrapes my job as a crime-scene cleaner had gotten me into in the last few months. But I knew the truth— Riley had turned down lucrative offers from several top law firms to start his own pro bono practice. He didn't have the money to pay me. Not now. Maybe not ever. Knowing Riley as I did, I could easily envision him going without his own pay in order to cut a check for me. I couldn't let him do that.

"Nah, this will be a piece of cake." I glanced at my cheap, Wal-Mart watch. "But I've got to run. I told the guy I'd be there in thirty."

"Be careful. You know snakes like to live under houses. It's been a warm autumn so they may not be hibernating yet."

I gripped my purse strap, well aware of the slithery creatures I might encounter. "Yeah. Thanks for the reminder."

I crossed Colley Avenue, the main street that cut through Ghent, an area of Norfolk, Virginia, that I considered to be the equivalent of Greenwich

Village in New York. The artsy neighborhood had lots of personality and a wide variety of residents. I loved everything about the community.

My white unmarked van waited in the parking lot in front of my apartment building, a huge restored Victorian that had been divided into five little homes. To most people, it wouldn't be much, but to me, it was a haven where every day was like a new episode of *Friends*.

My van roared to life, and I pulled out of Ghent, drove through downtown, and headed north toward Ocean View. The neighborhood rested on the Chesapeake Bay and had once been home to the famous Ocean View Amusement Park. People had traveled from miles around to experience the park's roller coasters and rides. A few tragic accidents had closed the place down in the '70s.

I turned away from the bay and down a residential street. Houses with crooked shutters, faded pink and turquoise paint, and sprigs of unsightly weeds cluttered the streets. Then I spotted my destination: a weathered ranch, broken front window, two rusty lawn chairs lying on their sides in the midst of knee-high grass and weeds. A new Toyota 4-Runner in the driveway stood out like a diamond in the rough. I parked behind the SUV.

No sooner had I stepped from my van than the front door opened. On one hinge. A balding man in his forties stepped out. Glasses covered almost half his face, and his T-shirt, stretched tight across his ample belly, read "Geek Inside." Classic techie. I'd have to see where he purchased the top so I could get one myself. I had a T-shirt collection that I was considering submitting to Guinness World Records. A shirt like his would be a nice addition.

"Miss St. Claire?" The man, Bob Bowling, offered his hand as I met him on the cracked sidewalk.

"The one and only." I gripped his soft fingers and suppressed a tiny shudder at the Pillsbury grip. Now I knew why the Doughboy didn't want to go under the house himself. He was obviously an "inside boy." I retrieved my hand as quickly as manners allowed.

"You don't look as creepy as I expected." He stared at me until I cringed.

"I know, when people hear crime-scene cleaner, they automatically think freak." Due to good genes, I had a sweet, heart-shaped face that belied my inner oddball.

He pushed his glasses up and looked back at the shack he'd emerged from. "I appreciate you coming out. If you can't tell, this house needs a lot of work if I'm going to sell it." His nasal voice reminded me of the high-pitched cry of the gulls I'd heard in Ocean View, only wimpier.

No joke. "No problem."

The Doughboy shifted, and goose bumps popped across his arms. "I wanted to hold on to the old girl. It's where I grew up, you know? But my parents wouldn't have liked seeing their place like this."

My estimation of his parents rose.

"It's time to move on." His lips—collagen puffy, though I'd bet they were all his—twisted into a faint smile. "At least that's what my wife says."

"I understand." The house reminded me of the home I'd lived in for a few years as a child. Let's just say my family wasn't rolling in the dough. We'd barely had enough for a homemade pizza, for that matter.

He pulled his gaze from the house. "Well, let me show you how to get underneath." He plopped a big Birkenstock-and-sock-clad foot into knee-high grass. He glanced back. "Sorry. I should have cut this."

"How long has the place been abandoned?" I followed him, thankful I'd worn long khaki pants. What's a safari without them?

"Ten years. My parents died in an auto accident, and I haven't wanted to touch it since then. The neighbors are starting to complain, though."

I pictured their showcase abodes but kept my mouth shut.

"They lived here for thirty-five years, back when this was the place to live. I guess you're too young to remember those days."

"Yeah, but I've heard about them."

He stopped by a boarded-up section of underskirting. "This is it. I pulled the boards off the other day to see what was underneath. That's when I called you."

I stared at the planks, which should have been marked with a Keep Out sign bearing a skull and crossbones. Did I really need the money this bad? "Where'd you hear about me again?"

I wasn't planning vengeance on any friend or former client who had recommended me. Not really.

"I saw your ad for Trauma Care in the phone book."

Done in by my own Yellow Pages ad. Great.

"I'd called a couple of restoration guys, but they wanted to charge thousands. I liked your ad and decided to give you a call. I don't have tons of money to put into this place, especially since I probably won't make much on it."

"I pride myself in being affordable." Note to self: up your prices.

"You said you want to go under there, then give me an estimate?"

Imaginary creepy crawlies danced across my spine. Two minutes from now, I'd be able to substitute the real things. "Yeah, let me take a look first."

"I put these boards back up so no stray animals would crawl in. I'll start taking them off."

I went back to the van and pulled on a disposable Tyvek suit. The white Teletubby outfit covered all my clothes so I wouldn't get grime on my "uniform"—khakis and a polo. I also tugged on a headlight and a respirator, then grabbed an extra flashlight and camera before joining Bob in the back yard. The foot-and-a-half opening under the house beckoned me like a visit to the gynecologist.

"I'll be inside whenever you're done."

I waited until Doughboy rounded the corner before lying on my belly, facing the rectangular opening. Grass shot up all around me, sharp and poking. The damp smell of decay drifted outward, reminding me of the time I'd gone spelunking in college. It smelled like an animal had already crawled under here and died. Too little, too late, Bob.

Riley's warning about snakes echoed like an alarm in my head. Snakes. What would I do if I came face to face with one? Blood I could deal with. Guts, brain matter, bone fragments—no problem. Snakes were a whole different story.

Suck it up, Gabby. Without money, you can't pay your bills. If you can't pay your bills, you get kicked out of your apartment. If you're kicked out of your apartment, you'll have to go live with your dad.

Dad! Finally I found a motivation that worked.

"Here goes nothing." I pulled the respirator over my mouth and nose and began army crawling forward, elbows and knees digging into soft mush. I flipped on my headlight and stuck my head into the tight, warm, damp space. I pushed myself slowly forward, not unlike reverse childbirth. I could see only about a foot in front me at a time. The slow progress was giving me lots of time to let my imagination run amok, and never let it be said I don't have a good one. Boa constrictors, overfed rats, puffy white maggots—the latter reminded me of Bob, which brought me back to task. I crawled on through the puddles of water soaking the ground.

Bob had said the mold was pretty bad. The house was one thousand square feet so the crawl space wasn't that large. I'd zip under here, figure out a quick estimate, and then hightail it out.

With my whole body under the house, shivers captured me. Claustrophobia had never been my psychosis of choice, but I was finding some latent tendency, and wasn't this just the perfect time for that? If I raised my rates, maybe I could afford rent and therapy.

I raised my head for a better look at my surroundings.

I'd crawled through the entrance to the underworld.

Nothing on earth would look like this. Alienlike mold and mildew draped in sheets from the floor beams of the house. Cobwebs plastered every surface not covered with fungi.

I fumbled at my hip for my flashlight and held it in front of me. A snake draped over my hand.

Screaming into a gas mask isn't all that satisfying, but sometimes it's all you've got. I threw the snake, and the flashlight went rolling with it, crashing against the cinderblock foundation of the house. The light arced wildly, and I saw the snake float to the ground. It was just a snakeskin.

Which means there had been snakes down here at one time. Which meant there still could be.

I scrambled toward the sunlight.

Stop, Gabby. You're being ridiculous. Do your job like a big girl. If you want to be a forensic investigator, you'll probably have to go places worse than this.

I took a deep breath. I had to look around the corner of the L-shaped house before I could give Bob an honest estimate. Do it, and do it quickly.

I crawled over to my flashlight like a snail on a caffeine high and tucked it back in my belt, using the headlight as I passed rusty pipes, sagging insulation, and industrial-strength mold. Note to self: never, ever venture into the realm of homeownership if this much decay could be hidden.

When I reached the other side of the house, I turned left and headed toward the second section, also known as "the mold center of the universe."

The fit was tighter here, hardly any room overhead as I scooted forward and checked the last corners. I could give an honest estimate now. Buh-bye.

Maneuvering carefully to keep from bonking my head, I turned to leave. My light shone on something white in the distance. What was that? And should I care?

Of course I cared. Some might call it curiosity. A few would say I'm a snoop who can't mind her own business. It's all semantics, and defining myself wouldn't stop me from checking on the lump. I inched closer. The floor overhead sagged until I only had an inch or two of room to maneuver.

Was the lump a dead dog? Was that the awful smell I'd gotten a whiff of before I put on my respirator?

Flat on my belly on the mucky ground, I tilted my head to shine my light down the length of the mass. Too long to be a dog. Maybe it was plastic that had been wadded in a corner. Probably. That made the most sense. But it wouldn't explain the smell.

Closer. I saw more angles and ruled out a rumpled plastic moisture barrier. A reflection on something shiny and small caught my attention.

I was almost close enough to touch it.

That's when I saw a button. On a shirt. A white shirt with a starched collar standing up around something dark, hairlike. A pompadour. And huge mirrored sunglasses.

I screamed.

I was face-to-face with Elvis. And indeed, the King was dead.

CHAPTER 2

PANIC SWELLED my body as I tried to wiggle backward. The more I struggled, the more tightly I wedged between a beam and the soggy soil.

I thrashed, choking on fear. I could be trapped under here!

My gloved hand caught a swag of mold, and the fungus clung to me like a needy boyfriend. I've always hated fungus. Like mushrooms. And to think people actually eat those things.

Elvis stared. I could have sworn I heard "All Shook Up" playing in the distance, mocking me. His limp body warned that this could be my fate, to die under an abandoned house where only snakes would mourn me.

I had to get out. I would not be conquered by the underworld.

A wooden beam dug into my hip. I seemed to be smothering, and only the memory of the smell of death stopped me from ripping off my respirator mask. Something, most likely a nail, snagged my suit, and I heard the sharp sound of plastic tearing. Cold air rushed at me, chilling any visible skin. I moved an inch toward the outside world. My fingers clawed the dank, sweaty ground.

I forced myself to stop. Calm down. Get a grip. I had to work with my body, not against it.

I am a scientist . . . almost. I can figure this out logically.

I hummed "Hakuna Matata." No worries. I could adopt that philosophy. I stretched my arms out and rested the side of my head against them.

Breathe in and out, Gabby. In and out.

Think happy thoughts.

I thought of The Lion King Broadway musical, which Parker had taken me to see last night at Chrysler Hall. I remembered Timon and Pumbaa singing my song. I nodded to the beat, imagining the two dancing on stage with Simba. Happy thoughts.

Then Timon began to gyrate his hips. He slipped oversized sunglasses over his eyes and tossed a handkerchief into the audience.

Elvis. Dead. Close enough to touch.

My heart rate sped again.

My fingers dug into the earth. Even with my respirator, my breathing labored. I shifted sideways, and my air tank caught on something, pulling the mask askew. Decay filled my nostrils. Rank, awful, the smell of death.

Nausea rose in me, choking me. Fighting it, I pulled my mask back in place and went all GI Jane, using my elbows to pull myself forward. One inch, then two, then a foot. I could see around the corner of the crawl space. The light at the end of the tunnel shone ahead. I could reach it. I had to reach that blessed freedom.

I dragged myself a few more feet. Almost there.

Something slithered into my path.

A snake in front of me, Elvis behind me. I felt like Clint Eastwood in an old Western. The good, the bad, and the slimy.

I didn't care if I was bigger; this little sucker had all the power as far as I was concerned.

I stared into his beady gaze, wondering what the creature was thinking. Would he strike? Was he poisonous? Would the Doughboy look for me if I didn't emerge within the hour?

Talk about a dilemma—die a slow painful death from poisoning or let Doughboy touch me with his lips to suck the venom from my blood.

Was this what Eve felt like when the serpent approached her in the Garden of Eden? So scared that she agreed to do whatever he said? Anything, just don't bite me. Even if it means sentencing the rest of humanity to toil the earth and have great pain during childbirth.

I had two choices: Elvis or the snake. Leather Face wasn't backing down, and I feared he might strike at any moment.

"Are you okay under there?" Bob's face appeared in the crawl-space opening.

I gasped as the snake slithered away, deeper into the abyss surrounding me. But away from my precious, life-carrying veins. I let out my breath.

Yeah, I showed you . . . you, you—future designer shoe. That will teach you to face off with me.

"I thought I heard a scream."

I reached my hands forward so Mr. Happy Home Owner could help me out. As soon as the sunlight hit my face, I pulled off my mask and tried to pace my breathing.

"Ma'am?"

I looked up at the man, at the concern etching his pasty face. I'd never been so happy to see anyone in my life. How would he take the news? As a great marketing pitch to sell his parents' home? Elvis Slept Here.

I rolled onto my back in the grass, loving the light and the breeze and the grass, now that I had something really disgusting to compare it with. I dropped my head onto the ground and closed my eyes, picturing the King's lifeless body.

Once I'd gathered my wits enough to speak, I looked up at the Doughboy to give him a really bad estimate of the damages. "Let's just say that Elvis has not left the building."

i i

I perched myself on an algae-covered picnic table, elbows to my knees, and watched as police officers swarmed the house. I saw a couple of cops start through the hole under the house. I resisted the urge to grab them and save them from entering that pit. The smell of death clung to me. It didn't matter if I pulled my shirt over my nose, I couldn't get away from it.

Now that I was safely out from under the house, I started asking myself questions. How had Elvis turned up dead in a crawl space? How had he died? Why, oh why couldn't he and Priscilla have worked things out?

Though I didn't see any signs of violence, chances were pretty stinkin' good that he hadn't checked into the Heartbreak Hotel by himself.

Obviously, I knew the man wasn't really Elvis. So who was he? And why was he dressed like the King of Rock 'n' Roll? Did that have something to do with his death? Did he step on someone's blue suede shoes?

"If it isn't Gabby St. Claire," a deep voice said.

I looked up to see Detective Adams, still looking like the same balding, stocky man I'd first met during a bomb threat a few months earlier.

"Detective." Just the guy to make a bad situation worse.

"For some reason, I'm not surprised you're here."

Well, that was him. Honestly, I was really surprised I'd crawled up to a dead man. "What can I say? Gabby St. Claire, crime-scene cleaner and first-class snoop extraordinaire."

He offered a tired grin. "I'm going to need you to tell me what happened."

I ran through the details.

"Mold remediation?" he questioned.

I shrugged. "Tight on money. Going back to college now, you know."

"Smart decision. College, that is." He turned away from me, his eyes on the forensic scientists disappearing under the house. "Can I contact you if I have more questions?"

"Of course. Or if you need an extra hand or if you want to give a nontraditional, or as some would say old, college student some experience." Twenty-eight, but those felt like dog years when I walked the halls of the university. I was a part of a group at the school who'd labeled themselves The Grateful Dead.

He chuckled. "You're a go-getter. I'll give you that."

I could still hear his chuckles as he walked away. I could officially go home, but now that my heart rate had dropped back to two digits, being at the scene of a crime fascinated me. One day, I'd be on the other side of this. I'd be one of those forensic scientists. I only had a few more credit hours before I could apply.

Until then, I had the market on the crime-scene cleaning jobs in the area. It was just me. Nobody else wanted the trouble I'd seen. Couldn't blame 'em. I'd experienced some pretty gruesome things in the three years since I'd been doing this. But the pay was decent. At least it would be if I didn't send almost half to my father every month. Long story.

My attention shot to a man walking into the back yard, obviously not a part of the police crew in his ratty jeans and white T-shirt. His eyes zeroed in on me, and he beelined my way. A slow, laid-back beeline.

"Excuse me. I'm looking for Bob Bowling?"

I glanced at Bob as he paced among the cops, looking like his eyes might pop out of their sockets with stress. "He appears to be a little busy right now."

The man, whom I guessed to be close to my age, followed my gaze to the flurry of activity behind him. "Looks like I missed some excitement."

"You could say that." I stared at him, trying to figure out why the man was here. The lean surfer dude obviously wasn't family or official. So why did he choose this moment to wander into the back yard? "Can I help you?"

He rubbed his chin, scruffy with the beginnings of a goatee. "Maybe. Bob asked me to come and check out his crawl space, to give him an estimate on cleaning it up."

Strange, Bob said he'd decided against restoration services. "Oh, did he? What company are you with?"

He shrugged. "My own."

"And what's that?"

"I don't have a name for the business yet." He extended his hand. "But my name's Chad Davis. I'm a crime-scene cleaner."

CHAPTER 3

CRIME-SCENE CLEANER? This man was a crime-scene cleaner? Who did he think he was? I was the only crime-scene cleaner in the area. I needed all the jobs I could find in order to pay my bills. It was called s-u-r-v-i-v-a-l, buddy.

"This area doesn't need any more grim sweepers." I refused to break my gaze with the man. He had to know I meant business.

He chuckled. "Grim sweepers, huh? I like that. But I only found one other company doing it in the area. Nothing's wrong with some competition, right?"

My jaw dropped momentarily. "Do you have any experience?"

He shrugged, like he had no worries, no concerns, no heart. "I used to work in the morgue. Stuff like blood doesn't bother me. Plus, crime-scene cleaning is a great way to make some extra money."

"Extra money?" I could feel my face turning red. "Does this mean you have another job?"

He shrugged again. "Wise investing, you could say. I moved here from Kansas and plan on surfing in the summer and skiing in the winter. I'll take on jobs whenever they come up."

"You . . . you . . ." The words just wouldn't emerge. My future flashed before my eyes.

"Are you okay?"

"You . . . you . . ." Finally, I stood, unable to formulate anything re-motely intelligible. I shook my head at him and stormed to my van. I had to get home.

Home, sweet home. I'd never felt so relieved to see my apartment building. I parked my van, grabbed my sparkly purse, and escaped into my sanctuary. The front door clicked shut behind me.

"Help! I've been stolen!" The little, white-haired woman stormed down the stairs of my Victorian apartment building. I had ten seconds before she rounded the last flight of stairs and spotted me.

I started to turn around and walk back out the door. Just go to the van and drive away. I had enough to handle without any drama from Mrs. Mystery, my upstairs neighbor and eccentric novelist extraordinaire. I leaned against the door, hand still on the knob. It wasn't too late to flee.

I just hoped Mrs. Mystery wasn't testing out her latest book plot on me. I drew in a breath just as I heard Riley's door opening upstairs.

"What's wrong, Mrs. Morgan?"

The frail woman was halfway down the last stairs. I'd missed my chance. She reached the bottom of the stairs. Her boney, age-spotted hands shook, and her white curls flew like they'd been charged with electricity. The wrinkles on her face vibrated as she clutched my hands. "Gabby, I've been stolen. What should I do?"

"Someone broke into your apartment?"

Her head swung back and forth vehemently, the wattles under her neck flapping until I thought I felt a slight breeze. "No, no. Stolen. Don't you see? I've . . . been . . . stolen." Her voice rose with each word.

Riley's feet pounded on the creaky stairs. He joined us and gave me a questioning look behind the mystery writer's back. "What's going on?"

"Mrs. Morgan has been stolen." I tried to keep any skepticism out of my voice. I pulled my fingers from her grasp and placed a hand on her shoulder. "Why don't we go upstairs and talk about this?"

"No time to talk. Someone's spending all my money. They're ruining my reputation! What can I do?"

I grabbed her elbow, saggy skin over bones on her frail body. Gently, but firmly, I urged her back up one flight to my apartment. "Let me make some tea. We'll get this all figured out."

"Oh, it's terrible. Terrible, I tell you. Why would someone do this to me?"

I didn't let go of her until we reached my door. Then I led her inside and sat her on the couch. Riley closed the door and sat across from her while I went into the kitchen to put some water on.

I shuddered as I crossed the vinyl floor to the oven, remembering the dead body and blood of the man who had been killed here. I hadn't killed him, of course, though I'd been the police's number-one suspect. The man had been my number-one suspect in a murder at a crime scene I'd cleaned. I'd found some evidence that pointed to him as the guilty party, and I'd tried—in vain—to convince the police that they were following the wrong leads.

The man's death had put a kink in my investigation, to state it lightly.

The events had unfolded a few months ago, but my first amateur investigation still remained fresh in my mind. The good news was that the case had a happy ending. The bad news was that I'd have to live with the image of a dead man in my kitchen for the rest of my life. When it happened in your home or to someone you knew, everything changed. It didn't matter that you dealt with death every day.

I heard Riley trying to calm down Mrs. Mystery in the other room. I turned the burner on and grabbed some miscellaneous mugs. One advertised a dry-cleaning service. Another was from a mini-marathon I had run last month. The final one, I purchased myself. It read: Princess. That one would be mine. Or if I felt especially devious, I'd let Riley drink from it.

I wasn't much of a housekeeper or a hostess. But I did the best with what I had. I pulled out a TV tray, put some sugar in a cereal bowl, blew the dust out of a gravy pitcher, and poured in some lowfat milk. It wasn't Martha Stewart, but then I'd never done any hard time, either, so things had a way of evening out.

I added some tea bags and spoons, poured the boiling water, and joined my neighbors just in time to hear Mrs. Mystery saying, "Next, they'll want my body. You'll see me, but it won't really be me, Margaret Morgan. It will be somebody else in my skin, living out my life."

She had quite an imagination. I had to give her that. I guess that's what made her a good writer. Not that I'd ever read—or seen, for that matter—any of her mysteries.

"Tea, anyone?" Using my foot, I pushed several issues of *Popular Science* and *Rolling Stone* to the floor in order to set the tray on the coffee table. My mother had to be frowning on me from heaven. I was raised with better manners than this, but what's a girl to do? I only had two hands.

"I would have helped you with that," Riley said, half his lip curled in a grin.

"I make do with what I have. What can I say?"

And this is why I could never be with Riley. A lawyer could never be married to someone like me. I'd be an embarrassment to all of his high-falutin friends. He needed someone cultured and elegant.

"Well, I think I've figured out what's wrong with Mrs. Morgan." Riley perched on the end of the burnt orange recliner. Okay, the awful decorating scheme wasn't all my fault. I had a very limited budget. Hand-me-downs and thrift stores had been good friends when I first moved in.

I fixed myself some Lipton tea—nothing fancy ever saw the inside of my cupboards—with lots of sugar. I noticed no one else seemed thirsty. Was it the gravy pitcher?

"I'm pretty sure you've been a victim of identify theft," Riley said. "We just need to make a few phone calls, and hopefully we'll be able to straighten everything out."

She grabbed his hand. I always knew Mrs. Mystery had Riley on her romantic radar. She seemed like the type who would go for a younger man. "Really, Riley? Is it that easy?" She looked at him like he was the hero to her damsel in distress.

"Identity theft is very common nowadays, Mrs. Morgan. We'll get this straightened out. It may take a few days." Riley explained that she'd received a cell phone bill for an account she had never opened.

"How did they get my information?" The eccentric woman's whole body quivered with tension. Come to think of it, I'd never seen her look relaxed.

Riley explained that sometimes thieves went through trash cans. "It's important to shred any papers containing personal information."

Mrs. Mystery's eyes widened. "I don't own a paper shredder. I've never heard of such a thing."

You'd think Riley had asked her to perform heart surgery with a dull spoon. Perhaps it was an excuse for Riley to take her shopping?

Riley promised to go upstairs and make the calls for her. He'd been lured into her web of seduction. I just knew it. I would sit back and enjoy the show as it played out.

When I opened the door to let them out, I spotted someone about to knock at Riley's apartment. The man turned and grinned when he spotted the lawyer behind me.

"Hey, Riley. I was hoping you wouldn't mind if I stopped by." The man had shaggy hair and a dopey grin, reminding me of, well, Shaggy from *Scooby-Doo*. "I can see I'm catching you at a bad time."

"You're fine." Riley stepped forward. "Randy, these are my neighbors Gabby and Mrs. Morgan. Ladies, this is Randy. He's the pastor at the church I attend."

We called out polite hellos. He certainly didn't look like any pastor I'd ever met. Of course, new churches were trying to appeal to a younger crowd, so I wasn't really surprised. Riley's church was supposed to be pretty cutting-edge, from what I understood. I still owed him a visit.

During a close call with death during my last investigation when I'd discovered the real killer—not the dead one in my kitchen—I'd promised God that I would attend church if I survived. Well, I still had blood in my veins and air in my lungs, but I hadn't been to church yet. Sometimes I felt guilty; then I justified it by thinking: Well, I didn't put a timeline on it. I still plan on going sometime.

"I was hoping I could talk to you later about some outreach events that might appeal to non-Christians in the area." Randy stuffed his hands into the pockets of his jeans.

I frowned at the pastor's word choice and stepped back into my apartment before I said something I'd later regret.

They all looked my way.

"I've got to get showered," I explained. "Spent the afternoon under a house with a dead body. A non-living body, you might say. I'll chat with you later."

Before they responded, I slipped inside and shut the door. Sometimes I liked working with the dead more than I liked listening to the living.

CHAPTER 4

PAGAN. HEATHEN. Agnostic. Unbeliever.

Surprisingly, I could handle those terms. But non-Christian? The word made the skin on my neck crawl. I guess if people were going to label me, a few more titles could be thrown into the mix.

Non-Rotarian. Non-Chinese. Non-space alien. Non-senior adult.

"Can I take your order?"

"Nonfat latte." The barista wrote my order on a paper cup, and I moved to sit down. My morning ritual was going in full swing. The routine wouldn't be the same without a visit to the coffeehouse.

Non-senator. Non-Olympian. Non-vegetarian.

Randy's comment still lingered in my mind. And bothered me. A lot.

I mean, why would you label someone for what they're not? I worked stinkin' hard to become what I am. A student. The owner of my own business. A fan of musicals. Someone who could annoyingly quote the lyrics to more than one thousand songs of all styles and generations. A girl in the running to have the most extensive T-shirt collection in the Mid-Atlantic region. And an avid lover of flip-flops.

For that matter, maybe I'd start labeling Christians for what they weren't.

"Hi, Gabby."

Riley. This was his morning ritual, also. I forced a smile, wondering why I felt hostile toward him. He hadn't labeled me. Not directly, at least. Who knew what he said around his church friends?

"Hi, non-heathen. How are you today?"

His eyebrow shot up as he pulled out the chair across from me. "What?"

"Never mind. Just feeling a little sassy today."

"Today?" He sat down and gave me his full attention. I loved that about him. "What's on your mind?"

I sighed, never one to mince words. "Your pastor really bugged me yesterday."

"I wondered if he did."

"I just thought he was rude."

"He was."

"I mean, he was talking about me—the non-Christian—like I wasn't even there."

"I know."

I paused. "You do?"

"He didn't mean any harm. He just wasn't thinking. But that's definitely not the way that we're going to win the lost—"

I leaned closer. "To what?"

"To reach the unsaved—" He shook his head. "I'm falling all over my words, Gabby. What I'm trying to say is that we want people who don't know Christ to come to know Him. It's easy to get caught up in the jargon."

"I can see that."

"The last thing I intended was to offend you. I know I've done enough of that in the past."

"It's true." I saw Riley's lips twitch at the harsh honesty of my agreement, and I smiled. "You have to admit, I don't have all the virtues of those in 'the Lord's army,' but at least I'm truthful."

"I'll give you that one, Gabby. And I'd never want to change it."

Why did he have to say sweet things like that? Didn't he know how his compliments tortured me?

My cell phone rang, a digital rendition of the song "Love Shack" by the B-52's. I smiled each time I heard the tune. "Excuse me." I grabbed it from my purse and answered. "Trauma Care."

"Gabby, this is Detective Adams. Do you have a minute?"

"For you? Any time." Really, I wasn't a suck-up or anything.

"Listen, I need you to do something for me. It involves the body you found yesterday. Think you might be game?"

"Is Elvis the King of Rock 'n' Roll?"

"I'll take that as a yes. This is what I need you to do . . ."

§ §

An hour later, I'd changed into some respectable black pants and a fitted red shirt. Yes, it's true. I might be the only redhead who actually likes to wear the color of love. I pulled up to the house where Elvis's widow lived. Okay, his name was actually Darnell Evans, but calling him Elvis was much more fun.

The house was average, a brick ranch in a fairly well-kept neighborhood about twenty minutes from Ghent. The yard could have used a little maintenance, but compared to Ocean View, this neighborhood was upscale.

I approached the front door and pressed the doorbell. I heard nothing, so I rapped against the wood. A few minutes later, a woman with circles under her eyes and dried, frizzy black hair answered. She reminded me of an older, ghetto version of Priscilla Presley. Weird.

"Can I help ya?"

"Hi, Mrs. Evans?"

She looked me up and down, a cigarette smoking between her fingers. "Depends on who's asking."

"My name is Gabby St. Claire. I'm the one who found your husband's body."

She frowned, not necessarily in a sad way. "Yeah?"

"I wanted to offer my condolences."

"Thanks." She started to close the door.

I had to think quickly. "Wait!"

She paused. "Yeah?"

"I just wondered what happened. Have you heard anything?"

She sneered and took a long puff of her cigarette. "Who are you again?"

"I'm a crime-scene cleaner. I was supposed to take care of some mold under a house in Ocean View, but instead . . ." I pointed back at her car, which had a magnetized sign on it. "I see you're a house cleaner."

"It pays the bills."

Keep her talking, keep her talking. "I understand how that is. How long have you been working that job? I've been at it three years now."

"Too long. Long enough that the fumes have gone to my head and made me a little loopy."

So I wasn't the only one who'd noticed. "I know of a great cleaning solution you can try out. It's unscented."

She nodded with a raise of her chin and a puff of smoke. "So why are you really here? I'm assuming you didn't come by to offer me cleaning advice."

I contemplated what to say. Detective Adams had wanted me to bond with the woman, said I might have better luck than the police did. So far, I guess they didn't have any leads in the death of the plumber-by-day and Elvis-impersonator-by-night Darnell Evans. The detective had shared that the man was forty-five and had been dead approximately a week. That was it.

Gabby the Truthful Gabber plunged ahead. "I want to help figure out what happened."

She eyed me. Took another puff. Flicked her hair behind her shoulder. "Why?"

I shrugged. "Because I'm weird. Because I like helping people. Because I found the body."

The chin nod again. "You're the chick who helped break that case with the guy running for senator a few months ago, aren't you?"

The detective said that sometimes people were more comfortable talking to people who weren't in uniform. At least I had that going for me. And the one mystery I'd solved. "That's me."

"Call me Jamie. Whatcha wanna know?"

"Did the cops tell you how he died?" I remembered the gunshot wound, but I figured the question might get her talking.

"He was shot, that's what they told me."

"Anything else?" Okay, I was supposed to be finding out information for the cops, not for myself. I might as well kill two birds with one stone, right?

"Yeah, there were some other suspicious signs. His throat was constricted, and he was swollen."

"Dead people swell up." I hated to break the news that the swelling wasn't all that suspicious.

"Yeah, there's more to it than that, honey. The police are doing some tests. The autopsy should be able to tell us more."

"More about what?"

"More information as to whether or not he ate a peanut before he died."

CHAPTER 5

"HE HAD a peanut allergy? Didn't Elvis . . . ?"

She snortled, as my best friend, Sierra, liked to say. "Yeah, Elvis loved peanut butter . . . with bananas, usually. Darnell knew better than to get close to the stuff, though. He had one bad attack as a child and never ate the stuff since then. Real pain in the butt if you ask me. Do you know how much stuff might possibly contain nuts?"

"A lot, from what I understand."

"You're telling me a lot. I had to read all the labels, trying to make sure he didn't get sick. Go figure that's the way he'd die."

I'd expected a grieving widow. This woman wasn't even pretending to be sad. Of course, her husband hadn't been reported missing, and he'd been under that house for at least a week. "How long were you married?"

"Twenty long years. I saw him singing 'Love Me Tender' at an old folks home I worked at, and that's what I vowed I'd always do—love him tender."

"Sounds like you were a big fan."

"I know I look young for my age, but I was alive to see the real Elvis in concert several times. I even have one of his handkerchiefs that he threw out when I had front-row seats. That man could capture anyone's heart."

I shifted. "Elvis or your husband?"

Snortle. "Elvis, sweetie. Elvis."

"I'm sorry if I seem insensitive but—"

"I don't seem sad?" She took another drag and slowly blew out the smoke. "I'm not. That sucker was cheatin' on me. I thought he'd run off to Vegas with that tramp. It's what he said he was gonna do."

"You knew the woman?"

"She's the president of his fan club."

"He had a fan club?"

"'Course he did. He was only one of the most popular Elvis tribute artists in this area. People called on him all the time to come and entertain. Lots of women wanted him." She threw open the door. "Come on in, sweetie. I like you. I'll jabber all you want about that loser."

I stepped inside the filthy house. The place smelled so strongly of cigarette smoke that I wished I had my respirator. You know what they say about secondhand smoke . . .

"Have a seat. Can I getcha a beer? Wine cooler?"

It wasn't that I opposed drinking, but my father was an alcoholic. I'd stayed away from the stuff since I was old enough to drink legally. "No, thank you."

She plopped onto a worn, blue sofa. "So, fire away. I'm all yours. Whatcha wanna know about dear old Darnell? You want to know about his snoring problem? Or how about the way I had to make him cut his nose hairs?"

I sat in a well-used La-Z-Boy across from her, repulsed by the thought. I had to get control of this conversation and fast. "Did your husband have any enemies?"

Snortle. Jamie looked at the ceiling. The yellow ceiling, I couldn't help but notice. Didn't this woman realize her lungs looked worse than that plaster?

"Where should I start? Let's see. There's Lynette, the woman he was sleeping around with. You see, I thought they were moving to Vegas together. Apparently, he wanted to go without her. I just found that out today, though."

"What's Lynette's last name?"

"Lewis. You want her phone number?"

Wow. Was it ever this easy? Detective Adams sure was going to be jealous. "Sure."

She grabbed a piece of junk mail from the end table and jotted something in the corner. "And who else? Well, then there was Hank Robins. He's another Elvis tribute artist in the area."

"There are more than one?" Call me naive but I don't keep track of the imitators.

"Oh yeah, sugar. Those two were always real competitive, but last week Hank and him got into an argument. Not sure what about, but I could hear 'em screaming from across the house."

"Hank came over here, to your house?"

"Yeah, looked real angry. And not a thing like Elvis. I always said he was an impersonator of an impersonator, that being my Darnell. My husband, he was the real deal. He even had the grin down." She poised her pen. "I'll write his name down too, just in case you want to check him out."

"Great."

"Let's see. Oh, there's his boss, Rodger Maloney. I called him Phony Maloney. He's a real pain."

"Why Rodger? Why was he an enemy, besides the being a pain part?"

"Darnell threatened to start his own business. Rodger was afraid he'd take away too many customers."

"When did that happen?"

"Oh, Darnell's been talking about going out on his own for years—but that's all it's been: talk. He mentioned it to his boss a month or two ago, just to get under his skin."

"What kind of guy is Rodger, besides phony?"

"He always reminded me of a wife beater. You know the type. All macho and wearing his white T-shirts like he had something to show off. A beer gut. That's what he had to flaunt. He's like a big, fat, pregnant man."

I pointed to the paper.

"Of course." Mrs. Evans smiled and began writing. "I know his business and home numbers."

I glanced around the house, surprised that no one was here to comfort the woman in her time of loss. Sure, the two had a weird relationship, but usually loved ones gathered after a death. Her living room didn't even have a box of tissues.

"Are you planning the funeral, Jamie?"

"Nah, his fan club is." Long drag. Long exhale. "Apparently, they want to have this huge shindig. They want the King to go out with some style, you know?"

"Of course." I paused, desperate to figure out their relationship. She acted like she hated the man one minute and loved him the next. "Were the two of you separated?"

"No, he still lived here. I mean, up until he left last week for Vegas. He was going to become world famous there, you know. I believed it. I always knew he would make it big time." For the first time, I saw a hint of sadness in the woman's eyes.

"Mrs. Evans, if you were so unhappy with Darnell, why did the two of you stay married?"

"Because, honey, he was Elvis. No woman can resist the King of Rock 'n' Roll."

CHAPTER 6

"GABBY? HELLO? You there?"

I looked up at Parker as shadows flickered across his face in the candle-light. I made myself smile and forget about Lynette, Hank, and Rodger. Not to mention Darnell and Jamie.

And Elvis.

"I'm here." I pointed down at the fancy tile floor and nodded adamantly. "Right here. Nowhere but here in this lovely restaurant you've taken me to."

Where I felt like at any minute I'd spill my water or trip or send some slippery escargot flying across the restaurant like Julia Roberts did in *Pretty Woman*. I'm not a five-star restaurant kind of gal.

But at least my sparkly purse felt right at home.

"You obviously have something on your mind." My boyfriend leaned closer across the dainty table, white linen cloth, and expensive china. "What's going on?"

The two of us had a deal—we couldn't talk about work. I couldn't use Parker's position in the police department to get any additional informa-tion about cases that interested me, and in return Parker wouldn't ask me any details about bloody crime scenes. I'm not really sure why Parker couldn't ask me questions about my job. I think it was because he didn't want to hear about my job. It wasn't like he could compromise my cleaning job like I could compromise his investigation.

Back to his question. "I just had an interesting day. I'm trying to get my mind off of everything that's happened, but it's hard."

Parker leaned back, and the side of his mouth curled in a half smile. "You want to talk about work, don't you?"

32

I shrugged and stared at the amazingly small amount of food on my plate for the price it had cost. I wondered how much blood I would have to scrub off walls to afford the meager portions. It's a good thing I wasn't paying. "Maybe."

The curl turned into a full-fledged grin across his Brad Pitt–like face. "That's just too bad. Remember our deal."

"How could you not want to know about my Elvis encounter?" I teased, batting my eyelashes. "I was thinking about selling the story to the *National Enquirer*. And when I make lots of money off my Elvis sighting, I'm not sharing any of it with you."

"What does Elvis have to do with crime-scene cleaning?"

"Well, since you asked . . ."

He moaned. "You were involved with the dead Elvis, weren't you? I should have known." He tapped his fist against the table and shook his head. "Only you would find a dead body while doing mold remediation."

I smiled, somehow feeling complimented. "What can I say?"

"How about: I'm not going to get involved, darling. I'm going to stay out of it, honey. I don't like to get involved with police work since I'm not on the police force, sweetheart."

I tilted my head in mock innocence. "You really want me to call you all those pet names, cupcake? I had no idea."

The space between his brows narrowed. "You're impossible."

"And that's what you love about me." The smile dropped from my face as my words echoed in my ears. "I mean, not that you love me. Don't misunderstand that I'm implying—"

Parker grabbed my hand. "Gabby, has anyone ever told you that you're adorable when you blush? Your face turns the same color as your hair."

I touched my red curls and frowned. "And that's a good thing?"

"It fits that heart-shaped face of yours."

I flipped my hand in the air as if brushing him off. The man has a way with words. At least he'd stopped calling me Nancy Drew as of late. It had been his favorite name for me when we first met. "Now you're flattering me."

His million-dollar smile flashed across the table. "You're a mess, Gabby. Not many men could handle you, you know."

Yeah, like Riley. Oh, wait. I couldn't think about my neighbor when I was out with my boyfriend. Besides, I was over Riley. My broken heart had healed.

And the Earth's ozone layer had begun to repair itself, even with all the pollution earthlings were creating.

I sounded like my best friend, Sierra. Scary. Very scary.

I leaned closer. "Well, I guess if I'm such a mess, then it's a good thing I've got you."

His smile was all the response I needed. Finally, he sighed and leaned back in his seat. "So, spill it. I know I won't have any of your attention unless you tell me what kind of trouble you've found."

I was tempted to correct him about me finding trouble when trouble had so obviously found me, but I didn't want to miss my opportunity to share about my day. I began telling him, detail by detail, about my experience.

"His wife actually gave you the names of all the people she thinks are suspects?" Parker's lip cocked back in what I could only call disbelief.

I nodded. "I told Detective Adams what she told me, and he couldn't believe it. I guess she was tight-lipped with him."

"And then after that, the good detective told you that you'd done your good deed and to let the police handle it from there, right?" He nodded as if hoping I'd agree.

"I don't think he used those exact words."

"Gabby, do I need to remind you what happened last time you got involved?"

Images flashed, and I shut my mind's eye against them. "No, I don't need reminding. I need help forgetting, actually."

"You don't need any more bad memories. So let the detective do his job, and you do yours."

I picked up my fork and nabbed a tender piece of salmon. I couldn't make a promise I couldn't keep. I took a bite. "Good fish. This is a great restaurant."

Parker's look let me know I hadn't fooled him for one second.

That's why they paid him the big bucks to be a detective.

◦ ◦

I let the door to the apartment building slam behind me. Normally, I'm very careful to let it close quietly so I don't alert my neighbors that I'm home. The residents of the house are like a freak show of social misfits—with the exception of Riley. My best friend, Sierra, was an animal rights activist. She lived on the first floor, right across from Bill McCormick, a conservative, radio talk-show host who never stopped talking about his evil ex-wife. On the second floor, there was Riley and I. And then in the attic apartment lived Mrs. Mystery.

Normally, I crept up the stairs, lest doors fly open and problems pour out. Sierra would start telling me about some horrific animal brutality going on somewhere in the world, and Bill would bemoan the evils of his ex-wife . . . and Democrats. Mrs. Mystery would proclaim she was stolen . . . and Riley, well, just his very appearance could send me reeling.

But I was over him. Really.

Tonight, I wanted my crazy, lovable neighbors to distract me. I mean sure, I talk trash about them, but my neighbors are family. I don't know what I'd do without them, especially on nights like tonight. So I stomped up the stairs. Paused. Nothing. Where were my neighbors? Was there some kind of outcast convention going on that I hadn't heard about? Not a single door opened, no matter how many times I knocked into the wall or jangled my keys.

Weird. Very weird.

Maybe some kind of misfit rapture had occurred and all my friends had disappeared for good. Maybe the building had another bomb threat and everyone had been evacuated except me. Maybe I'd developed really bad BO and no one had the heart to tell me so they avoided me instead. But if they'd been eager for my company even when I smelled like rotten blood, then BO shouldn't be a problem.

I turned the handle to my apartment door and twisted several times for effect.

Nope, still nothing.

I finally sighed and pushed into my apartment. Maybe being alone would be good for me. After all, if I were really desperate for company, I could have invited Parker up. He was my boyfriend, and he'd seemed interested. But I'd feigned a headache instead.

What was wrong with me? Here I had a gorgeous man interested in me, yet every time I was with him, I thought about Riley.

I needed to have my head examined.

I mean, Parker looked like Brad Pitt. He drove a Viper. He was a dashing detective, making the city a safer place at the expense of his own physical safety. What more could I want? Would there ever be a man that I didn't compare to Riley, a man who had broken my heart when his fiancée had shown up unexpectedly? What was so Prince Charming about that?

Hello? Nothing.

Still, Riley had a gentleness about him, yet he was masculine. His eyes perceived things in me that no one else did. I felt safe in his presence.

But I would never be with someone who'd broken my heart. Men had one chance with me. I wouldn't be anyone's fool. No man would play me more than once.

I hit the blinking light on my answering machine, and dear old dad's voice rang through the small speaker. Slurred, like he'd been spending time with Jack Daniels again. Surprise, surprise.

"Hey, Gabby. When are you going to come over and see your old man? What's it been? Two, three months? Give your papa a call sometime."

I hit delete and hurried into the bedroom, where I changed out of the fancy little black dress and into some sweats and a T-shirt that read "Grumpy." It seemed fitting.

I plopped on my couch and reviewed my conversation with Jamie. She had some definite ideas about who had killed her husband. Impulsively, I grabbed my purse and retrieved the list she'd given me. Names and phone numbers. Does it get any easier than this?

I stared at the list and tapped my finger against my chin. Detective Adams had insisted the police department didn't need my help anymore. But Jamie did. She needed to know what had happened to her husband, and she didn't trust the police to find the answers. What had she said? No one in her circle trusts the Five-O's.

But they might trust me.

I sighed, and my gaze wandered to the textbook on the end table. I pushed my head into the fluffy cushions of the couch. I couldn't wait until I could give up the crime-scene cleaning business in favor of becoming an actual forensic specialist. Then there wouldn't be any guilt when I snooped. It would actually be my job to snoop. Parker couldn't lecture me. Riley wouldn't have to give me warnings about safety. Detective Adams would ask me to get involved because it was my job.

Soon enough. I only had one more semester's worth of classes. At the rate I was going, however, that one semester might take me three years.

I couldn't afford to take too many credit hours at once. If I did, then I'd have to turn down too many jobs, which would mean I wouldn't have money to pay my bills, or my father's bills.

Really, more than even helping Jamie out, the case intrigued me. Why would Darnell's body be left under the house? What had happened to the man? Had someone given Elvis a fatal taste of peanut?

CHAPTER 7

"I SMELL dead people." I said it with that same rakish whisper of the boy from *The Sixth Sense.*

Even better, I was alone, so I said it to myself.

Nothing smells worse than a body that's been decomposing for two weeks in a closed space. Take my word for it.

I pulled on my respirator and wondered why I'd decided to do this job. I hated crime scenes that weren't really crime scenes. This was a forty-nine-year-old hermit of a man who'd died of a heart attack. Since he was a hermit, no one had thought to check on him. Finally, his landlord had reported a foul order escaping from the house. The police found the man dead in his recliner. After a while, the body just begins gelling and . . . well, I won't get into too much detail. Let's just say it's really gross.

As I mopped up the glop into hazmat bags, sweating beneath my safety suit, I realized just how much I missed Harold. Harold had been my assistant for a short time until he'd been accused of a crime he didn't commit. After he was cleared, he decided to retire and spend time with his family.

I really wanted to hire another assistant. Jobs like this took a long time, and having someone else there to chat with while you worked really made the time go by so much more quickly.

Looking at the room before me, I wondered if I'd get everything done in a day. This was a big job. It would require fumigation. I'd have to tear out the carpet, haul away the recliner. I'd possibly have to find someone to replace the subfloor. And the landlord wanted the walls painted. Normally, I'd subcontract that job out, but with money being tight, I decided to do it myself.

The chair was soaked with body fluids that had oozed from the skin. Just seeing it almost made me gag, and I see pieces of people's brains all the time, if that tells you how bad it was.

I made a mental note to never take a job like this again. Some things a person just couldn't handle.

Besides, now people could also call Chad Davis.

I frowned as I thought of the other crime-scene cleaner.

I couldn't afford for someone else to take all my business. I needed the money. Riley might be kind and ask me to do some filing, but I knew he really didn't have the money. I could work at the Grounds, but getting paid minimum wage would stink. Still, if it paid the bills . . .

I'd have to start thinking of ways to cut back. Starting with, I'd have to cut out my morning coffee at the Grounds. I used to be really good about setting the timer on my coffeemaker and sipping some java at home. I would hold off on buying any new flip-flops or T-shirts.

I could stop sending Dad money.

I know it sounds weird—that I'm paying my father's bills. Let's just say it's my way of paying off guilt. Ever since Mom died, Dad had gone downhill even further. Sure, it would help if he stopped drinking. But I didn't want my father to be homeless. After all, he was my father, my one family member left in the world. Ever since my brother was kidnapped under my watch when I was ten years old, I'd felt the need to make it up to people, that if I somehow earned their forgiveness, maybe I could forgive myself.

I spent five hours shoveling glop into hazmat bags. My bones ached, my back throbbed, my gag reflex wanted to purge.

For other jobs, I would stay late, trying to get them done quickly, but today I had to call it quits. I'd come back in the morning.

I waited until I was outside on the porch before stripping off my hazmat suit. I couldn't risk smelling like body rot. No way. I stuffed the disposable suit into a hazmat bag. I had to drop these by the hospital before calling it a day. Otherwise, I'd be fined for improper disposal. An hour later, I was ready to head home.

But somehow, autopilot kicked in, and I headed toward Ocean View. I wanted to see Elvis's shoddy, crawl-space grave once more. I don't know what I thought I might see, but his death was on my mind. I couldn't distract myself from the case, no matter how hard I worked.

I drove past rundown hotels and weatherworn beach houses and watched as peeks of the ocean slipped in between the buildings. I felt like mourning every time I came into this area of town. It was kind of like the Beatles breaking up—why do good things have to come to an end?

I was surprised to see a vehicle in the driveway when I pulled up to the crime scene. It wasn't the owner's car. It was a vintage VW van. An orange, boxy, hippie van. I parked behind the vehicle, climbed out of my van, and stuffed my keys into the pocket of my boot-cut jeans.

I rounded the corner of the house just as Chad Davis knelt in front of the crawl space, apparently about to open it up. He obviously didn't hear me coming. Where were my stealthlike movements when it counted? Like when I wanted to sneak up on someone?

I cleared my throat, and his head shot up. He stood, shaking the dirt from his baggy jeans. A sheepish smile pulled at his lips, and he took a couple steps my way. I stopped and waited for him to reach me, plastering my arms across my chest to show disapproval.

"I don't mean to intrude on your family's property."

My head jerked to the side, like it always did when I tried to hide my confusion. "My family's property?"

"I just thought the crawl space may still need to be cleaned up after this whole Elvis fiasco passes. I wanted to let you know I was still available to do the work."

He stood in front of me now, the same beach-bum good looks kissing his tanned face. The goatee was gone now in favor of a small patch of hair in the center of his chin, a soul patch, I think they're called. And this little surfer boy thought I owned the place.

Should I correct him? My conscience said yes.

Unfortunately.

"I'm a crime-scene cleaner, also," I blurted, as bluntly as possible. I wanted him to know that I didn't appreciate him stepping into my territory. Just call me a Doberman. Now all I needed were some pointy teeth and growling lessons.

His face morphed from blank, to processing, to a wide, welcoming grin. "A colleague. Cool."

I scowled. "Unlike you, crime-scene cleaning pays all of my bills. This isn't fun. It isn't a hobby. It doesn't earn me any extra income. It's . . . my . . . livelihood!"

The grin slipped from his face, but reemerged a moment later as a smirk. "I see."

I continued to scowl, just to make sure he got the point. "So, what are you really doing here?"

He crossed his arms, the smirk still present. "I came to secure the job for myself by following up. Of course"—he threw me a pointed look—"if this is your livelihood, I'm surprised you weren't here fighting for it earlier."

"I shouldn't have to fight for it! I've been establishing my reputation in this area for the past three years. That has to count for something!" The decibel of my voice rose steadily.

His chuckle told me I'd given him just the reaction he wanted. I mentally scolded myself for letting him win.

Suddenly, he waved his hand in front of his nose. "Speaking of crime scenes, you must have just come from one. What's that awful stench?"

Why did people always say that to me? Just because the smell of death infiltrated my every pore and even attached itself to my nose hair was no reason to be rude. A woman's got to make a living. So the job did nothing for me in the pheromones department. A girl couldn't have everything.

"This job will be mine," I announced, stomping my foot into the ragged, needlelike grass that crawled up my jeans.

"You'll have to fight me for it."

"The estimate I originally gave the homeowner just went down about two hundred dollars." I forced a little-too-bright smile.

"He likes me more."

My hands went to my hips. "Says who?"

"Says me."

"How do you know?"

He stepped closer. "I have a sense about things."

"That's still a crime scene. Why were you about to go under there?"

"It's no longer a crime scene, thank you very much, and it's none of your business."

"That's my crime scene, so yes it is!"

He stepped back. "Your crime scene?"

I rolled my eyes. "I discovered it, didn't I?"

"I could ask you the same question. What are you doing back here?"

Oh yeah, maybe I shouldn't have brought the subject up. I shrugged. "Nothing."

His jaw cocked to one side, and he nodded, like he had me pegged. "You were totally snooping."

"Why would I do that?"

"Because it's, like, your crime scene."

"You're being ridiculous." Right on the nose, but ridiculous. "And presumptuous."

"You said it."

"The truth is I think I left something under there when I was crawling around." I chomped down, hating myself for lying. Riley would never lie.

Except about having a fiancée. Okay, he didn't really lie. I mean, they had broken off their engagement when his ex-fiancée swept in on my territory and somehow they became engaged again. Good old honorable Riley just had to give their relationship one more chance before calling it quits for good.

Chad swept his hand toward the entrance with enough flourish that I wanted to tell him that he should try out show business. "Well, why don't you look for it?"

I squirmed. No way did I want to go under that creepy house again.

Unless I got the job, and right now the foremost reason for me wanting the job was just so Chad wouldn't get it. I wanted him to keep his grimy hands away from my crime scene . . . and my business, for that matter.

I threw my shoulders back. "I think I will."

Why did I have to say that?

Chad watched me with expectant eyes, so I couldn't turn back now. And it was no longer a crime scene—at least that's what Chad had said, so I wouldn't be disturbing an investigation. Yikes, would Parker be all over me if I did.

I squirmed as I thought of Parker. He would not be happy if he knew I'd come here. I could hear his lecture now.

I cast those thoughts aside and marched over to the entrance of the netherworld. With steady hands, I pulled the boards off, then got on my knees and peered inside the space. It took my eyes a moment to adjust to the darkness. When the black finally became normal, I squinted. I had to at least pretend to search for something.

I didn't have to search for very long.

Right in front of me was a very big something that I'm sure the police hadn't seen.

Another dead body.

CHAPTER 8

I SCREAMED so loudly that even my nemesis decided I needed help. I felt a jerk on my legs, and before I knew what was happening, my elbows collapsed. My face hit the coarse lawn.

I tried to gain some control, only to end up with a mouthful of grass and dirt and who knows what else. Yummy.

"What's wrong?" Chad Davis sounded truly concerned.

I spit out some gritty blades of grass before flopping over onto my back. "There's a dead person under there." My words collided with each other as I pointed to the house.

"You mean, there *was* a dead person under there." He said it slowly, as if I had a mental problem of some sort.

I pulled myself to a sitting position and rubbed my elbows. "Look for yourself."

He eyed me another moment before rubbing his hands across his 17th Street Surf Shop shirt and taking tentative steps toward the house. He bent down and a moment later I heard, "What the . . . ?"

I already had my cell phone out and dialed Detective Adams, whose number I knew by heart. He recognized my voice.

"Gabby, can I call you back? I'm in the middle of something."

"You can call me back, but I thought you might want to know that there's another dead body under the house where you found Elvis."

Silence. Then, "Say again?"

I repeated what I'd told him.

"Are you there now?"

44

"Yes, sir."

He sighed. "Stay where you are. I'll be right there."

I flipped my phone shut and looked at Chad. "They're on their way."

"So . . . we're supposed to wait here?" Chad snapped his fingers and then clapped, as if nervous.

"You should be used to dead bodies. You used to work in a morgue, right?"

"I'm used to dead bodies that come into a funeral home. I'm not used to finding them under houses."

Point taken.

"Well, I'm just going to make myself comfortable." I nodded toward the dirty picnic table beneath a massive oak tree. Chad followed me to the green table. It had once looked like wood, but now various fungi grew all over it. It didn't matter to me anymore. I plopped on top. Chad plopped beside me, and we sat in silence for several minutes.

Another dead body. Chad had seen it too, so I wasn't imagining things. I could only guess that Chad was thinking the same thing.

"Maybe it's haunted," I finally offered.

"I don't believe in ghosts."

"Me, neither. Maybe it's cursed."

"I don't believe in curses."

I sighed. "Yeah, neither do I."

"You've got a grass stain on your cheek."

Great, I smell like rot. I look like the Jolly Green Giant's starter wife. I was perfect fodder for a comic book. A superhero comic book, for that matter. Maybe people could call me Septic Woman. It had a nice ring to it. My secret power? Cleaning stains. I'd have to approach Stan Lee with my idea. I'm sure he'd jump right on it.

Sigh.

I rubbed my cheek.

"I guess I should thank you for pulling me out."

"No problem."

Chad looked at me for the first time since we'd seated ourselves on the table. He must have known about the grass stain from memory. "Oh, and you've got some black stuff between your teeth."

It was a good thing I didn't try to look perfect all the time. I would be severely depressed if that were the case. I was a walking train wreck.

"Here." He handed me a tissue from his pocket.

"Is it clean?"

His lip curled. "Of course."

Silence stretched. Sometimes I hated silence and babbled to fill the space. Not always the smartest thing to do, I know.

"You ready for summer so you can surf again?"

"Yeah, you could say that. Next winter, I plan on going to West Virginia for some skiing. I figured I'd stick around here this year, just to get myself, like, established."

Just to steal my business, in other words.

Silence again.

"My dad used to be a professional surfer," I volunteered. It actually sounded like I was bragging on my dad. I'd never done that before. It left me feeling off balance.

Chad seemed to perk. "Really? What's his name?"

"Tommy St. Claire."

Chad's eyes widened. "Your dad is Tommy St. Claire? He's, like, a legend."

"That's what I've, like, heard." I kept my words crisp, wishing I hadn't brought the subject up. What had I been thinking?

Thankfully, I saw a police car pull to the front of the house. Now it was time for the real fun to begin.

        ● ●

The coroner took the body away as Chad and I watched in the distance.

"So, it looks like the homeowner decided not to use either of us," Chad said.

"What do you mean?"

"That man was wearing coveralls. It had the name of a mold remediation company on it."

My mouth dropped open. "Are you sure?"

"Yeah, I just talked to some guys from that company yesterday, letting them know about my services."

"You were trying to drum up business like that?" Great idea. Why hadn't I thought of it?

"Anyway, their logo is pretty distinctive. I'm pretty sure I saw it on that guy's suit."

"How could he not pick one of us? He said the other people were too expensive."

"Good question." Chad shrugged and pushed himself off the table. "I guess we're not needed anymore, so I'm going to take off." His eyes caught mine. "It was good sparring with you, Gabby. Maybe we'll get to do it again sometime."

"May the best cleaner win."

"I'd say the same, but I know you need the money to pay your bills. I'd hate to see you obliterated."

I scowled at his figure as he walked away. How dare he?

I told Detective Adams goodbye. I was ready to go home. The day had been long, and I wanted to take a shower and crawl into bed. As my van bounced along the road, I replayed the scene in my head.

I remembered walking up just as Chad was bending over the crawl-space door. I remembered the way he'd goaded me—

Chad had been bending over the crawl-space door. What if he hadn't just gotten there, as I'd assumed? What if he was putting the door back on after he had deposited the body under the house?

I shivered. Had I been face-to-face with a killer?

CHAPTER 9

"MAYBE HE'S one of those killers who come back and see how people are reacting to the death. I've read about people like that. What if Chad Davis is one of them?" In my excitement, I smacked the table with my palm. My coffee leaped out of its ceramic mug and pooled on the table. I ignored it for the time being and decided to clean it up before I left the coffeehouse.

Parker narrowed his eyes and leaned back in the chair, like I was annoying him. What was new? It's what our entire relationship had been built on at first. Every case lead I'd come up against, Parker had been there chiding me for getting involved. Rolling his eyes. Calling me Nancy Drew.

Were the two of us really supposed to be together, or did I just want a boyfriend? The painful question had to be addressed. Every woman should ask herself that question, lest she end up in an awful relationship . . . like my mom. I'm sure she and Dad had loved each other at some point, but their marriage probably had more to do with the fact that they conceived me out of wedlock than it had to do with true love.

Parker shook his head, his expression void of a smile. "Gabby, please don't make me an embarrassment to my colleagues."

I jerked my head back. "Excuse me?"

He leaned closer and brought his voice down low, as if doing so might take the emotional smack out of his words. "If you stick your nose into another investigation, it's going to get around. Then I'll be known as the guy who's dating the nosy redhead."

Blood rushed to my ears. Probably to my cheeks too. "Is that right? I thought you might be proud of me. After all, I did help solve that last murder investigation." I started to stand, but he grabbed my wrist.

"Sit back down, and don't get your feathers ruffled." He looked from side to side, and I knew he didn't want me to make a scene. Most of the people in the coffeehouse were regulars, so I didn't care if they knew what a jerk my boyfriend was acting like.

Nonetheless, I hesitantly lowered myself back into the chair and listened for a moment to a singer on a stage in the corner singing Lisa Loeb's "Stay." I tried to let the song speak some wisdom—or not—to me.

Parker grabbed my hand. "That didn't come out completely right."

I kept my gaze focused on the singer in the distance. "Then, as someone once said to another nosy redhead, you have some 'splaining to do."

"Gabby, respect is hard to find."

I thrust my jaw out and took the opportunity to scowl at him. "This isn't getting better, Parker."

He sighed. "I just want you to stay out of trouble."

That was just a cover for how he really felt. What he really meant was that I embarrassed him.

"I need to go." I stood.

"Gabby."

I stepped away. "I don't want to talk right now."

"Gabby, I'm tired. I'm not thinking straight."

"Well, don't call me until you get some sleep and decide just how you really feel."

I stormed out of the coffeehouse and into my apartment building. Sierra's door opened as I passed, and my cute Asian friend with the trendy glasses and pierced eyebrow stuck her head out. "Gabby—"

"Not now. I'm not in the mood." I shouldn't have been short with her. I really did love her like a sister. I'd apologize profusely later and beg for forgiveness.

Right now, I charged upstairs and slammed the door to my apartment.

I would never, ever date someone who was embarrassed to be with me.

Was I really this hopeless? I couldn't get my mind off Riley, a man who had led me on, all the while having a fiancée . . . off and on. I was dating Parker, a man who was ashamed of me. And I felt strangely attracted to a man who just might be a killer.

First thing in the morning, I was going to find myself a shrink. I obviously had problems. Maybe I should just call off dating altogether until I got my head on straight.

But would my head ever be on straight? Being born into my messed-up family, I had serious doubts. Maybe my screwed-up emotions were hereditary.

I fell into the couch and buried my head in a pillow.

Did I want so desperately to be loved that I'd date a man who treated me poorly? I'd always prided myself that I was stronger than that. On second thought, maybe I did need to talk to Sierra. She'd be straight with me.

I stood and stepped toward the door. The phone rang.

I stopped and stared at it. I really wished I had caller ID. What if it was Parker? Was I ready to speak to him yet? No.

I picked up the phone anyway, being sure to keep my voice even and emotionless. "Hello."

"Gabby?"

Parker. Go figure. "What do you want?"

"I just talked to a colleague of mine in Norfolk, and I found out something I thought you might want to know."

I sucked my cheeks in and nibbled on them, trying to control my tongue. "Did you?"

"The homeowner had just hired this man to do the mold remediation."

"I knew that."

"The mold guy was shot."

I released some of the suction on my cheeks. "Really. And then his body was placed under the house?"

"No, Gabby. He was shot under the house."

I let my head fall back into the couch cushion. The man had been murdered? Why?

"Motive?"

"They don't have any yet."

This was Parker's peace offering. Most guys brought roses or chocolate. Parker gives me information on an investigation, which was really much sweeter than your traditional "I'm sorry."

"Gabby, don't you realize what this means? It means that if you get involved with this case, your life could be in danger. What if you'd been the one the homeowner had called to come out and do the work? That body discovered today could have been yours."

I shivered. I wasn't ready to die yet.

But I wasn't ready to let this drop either.

"Do you forgive me for being stupid?"

"I haven't decided yet."

"Will you think about it?"

"Maybe."

"Can I call you tomorrow?"

"I can't promise to answer."

"I really am sorry, Gabby. I know I was a jerk. That's just what stress and lack of sleep does to me sometimes."

"I hear you."

I started to hang up when I heard Parker's voice coming from the receiver.

"Gabby?"

"Yeah?"

"I love you."

I hung up and purposefully knocked my head against the wall, wondering why my life had to be so complicated.

CHAPTER 10

AS SOON as I hung up, the phone rang again.

I couldn't keep the irritation from my voice. "What now? I said tomorrow. You know, the day after this one."

"Gabby?"

"Riley?" I closed my eyes, wanting to end this nightmare. I just wanted to turn off this day like you turned off the radio. If only it were that easy.

"Everything okay?"

"Just a little spat between Parker and me."

"Oh, I'm sorry to hear that."

Unfortunately, he was probably telling the truth. I guess part of me wanted Riley to be jealous, to be secretly hoping that the two of us would break up so he could pursue me. Again, am I desperate? I really needed to examine that because I definitely didn't want to be desperate.

"I was just calling to see if you wanted to go to church with me tomorrow. I know it's been a while since we talked about it, but I figured now was as good a time as any, right?"

"Right." I looked at my ceiling, trying to think of an excuse. Then I remembered the truth. "I have to finish a job tomorrow morning. I wanted to finish today, but I was just too tired."

"You could go to church with me and then I could help you afterward."

"Or you could go to church without me and then help me out afterward anyway." I wanted to punch myself for being such a jerk, but I wasn't in the mood to go to church right now. I didn't want to face something else that was destined to disappoint me. I didn't want to pretend there was actually a God out there when I knew good and well there wasn't.

"I'd be happy to help you afterward, Gabby."

Why did he have to be so sweet? "Really?"

"Of course. Just tell me when and where."

I swallowed my guilt and gave him directions. As soon as I hung up the phone, I rushed out the door, down the steps, and pounded at Sierra's apartment. As soon as she opened her door, I pushed through the orange beads clacking from the frame and faced my friend.

"Am I desperate?"

My Asian friend jerked her lip back in confusion. "Huh?"

"You've got to tell me the truth—am I a desperate female?"

She closed the door and glanced around the room with wide eyes. "I've never thought of you that way."

"Am I boy crazy? Because I'm feeling boy crazy lately."

"Can someone with a boyfriend be boy crazy?"

I buried my face in my hands. "I don't know. I don't know anything."

She sat beside me and, in a strangely comforting action, placed her hand on my back. "Is everything okay?"

The only thing I'd ever seen Sierra comfort was an animal. Was she equating me with one of her defenseless mammals that she fought for tirelessly? Don't get me wrong—I admire her passion. But I still hadn't completely figured my friend out. I just knew that Sierra had always been there for me and she'd be straight with me.

I began pouring out everything that had happened, and she just listened, nodding every so often.

"It's going to be okay, Gabby." Sierra held out a brownie for me. The last brownie I'd taken from her had been made from acorns. I repressed a gag and politely declined.

I looked her dead in the eye, silently begging for truth. "I don't want to be screwed up, Sierra. I've worked my entire life not to be screwed up like the rest of my family. But maybe it's inevitable."

"You're not screwed up, Gabby. I mean, not any more than anyone else."

I wasn't sure if that comforted me or not.

My shoulders slumped. "I don't know what to do about Parker."

"I've never really liked the two of you together anyway."

I swiveled my head toward her. "Why didn't you say anything?"

"People usually have to find their own way. Besides, would it have mattered?"

My shoulders slumped more. "Probably not."

"You'll figure things out, Gabby."

"Why do you sound so sure?"

"Because you always do. That's what I like about you—you rise above circumstances. You're a fighter, and you always come out on top."

"Right now I'm feeling like a failure."

"I have some lactose-free chocolate ice cream. I even have some nuts to put on top. Would that make you feel better?"

I didn't even bother to ask what kind of nuts. Bring on the acorns. "Sure."

◦ ◦

I arrived back at Mr. Hermit's house just as the sun was rising the next morning. I pulled my unmarked white van to the back of the house, so neighbors wouldn't see me. No one likes to be reminded of tragedies that they're somehow connected with. A man dying alone in your neighborhood and no one discovering his body for two weeks was the ultimate tragedy. No one wanted to think about their life ending like that. No one wants to think that they weren't a friend to someone who had no one.

I knew that I didn't want to think about my life ending like that.

As I hauled in equipment, I pictured my life, flashed-forwarded thirty years. I'd be almost sixty. As the Beatles once said, would anyone still need or feed me when I was that age? And would dear old Dad still be around? If so, what would our relationship be like? He probably wouldn't be able to afford a nursing home, so he'd come to live with me. Otherwise, he'd be a ward of the state. Like I'd let that happen. This cycle that had started when Mom died would continue. Then after Dad died, it would just be me.

Alone.

I hated being alone.

Sure, I had friends. I had great friends, friends who would risk their lives for me. But sometimes I just wanted something deeper, more permanent.

Maybe that made me desperate.

Or maybe that was just human nature. Maybe throughout the evolution of our species, we'd come to depend on others. We were like dogs—we liked to run in packs.

Of course, Riley would say we were designed with the desire to be around others. He would remind me of the story of Adam and Eve. How Adam was lonely so God created Eve as a soul mate . . . or something like that. I hadn't heard that Bible story since I went to vacation Bible school as a youngster. I preferred to keep it that way.

Guilt still stabbed at me that I hadn't gone to church with Riley this morning. I had promised, and I liked to keep my word. I pushed aside the guilt to focus on my job.

Darkness filled the living room. Mr. Hermit had kept heavy brown drapes across the windows. I decided they should come down. I pulled a hefty wooden chair over to the picture window and tugged at the curtain rod. I sneezed as dust poofed from the thick fabric. Lifting the rod like a barbell, I climbed from the chair and dropped the curtains in a heap. Dim sunlight flooded the room.

The place already felt friendlier with a little sunshine brightening it.

I glanced at the huge entertainment center stacked against one wall. A monstrous TV centerpieced the unit. Shelves around the boob tube were filled with videos and DVDs. No pictures of family members hugging each other or smiling with mountains in the background. Just videos. Things to fill your day and help you forget how isolated you are, I supposed.

I needed to move the furniture out of the room in order to get the carpet up. I got the trolley from my van and began moving outdated end tables and scraped up wooden chairs and a dead house plant into the dining room. Then I piled videos—some so naughty that I didn't even want to touch them—into my arms and formed a miniature city of them on the kitchen table.

After some manipulating, I managed to get the soggy recliner where Mr. Hermit had died onto my trolley. I pushed it outside. Later, I'd put it into my van. It couldn't simply go out to the trash. I had to take it to an ECP incinerator.

The room was mostly clear now, except for the huge entertainment center. I'd move it once Riley got here. What would I have done if he hadn't said he'd help? I couldn't do this job by myself.

I sighed. I was going to have to hire another assistant. The thing was, I needed all the money for myself.

The AirScrubs I'd left in the house overnight had helped with the smell some. I'd leave them here for a couple more days to clean the interior atmosphere of the house. Today, I had to tear up the carpet. It couldn't be salvaged. The landlord would have to pay someone else to replace it if the subfloor looked decent.

I pulled thick gloves on over my disposable ones. Starting in the corner, I tugged at the carpet. The matted, pea-green floor covering peeled up like rind from a moldy orange. Cat dander, crumbs, and dirt blanketed the air and I was glad for my respirator. I worked the carpet like someone rolling cigarettes—slowly and carefully, trying to keep all the grit inside the carpet wrapper.

Once the carpet in the living room was left to the side, I examined the subfloor. A few stains blotched the wood, but the floor still felt sturdy. With a new rug, it would be fine.

I grabbed a hammer from my tool chest. I would pull up the tacks and throw them away. The landlord only wanted the carpet in the room Mr. Hermit had died in replaced. The rest of the matted gold, orange, and brown carpet throughout the house was to stay, cat dander and all.

I pulled up the tack strips and glanced at a wood-encircled clock on the wall. Riley should be here any minute. I'd get him to help me haul the carpet to my van. I pulled up my respirator mask and let the hood on my Tyvek suit fall around my shoulders.

How did someone's life end up this way? Dying alone, with no one to care about the possessions dear to you.

And why did Parker have to say that he loved me? Didn't he know that's what I wanted to hear? That it made me weak?

I sighed. I couldn't think about it anymore. I'd tossed and turned thinking about it all night.

All that was left was to paint. A fresh coat would do wonders for the smell.

As I walked out the back door to my van to grab the white paint, I saw Riley's beat-up Toyota Corolla pull into the drive. I crossed my arms and leaned against the van as he approached wearing jeans and a plain gray T-shirt.

"Hey, Space Girl."

I looked down at my white suit and grinned. "I've been called worse. Although, I do prefer Teletubby."

He tugged at my hood. "Cute."

"I'm thinking about submitting a design based on this very outfit to Project Runway. What do you think? Could I be America's next big trend-setter? Will I take the fashion world by storm?" I began singing Madonna's "Vogue" as I struck various poses. I was sure I'd look back on the moment one day in embarrassment. Did I have no pride?

"You could set some trends alright." He chuckled.

At least he didn't seem embarrassed, like some other unnamed man.

"I'm at your service. What do you need?"

I pulled out another suit from my van. "Put this on first. Otherwise, your clothes will be ruined."

As he climbed into the suit, I pulled the paint cans out. I motioned for Riley to grab a couple and follow me inside.

"Wow, this place reeks." He scrunched his nose up.

I fought a grin. "Yep."

"How can you stand it?"

"It's just part of my job."

We deposited the cans in the hallway. Then I instructed Riley that we needed to move the entertainment center. As we began inching it into the hallway, my fingers burning under the cabinet's weight, I found myself asking, "How was church?"

"It was great. I wish you could have come."

"And what did you learn about today?"

"Why humans need God."

We worked in silence for several minutes. I wondered if I would have gotten anything out of the sermon. I was interested in finding out why I needed God. To get to heaven? That seemed like a pretty selfish reason. Was I supposed to need God because of what he could do for me? Or was it supposed to be about what I could do for him? I didn't want to ask, not yet at least.

"So, did you and Parker make up?"

Did I really want to talk about my love life with someone who had broken my heart? No, but I found myself doing it anyway.

"Not really. I'm supposed to be thinking about it."

"Are you?"

"I guess."

"And?"

"And nothing. I mean, how do you know if a person's the right one for you? And if you don't think a person's the right one, should you be with them? How long does it take to figure it out?"

"I've heard that when you know, you know."

"Maybe I'm supposed to know, but I don't because my emotions are getting in the way. Or maybe I'm looking for someone perfect, and I'll never find that person because he doesn't exist. Or maybe my expectations are too high, and no one will ever be able to meet them because I'm being unrealistic."

"How many cups of coffee have you had today, Gabby?"

"A lot. A whole pot. Why? Am I talking too much?" He couldn't possibly understand how hard it was for an extrovert like myself to work alone.

He smiled. "No, you're not talking too much. Just fast."

Was that his only response? I'd poured out my heart, dug in, and asked the hard questions, and all he had to say was that I talked fast? Why did I even bother?

"I'm not a good one to ask about dating, Gabby," Riley finally said.

"You're not?"

"I don't have anything figured out. I'm just as confused as you are."

I remembered the whole Veronica fiasco and mentally agreed with him. Of course he didn't have the answers. He was just as screwed up as I was. For some reason, that made me feel better.

As we started to paint, I even found myself whistling. I loved knowing I wasn't the only imperfect one around here.

CHAPTER 11

EVEN AFTER Riley helped me, I still wasn't finished with Mr. Hermit's house. I'd called the landlord, and he'd offered to pay me to pack up Mr. Hermit's belongings and take them to Goodwill. Apparently, the man had no family or friends, period. Who would attend his funeral? Would he even have a funeral? Didn't everyone deserve a funeral?

The good news was that I'd have a job for the rest of the week and a decent paycheck. I could really use a decent paycheck.

After Riley and I dropped off the contaminated items, I offered to fix him dinner. He agreed. I just had to shower and get cleaned up before he came over. It was the least I could do to thank him—the shower and the meal. Before I hopped under the spray of water, I called a nearby Chinese restaurant for delivery. When I said "fix dinner," he couldn't possibly have imagined I meant I'd cook.

After I showered, applied apple-scented lotion, and put gel in my hair, I threw on jeans and a long-sleeved "Meat is Murder" T-shirt that Sierra had given me for my birthday last year. Ironic when I'd just ordered beef and broccoli. Needless to say, I wouldn't be inviting Sierra up.

The delivery man came with my food. I'd just taken everything out of the bags and pulled down two plates when someone knocked at the door. A freshly showered Riley stood on the other side. His still-wet hair clung to his forehead. I could smell Ivory soap. He smelled so good I could just reach up and—

"Am I too early?" he asked.

I brought my thoughts under control and stepped back. "No, come in. I've been slaving away, trying to get some food ready for you."

"So you called Chang's?"

"How'd you know?"

"I can smell Chinese food. It smells like Chang's."

"You know I'm not much of a cook."

No sooner had we filled our plates and sat down at my dinette, when someone else knocked at the door. Now who?

I opened the door and saw Parker standing there, a dozen roses in his hands.

"Parker."

He kissed my cheek and pushed inside. "Hey, darlin'. I know I said I was going to call, but—" He stopped and stared at Riley. "What's he doing here?"

"Riley helped me out on a job today, so I offered him some dinner."

Riley stood, looking back and forth from Parker to me. Can you say "awkward"? "Why don't I just take my food back to my apartment?"

"No, stay here and eat. I insist." I placed a hand on Riley's shoulder and pushed him back down.

Parker scowled.

"Why don't you join us? Make yourself a plate while I put these roses in some water. They're beautiful." I hurried into the kitchen before Parker could object.

Call me Miss Intuition, but I had the distinct impression that those two men didn't care for each other. But that wasn't my problem. Riley didn't want me, and Parker did. End of story. What was so complicated about that?

The phone rang. I grabbed it and ducked into the kitchen.

"Is this that crime-scene cleaner?" The woman's nasal voice made me cringe. Could I even bear to listen to it for the continuation of this conversation? She was probably calling about a job, which I needed, so I'd have to grin and bear it.

I drew in a breath. "Speaking."

"It's Jamie, Darnell's wife."

Jamie, Jamie, Jamie. Why was her name familiar?

"You know, Elvis . . . the man you found dead under that house?"

I straightened. "Oh, Jamie. How are you?"

"Did you talk to any of those suspects I gave you yet?"

She was expecting me to? "Uh . . ."

"Listen, honey, I need your help. I need you to find my Darnell's killer."

Though excitement washed through me, I kept it under control. "Aren't the police working on it, Jamie?"

"Police-smeesh. I don't trust them one bit. I need you to figure this out for me. Darnell deserves some respect. I want whoever did this to be behind bars. They can fry 'em for all I care. I just want justice."

"You really want my help?"

"Yeah, I've even got some cash saved up. I'll hire you. You can be like a PI or something, you know?

"I'd be happy to look into it." I felt myself smile, satisfied. Finally, an excuse to get involved. I quickly erased my grin when I saw both Riley and Parker staring at me from the other room. I scooted around the corner, out of sight.

As soon as we hung up, the phone rang again. I was never going to get to eat my moo goo gai pan.

"Hey," a male said on the other line.

"Um . . . hello."

The male laughed. "You don't know who this is, do you?"

What's up with people thinking I'm going to recognize their voices? "Nothing gets past you . . . whoever you are."

"It's Chad. Chad Davis."

I leaned against the kitchen counter. "Oh, you. How'd you get my number?"

"The Yellow Pages. What do you know—you are the only crime-scene cleaner listed. Until I get my ad in there, at least."

I scowled at the coffee ring on my countertop, pretending it was Chad Davis's face. "Did you call just to antagonize me?"

"Of course not. I just heard on the news that that guy we found was shot."

"Yeah, I heard."

He lowered his voice. "That could have been one of us."

"I know." I shuddered and briefly wondered about the silence I heard in the other room. I could only imagine the awkward glances Riley and

Parker were giving each other. The two had nothing in common but me, and I'm pretty sure I wasn't a good topic of conversation. I should be a saint and try to make them feel more comfortable. I would—after I found out what Chad Davis wanted.

"Why would someone want a clean-up guy dead?" Chad asked, as if I had the answers. Sure, I liked to refer to myself as the all-knowing one, but who actually believed it?

Besides, Chad Davis had been at that crime scene first. Maybe I should be asking him that question. "How do I know you weren't the one who shot him?"

"The police already tested my hands for trace evidence. They didn't find anything. Ask your detective friend."

I stared at my vinyl floor, making a mental note that I needed to mop it soon. I could still see splatters of tomato sauce from when I'd attempted to make spaghetti last week and dropped the whole pot. Can you blame me for ordering Chinese? "You could have been wearing gloves."

"Did you see any when you ran into me?" His voice didn't change pitch, as it might if my insinuation bothered him. He still sounded laid-back and surferish.

"You could have hidden them, stuffed them into your pockets even."

All the teasing left his voice. "I didn't do it, Gabby."

"That's what they all say."

"'They all' being who?"

"Killers."

"You think I killed the man? You really think that?"

Actually, no, I didn't. But I didn't want to freely admit that. Better to keep Chad guessing. Maybe he'd move his business to West Virginia. "I heard the man had been dead for less than an hour. If you didn't kill him, you must have brushed elbows with whoever did. If you're the one behind this homicide, I'll find out."

"What do you mean 'you'll find out'?"

"I mean I've been hired to investigate the death of Darnell Evans, the Elvis impersonator. Whoever killed him most likely killed the mold reme-diation man too."

"Hired you? You're not a private investigator, are you?"

"It doesn't matter. I've been hired."

"You want company?" he asked. "I can't get that man out of my head. It could have been me."

What if Chad Davis was the killer? It was true—I didn't see any gloves or a gun when I walked up on him at the house. Still, he could have hidden them. But what motive would he have? Of course, if he helped me with the investigation, he wouldn't have as much time to steal my crime-scene cleaning jobs. And I could keep an eye on him.

It almost seemed too good to be true.

Providing he wasn't the killer, of course.

"If any evidence points to you, I refuse to ignore it," I finally said.

"So that's a yes?"

I wouldn't mind some help. I wouldn't get it from Parker, and I didn't dare ask Riley. And let's face it, Chad was cute. This could be a win-win situation. "I guess."

"Even if the company is competition?"

I leaned against the kitchen counter and considered his words. "Don't expect any special favors in the job market."

"Let's meet tomorrow at the Ocean View Café. Three o'clock sound good?"

"I'll be there."

I hung up, feeling smug about the open invitation to snoop, and saw Parker and Riley staring at me with blatant exasperation. They both knew me too well.

I tried to hide my smirk, but I realized the only way I'd be more obvious was if I had pointy ears, whiskers, and some canary feathers sticking out from my mouth.

CHAPTER 12

PARKER STEPPED into the kitchen and crossed his arms over his broad chest. "What kind of trouble are you getting yourself into now, Gabby?"

I offered my innocent smile. It was a good one. I'd been perfecting it since third grade when I, being of curious mind, blew up a box of matches with a battery and a wire coat hanger. Looking back, I never should have included the lighter fluid, but the pursuit of science carries some risks, right? Ask Einstein. You think his hair got like that naturally?

I laid my hand, delicately dramatic, over my heart. "Trouble? Who said anything about trouble?"

He didn't back down. Maybe Parker and I were good together. He was one of the few men who could handle me. He flicked his hand at the phone. "What was that conversation about?"

"I was simply chatting with a colleague."

Riley stood behind Parker. They both stared at me until I sighed and dropped my fake smile. "If you both must know, there's a new crime-scene cleaner in the area. We're just exchanging trade secrets. What can I say?"

Riley did the eyebrow cock. "'Fess up, Gabby. What's going on? There's more to the story than that."

I brushed past them and sat down—hard—at the table. I refused to take the opportunity to rub my bum. "Nothing. Now, let's eat."

For the first time, Parker and Riley looked at each other as if they saw eye-to-eye on something.

The next morning, I finished up in the living room of Mr. Hermit's house. I ordered new carpet, by permission of the landlord. I purchased boxes from a moving company so I could begin packing. By the time I finished, I had to meet Chad.

I pulled my red sweater closer as I hurried out to my van, but it didn't stop the November wind from stinging my skin. Soon, I'd have to dig out my winter coat.

And start thinking about Christmas shopping.

Could it be that time of year already? Thanksgiving was only two and a half weeks away. Would Dad want to get together this year? It was hard to refuse him on a holiday. Last year, he'd invited me over to his place. He'd bought two TV dinners with turkey, mashed potatoes and gravy, and corn. That was our Thanksgiving dinner.

My family is so classy.

I pulled up at the Ocean View Café ten minutes later. The restaurant was snug between a Laundromat and a pizza joint. Inside, the lights were low, the wood dark, and the people quiet. I could tell by the way everyone murmured to each other at the bar that the place had regulars. I wasn't one of them. Just ask everyone who turned to stare at me when I walked inside.

I spotted Chad sitting at a table in the corner. He waved me over, and my chunky black shoes clunked against the shiny wood floor. I pulled out a seat across from him.

"Thanks for meeting me," he started.

His hair looked wind blown, although he probably styled it that way. The bed head look—was that still in style? I wasn't sure. He had slow, lazy movements that fit his drawn-out surfer drawl.

I had to ask the question I'd been thinking about all morning—even though I already knew the answer due to a conversation with Detective Adams earlier in the day. "Level with me—do the police think you did it?"

His lips twisted into a messed-up frown. "No, the police don't think I did it."

"So, why are you still interested in this case?"

"Why are you?"

I jabbed my thumb into my chest. "Me? Because I'm nosy."

"If it's good enough for you, why not for me too?"

"Because I'm the weird one. Normal people don't do what I do."

He leaned back in his chair, put his hands behind his head, and grinned. "I heard about you."

My eyes narrowed. "Heard about me? Heard what about me?" The word couldn't be out about the matches and lighter fluid. Was it about the time I made my high school chemistry lab explode? Or maybe the fact that I always fell for the wrong guy? Or maybe even the embarrassing detail that my mom used to dress me just like Little Orphan Annie?

"I heard that you solved some big case a few months back. That's why you're on friendly terms with the detective. You're, like, legendary."

Relief.

"Legendary?" I laughed. "Me? Hardly."

Flattery. It was going to get him everywhere.

I fidgeted in my hard wooden chair before locking gazes with a possible killer who could single-handedly run me out of business. "Look, I'm going to go question someone, a suspect. Do you want to come?" I must be losing my mind.

"I thought you'd never ask."

I stood up before my logic got the best of me. "You're impossible."

He grinned. "So I've heard."

"We're taking your car."

"Absolutely."

I flipped my keys in a circle around my index finger. "And I'm not reimbursing you for gas." I needed to save money every chance I could get.

"I would never expect it."

"And I left notes with your name on it scattered in several places so that if I turn up dead, the police will know where to look."

"I love a resourceful woman."

I stopped and turned around, causing him to slam into me. "And whatever you do, don't ask about my father."

He held up his hands in surrender. "Whatever you say."

I pulled a piece of paper out of my purse. The first person of interest was Lynette Lewis, the woman having an affair with Elvis.

• •

I took a quick inventory of Lynette Lewis as she pulled open the bright pink door to her house. Bleached blond hair that needed a root touch-up, like, yesterday. Yellow but straight teeth. Fake tan. Tight clothes on a skinny body. Premature wrinkles. I was sure she'd been pretty at one time in life. Now she just looked like she tried too hard.

I expected her tone to be obnoxious to match her looks, but she sounded surprisingly subdued. "Yes?" She blinked and looked from Chad to me.

I extended my hand, deciding to go the professional route. "Lynette, I'm Gabby St. Claire, and this is my . . . colleague, Chad Davis. We're investigating the death of Darnell Evans and understand that you were the president of his fan club."

Water pooled in her bloodshot eyes. She quickly wiped the moisture away with the back of her small freckled hand. "That's right."

"Can we come in and ask a few questions?"

She opened the door. "Of course."

Inside, the house was decorated respectably in gentle hues of white and beige. This woman seemed like one big contradiction. Her neighborhood with its moderate-sized, two-story, brick houses that all mirrored each other looked respectable enough. But then she had to have a pink door and an artificial plant in the pot on the porch. And who could miss the clash between her cultured voice and her redneck appearance?

Lynette instructed me to have a seat on a cream-colored leather couch. I perched on the edge, careful not to relax too much or the cushions would swallow me whole. Chad stood beside me, and Lynette wrung her hands together as she walked to a chair across from us. Her big brown eyes blinked rapidly, their watery surface mirroring the shine of the glass coffee table separating us.

"What do you do for a living, Mrs. Lewis?" I pulled out a notepad and pen from my back pocket. I clicked the pen and sat poised to take notes.

"I sell Avon."

I stared at her a moment, waiting for more. When she said nothing else, I simply nodded and jotted "freeloader" on my notepad.

"Are you married?"

"Divorced."

"Children?"

"Grown."

Was her husband paying her big-time alimony? Otherwise, how could she afford this house? This wasn't a living quarters that someone who sold makeup out of a catalogue could buy. Believe me.

I cleared my throat and moved on. "When did you first meet Darnell?"

She smiled, somewhat sadly, and pulled her arms across her chest. The too-long sleeves of her bright blue sweater covered her hands. The action made her seem young and vulnerable, but I doubted both.

"Five years ago. I saw him at a concert down at the beach. Then I started going to all of his shows. A year later, I'd started his fan club and became his manager."

"How long have you been divorced?"

"Three years."

Ah-ha. Had Darnell been the reason for the divorce? I needed a tactful way of finding out.

"Did you get divorced because of Darnell, ma'am?" Chad asked.

Well, that was one way.

"I can't say that didn't have something to do with it, but honestly, my husband and I were just drifting apart. It was inevitable."

I tried to mirror her motions so that she'd open up. I'd learned about it in class the other day. I brought my hands together in my lap and hunched over. "Mrs. Lewis, I heard that you and Darnell were having an affair. Is that true?"

She collapsed into tears. "Yes, it is." Her voice broke. "Or was."

Chad crossed his arms over his muscular chest. Not that I'd noticed those pecs or anything. I mean, I wanted to be an investigator. Being observant was simply par for the course. He eyed Lynette. "What happened?"

She wiped her eyes with the sleeve of her shirt and left a streak of mascara on the blue wool. "Darnell was wonderful. He treated me like gold."

I had to point out the obvious. "He was married."

Lynette looked at her fingers as they twiddled in her lap. "I know. I knew it wasn't right. But when you meet the person that's right for you, you just know."

I leaned forward. I'd always wondered if that was myth or not. "You just know when you meet that person? Really?"

Chad nudged me, breaking me from my fascination with her answer.

I cleared my throat and regained my focus. "Go on."

"We were going to move to Vegas. He was going to be the next big thing, the top tribute artist in the country."

Not bad. Eighty million Elvis impersonators, and he was the king. Pretty ambitious. "And you were going to be his Priscilla?"

"I would have followed him to Antarctica."

It would have been sweet, had the woman not been having an affair. "When were you supposed to move?"

"Today."

I bit down, not wanting to feel sorry for the woman. Regardless, I did feel a surge of compassion as she wiped away tears. Poor sweater. I glanced around for a tissue before drawing in a deep, nonjudgmental breath. "Lynette, do you have any idea who might have killed your . . . boyfriend?"

Her eyes cut straight to mine, all sadness erased. "His wife. She couldn't stand that he was cheating on her."

"Did he ever mention anything about her? That he was afraid she might hurt him?"

She shook her head, back to being solemn. "No. He would have never spoken ill of her."

I stood and snapped my pad of paper shut. "We're almost finished here, but would you mind if I used your restroom? I have a sensitive stomach." I tried to look embarrassed as I said it.

"Second door on the right."

Was this the oldest trick in the history of snooping? Probably, because it worked. I bypassed the bathroom and tiptoed down the hallway. The first room was painted brown and blue. Nothing remarkable there. Just a spare bedroom, it appeared.

The next room had a lacy white bedspread and matching curtains. Very Victorian. Probably the master bedroom.

Lynette seemed so normal except for her bad taste—in fashion and in men. My gut told me she wasn't guilty.

There was one more door on the hallway. Another bedroom? Just to be sure, I pushed the door open.

I gasped at what I saw inside. The room was wallpapered with pictures of Elvis—not the real Elvis, the fake one. The dead one. Well, they were both dead, but the most recently dead one.

A mannequin in the corner wore an Elvis outfit. A model of a pink Cadillac remained parked on a table. A handkerchief rested in a glass encasement.

Was this woman really dating Darnell? Or was she delusional?

CHAPTER 13

"I'M TELLING you, that woman was obsessed with Darnell."

Chad threw his hands in the air and off the steering wheel as he drove down the road. "They were dating. She was his manager and the president of his fan club. It's not that unusual."

I waved my finger in the air, wanting to make my point and to make it clearly. "You didn't see the room. It was a shrine."

His hands went back to the wheel. "She was, like, mad crazy about him."

I rolled my eyes. "When you're, like, mad crazy about a girlfriend, do you decorate an entire room with all of her things?"

He shrugged. "No."

"Okay then."

"It doesn't make her a killer."

"It gives her motive."

"What?"

"What if Darnell decided to stay with his wife? What if, in anger, Lynette decided to off Darnell for breaking her heart? You know, one of those 'if I can't have him, no one can' kind of things."

"It's cliché. Besides, Lynette would have had to drag him under the house. She's too small to have done that."

Point taken. I never did find out if Darnell was at that house because of a job or if it was random. That would be next on my list of things to investigate.

I thought of Lynette Lewis for the rest of the drive back to my van. I thought of her living in that big house alone with just the memories of her deceased lover. I remembered the forlorn look in her eyes. Killer or not, she was one hurting woman.

Inside my head, I could hear the Beatles singing "Eleanor Rigby." I agreed with them—where did all the lonely people come from? First, there was Mr. Hermit, with no one to love him enough to check on him. And today, there was Lynette, a woman who loved a married man. Would she have pursued a married man if she weren't lonely?

Chad dropped me at my van. I promised to contact him in the next couple of days. It was a little strange. He did seem overly interested in the case. But then again, so did I, and that didn't make me a killer. I'd have to be careful as I practiced the "keeping my enemies closer" rule.

I drove through rush-hour traffic to reach my apartment. I wanted to do some more research, and if I got home early enough, I could avoid all of my crazy neighbors.

The only other car in the parking lot when I pulled in was Mrs. Mystery's, and the only reason she'd make an appearance was if she thought she'd been stolen again. I hurried up the stairs into my apartment and plopped down at the computer in the corner of my living room.

What did people do before the Internet? I typed in Darnell's name on a search engine and watched as pages of results came up.

Apparently, he was quite popular in the Elvis tribute-artist community. He had won awards. Played at tons of venues. Really made a name for himself.

I didn't find anything interesting, case-wise.

Out of curiosity, I typed in Hank Robins. He was the other Elvis tribute artist that Jamie had mentioned. My eyes widened when I saw that he was performing tonight at the beach.

I glanced at my watch. I had just enough time to get there.

If I wanted to miss my evening college class.

I bit down. I couldn't miss my class. I had to finish up with my degree so I could get a real job. I had to do the responsible thing.

I grabbed my book bag from the corner and headed out the door. I was ready to learn more about forensic science.

👣 👣

Missing one class wouldn't hurt.

I veered off the interstate and headed toward Virginia Beach. This was my one chance to observe Hank Robins without being given any weird looks. What had Darnell's wife said about him? That he and Darnell had gotten into an argument at the Evans's house. What was he doing at the house? And what had they argued about? If I had those answers, would I be able to solve this case?

It couldn't be that easy, but at least I might have more clues.

So far, I had two possible suspects. Lynette Lewis, who may have killed him because he tried to leave her. Or Jamie Evans, who might have killed him . . . because he tried to leave her?

I wasn't sure either of the suspects or their motivations were satisfying. I needed more. I had to dig deeper—without getting in the way of the police. It would be tricky, but I could do it.

At the oceanfront, I found a parking space in a nearby garage and then walked three blocks until I reached the courtyard. The wind coming off the ocean made it seem ten degrees cooler. But I loved the smell of salt air. Of course, just the scent alone made my hair frizz. Okay, just the thought of it made my red hair take on a mind of its own.

A good-sized crowd had gathered around the outdoor stage, surprising for such a chilly night. In the summer, throngs of people filled these spaces. The boardwalk and sidewalk and storefronts were full of people, elbow to elbow. There were sailors looking for dates; families vacationing from faraway, exotic places like Kansas; and teenagers looking for mischief.

Tonight, there were no sounds of sidewalk bands. There were no smells of vendors selling hot dogs, funnel cakes, and boardwalk fries. But there was the sound of someone singing, "You ain't nothin' but a hound dog."

As I got my first good look at Hank Robins, I thought having him sing about a hound dog was rather fitting. How did someone with droopy cheeks, saggy eyelids, and earlike sideburns get to impersonate Elvis? They looked nothing alike. The man didn't even sound like the King of Rock 'n' Roll.

The crowd didn't seem to mind. Several people were dancing on the grass in front of the stage. It would have looked much more romantic if they hadn't been bundled in huge winter coats. And if there wasn't a hound dog singing.

I pulled my sweater closer and wrapped my arms over my chest. The wind nipped at my nose and ears and anything else it could get its frigid little hands on. I really should have planned better. I should have brought a coat and a hat and ear plugs. How was I to know I'd ditch class and go to the beach?

I mingled, throwing in a little two-step now and then so I wouldn't look out of place. I wanted to get a good look at the people present. I wanted to catch Hank after the show and grill him like a hot dog.

Wouldn't Sierra have a fit if she knew my carnivorous thoughts?

The song ended. Everyone in Elvis's dog pound applauded. I gazed up at the stage. Elvis needed to lose a few pounds before wearing his hip huggers again. I wanted to look away but felt morbidly curious. Despite the man's imperfections, he didn't seem to have a confidence problem. He smiled broadly at his fans. He wiped his sweaty brow with a handkerchief.

Before I realized what was happening, the limp fabric landed on my forehead. Hands surrounded me. In self-defense, I grabbed the sweaty kerchief.

The lady beside me scowled. I really didn't want the soggy memento, but I wasn't about to give it away to people who obviously despised me. Instead, I stuck it in my sweater pocket.

DNA, baby.

Elvis grinned at me. And continued grinning at me. Was he waiting for a reaction?

To make him feel better, I let out a fake squeal and threw my hands in the air.

Satisfied, he turned his attention to everyone else. About time.

"This next song is dedicated to a colleague of mine, Darnell Evans. This community lost a great entertainer when Darnell passed. May he rest in peace."

He started singing "Love Me Tender." I crept to the corner of the stage and turned to get a better look at the crowd. These were true fans, coming out on a night like this to hear the man. What caused people to idolize a man like Hank? Did they truly appreciate his talent? Or maybe they were just hanging on to a time in their life when they felt happy and carefree. Maybe they'd take what they could get. And with Darnell out of the picture, what they could get boiled down to one man: Hank Robins.

Some couples swayed to the music, arms wrapped around each other and eyes misty. My lip jerked back in a half-frown when I saw the happy couples. Did people think Parker and I were happy? Were we? Or was I just getting my feathers ruffled for no reason? I didn't have time to think of it now.

The gathering consisted mostly of people over forty. Probably about fifty of them all together. I cast aside my judgments and got to the task at hand. I started at my left, looking for anyone suspicious. Nothing even close, unless you counted the man with the comb-over. Did he think he was fooling anyone? You're going bald, dude.

At the very thought of the word dude, my thoughts jerked to Chad with his laid-back beach lingo. Should I have told him I was going here tonight? Nah. Keeping him close was one thing. Having him attached to my hip was another.

My gaze skidded to a halt at a blond standing on the fringe. Even from where I positioned myself, I could see that her roots were in major need of a touch-up.

Lynette Lewis.

CHAPTER 14

AS SOON as Hank sang the last song, I released the breath I held. I couldn't take any more of this torturous butchering of classic songs. Finally, I could question the man and go home.

Except the crowd started screaming for an encore.

Were these people insane?

If they considered Hank Robins to be entertaining, then yes.

I rubbed my temples as he started into "Jailhouse Rock." Could this be a sign of things to come for Hank?

Finally, the song ended. I mentally pleaded with the crowd not to call him back for more. Elvis waved and began exiting the stage. This was my chance!

I hurried in front of the stage to the steps where he departed. I pulled my wallet out and shouted, "Hank Robins?"

He stopped. His eyes narrowed as if trying to place me. Finally, he grinned. "Would you like an autograph, pretty lady? Perhaps on that handkerchief you caught?"

I found his flirtatious undertones repulsive and hoped it didn't show on my face.

I flashed my driver's license and then stuffed my wallet in my pocket fast, hoping he'd think I'd shown him a badge instead of my right to drive. "I'm investigating the death of Darnell Evans. I'd like a minute of your time."

"I'm afraid I'm busy."

"I'm afraid it's not an option. I need some answers."

He fidgeted. Looked beyond me at his adoring fans. Glanced back at me and scowled. "Come on. Let's go behind stage where no one can see us."

Before anyone else could reach him, we ducked in the back. He crossed his arms over his chest. "Now really, miss. I'm quite tired, and I have to be at work early tomorrow morning. Can we make this quick?"

"Why were you at Darnell Evans's house the week before he died?"

He chuckled forcefully and wiped his hand over his sagging brow. "At his house? You know about that, huh? We were just having a friendly conversation."

"I heard it was anything but friendly."

"Look, it wasn't a big deal. Our friendly conversation turned into somewhat of an argument. Adults do argue sometimes."

"But you were competitors, also."

"Nothing wrong with some competition. Makes you stronger, better."

"So, about your argument . . ."

He sighed. "We were both competing for a spot at a summer festival. I heard he paid off the judges in order to be the one."

"What summer festival was this?" I pulled out my handy dandy pad of paper.

"Sum-derful."

I'd heard of the event. It took place at the oceanfront every summer. And it was wonderful. How cute.

Gag.

"Do you need anything else?"

"Mr. Robins, when was the last time you saw Darnell Evans?"

"The day of our argument. That was it." He cut his hands in the air like an umpire calling "Safe."

"Now I wish we had a chance to make good with each other, but that won't be happening."

I snapped my pad shut. "Thanks. I'll be in touch if I have more questions."

"Who did you say you were with?"

I walked away without answering. He didn't need to know all of my secrets.

The next morning, I pulled another box out of Mr. Hermit's closet. So far, I'd found a box full of pink flamingos, a rock collection, and tons of comic books. Some of the stuff could probably be sold on eBay for a good chunk of money. But who would get the cash?

This was the last box in the closet of the master bedroom. I blew dust off the top of the two-by-three-foot box. What kind of treats would I find in here?

I'd already packed up all of the man's clothing and shoes. A thrift store was coming to pick them up in a couple of hours. A charity would get his furniture to auction off for the less fortunate. His food had been thrown away. It was all bad-for-you junk food anyway and better if no one ate it, even the homeless. Tomorrow, I'd start on the nonfood portion of the kitchen.

I plopped on the floor and stared at the top of the box, at the sides that were neatly tucked into each other. Would this be another fun collection? Maybe butterflies or postcards or stamps. Was it only reclusive people who collected things? I paused. Maybe I should ease up on my T-shirts and flip-flops.

I pulled the ends out from each other. Inside, I stared at another box, this one with a floral print decorating the fabric around it. This was the first feminine-looking item I'd seen in his house. My pulse raced in curiosity. What would be inside?

Carefully, I took the box out and set it on the floor in front of me. I stared at it a moment, wondering if it would be perfume. Maybe he had a fetish for wearing women's cologne. Or maybe it was a memento of his mother. Of a past lover? What would this box tell me about Mr. Hermit?

I tugged the top off. Holding my breath, I peered inside.

Pictures. Lots and lots of pictures.

Pictures of Mr. Hermit, I think, when he was younger and thinner and happier. His arm was draped over a thin blond. The wall behind them was lined with portraits. They looked happy. I flipped to the next picture. Mr. Hermit holding up a fish, a huge, proud grin on his face. Mr. Hermit with a little boy sitting on his lap, a Christmas tree in the background. Mr. Hermit cradling a new baby in his arms.

Mr. Hermit hadn't always been a hermit. What happened to make him this way?

My cell phone began singing. I jumped, then scolded myself for getting lost in the moment. I was being paid to do a job, not to daydream. I grabbed my cell from the clip at my belt.

"Gabby St. Claire."

"How's it coming?" I'm not great with voices, but I automatically recognized the landlord, whose name I couldn't remember. I'm sure it would come back to me when it came time to collect payment.

"It's . . . okay. I've made quite a bit of progress. I should be finished by the end of the week."

"I'll pay you the second half as soon as you're done. I have another renter interested in the house, so the sooner, the better."

"Understood. Time is money, right?"

"You said it. Now, back to work."

I took one more glance at the picture of Mr. Hermit with the pretty blond. I couldn't get rid of these pictures yet. I stuffed them back in the closet and decided to start on the bathroom.

As I worked, my mind drifted to the other things on my to-do list.

I needed to call Lynette Lewis, see what she was doing at Hank's show last night. I needed to go back to Ocean View and question the neighbors to find out if they'd seen anything suspicious. I needed to talk to Darnell's boss, the baloney guy.

Most of all, I needed to keep an eye on Chad Davis to make sure he didn't steal any of my business.

CHAPTER 15

JUST AS I climbed into my van, the cell phone rang again. It was Parker. I knew because of the special ring I programmed in just for him—the tune of "I Will Survive."

Did I want to talk to him? I still hadn't come to any conclusions about our relationship. Did I even have time for a relationship right now? I had mysteries to solve, crimes to clean up, and money to be earned. Oh yeah, and a degree to complete.

I sighed and put the phone to my ear. "Hey, you."

He chuckled, a mellow, throaty sound. "Hey, Gabby. Whaddya doing?"

"Just leaving my job, heading home."

"Let's do dinner."

"I'm not sure if I have time." I remembered all the things I had to get done. Plus, I still didn't know what I wanted to do about our relationship, and being around Parker would only confuse me further.

"You can make time for me."

He sounded so convincing. "Well, normally, but I really do need to do—"

"Need to do what?"

I couldn't tell him about my side job. "The normal things. You know, study and stuff."

"How was class last night?"

I cringed. I couldn't lie. But I really wanted to. "Class?" I tried to buy time as I figured out a good way to word my excuse—my truthful excuse.

"You know, the place you go to learn?"

"Oh, that class. I . . . um, I, well—I went to a concert instead."

80

"A concert? Gabby, you've got to buckle down. You're so close to finishing."

"I know. This is the first I've missed. I won't miss any more."

"So, about dinner?"

I had to eat, didn't I? And it seemed like a good way to get the subject off my truancy. "Name the place."

He threw out the name of a restaurant in downtown Norfolk. I'd have just enough time to go home and get ready before he picked me up.

As I wandered up the stairs to my apartment, I realized how much I missed my apartment-mates. Riley's job had been keeping him busy. I didn't see him all that much anymore. Sierra was in the middle of a big "save the whales" campaign. I wouldn't see her until that was over. The conservative talk-show host across the hall from Sierra was doing a mini-tour for his radio program. And Mrs. Mystery hardly ever emerged.

I felt like I had empty nest syndrome, and I didn't even have any kids.

Maybe I was the one who flew over the cuckoo's nest.

I quickly got ready. Just as I stepped from my bedroom, a knock sounded at the door. Parker. He grinned his million-dollar smile from the hallway, one arm leaning casually against my door frame. He pecked my cheek with a kiss and grabbed my hand. "You look beautiful. You ready to go?"

Man, he was in a good mood tonight.

"Just let me grab my purse." My sparkly purse. I snatched it from atop the TV and joined him on the stairway. A few minutes later, we pulled up to the Freemason Abby, the first restaurant we ever ate at together. Back then, it was for police business . . . kind of. Let's just say no sparks flew between us. I was hung up on Riley, and Parker was convinced I was trouble for his investigation.

After we ordered, I looked at my boyfriend from across the table. "How does a person become a hermit?"

His lips twitched, as they always did when I amused him. "Say again?"

"A hermit. How does someone become one?"

"You thinking of applying for the position?"

I played with the napkin in my lap. "No, I'm just wondering how a person goes from a life full of family and friends to dying alone with no one to mourn for them."

He shrugged and looked out the window. "I guess you separate your-self, for whatever reason. You stop returning calls and answering the door. You find excuses to stay home."

"But why? Why would a person do that?"

Parker shrugged. "Why not? Hurt, pain, embarrassment, loss. Maybe they're afraid to risk. They put up walls and rationalize that it's better to be alone than to face rejection or hurt."

"It's so sad."

"What's this all about?"

I explained Mr. Hermit's situation.

"This isn't like you, Gabby. Letting the job get to you." He paused. "I mean, it's like you if the job involves murder or a crime. But this isn't a crime."

"It's worse. It's a crime against humanity."

"Being alone is a choice everyone makes for themselves. Even the freak-ish people can find other freaks who understand them. It's just a matter of effort. Believe me—I could tell you about some cases I've worked that would prove that. The fetishes some people have . . ." He shook his head.

I leaned forward, curious. "Like what? Modern-day vampires? Forty-year-olds who pretend to be infants? People who claim to be space aliens?"

Parker sighed. "I'm not in the mood to have this conversation. Can we please talk about something else?"

I sighed this time. "Of course we can." What else could we talk about? Oh, I had a bright idea. Brilliant to the utmost degree. "How was your day?"

His eyes lit up, but the sparkle quickly faded, as if he were trying to hide his excitement. "I got a new partner today."

"Did you?" I never thought I'd see Parker look happy to have a partner who could potentially steal all of his glory. That was Parker—he wanted to be a one-man show. Depending on other people? Not something he was very good at.

"Yeah, I think we're going to get along pretty well."

"And your partner's name?"

"Charlie."

I pictured an older man with a receding hairline and oversized glasses. "Cool. I hope it works out for you." What I really hoped was that Charlie didn't curse the day they were assigned to work together. Apparently, Parker had that effect on his partners. He'd never told me that, but somehow the information had trickled down to me when I attended Parker's birthday party two weeks ago.

I stared across the table at Parker. Man, he was handsome. Could totally be a body double for Brad Pitt, I kid you not. Brad Pitt from *Ocean's Eleven*, not the Brad Pitt from *Fight Club*.

"What are you thinking about?"

"Have you ever seen *Fight Club*?"

"Huh?"

"Never mind." Why boost his ego even more? Any time someone said a word like handsome, great, dashing, heck, even Mrs. Dash, Parker turned to them, assuming they were talking about him.

The rest of dinner consisted of conversation about football, movies, and—lo and behold—video games. Were we on the fast track to a deep, committed relationship or what? I counted down the minutes until Parker dropped me off at my apartment. As soon as he did, I hurried to my van. I needed to pay Lynette another visit. Sure, the sun had set a few hours ago, but most people were still awake at nine. Right?

I pulled up to her house, and she opened the door, wrapping a thin, hot-pink robe around her tiny waist. She blinked when she saw me, mascara still caked around her eyes.

"Yes?"

"Lynette, can I have a few minutes of your time?"

"It's a little late, isn't it?"

"I saw you at Hank Robins's concert last night."

She blinked again. "Is that a crime?"

"I find it suspicious that someone who's not only the president of Darnell Evans's fan club, but also his lover, would show up to see another Elvis impersonator—"

"Tribute artist. He was an Elvis tribute artist."

"Whatever. I find it strange you would go to his concert. I'd like to know why."

The woman pulled the door open. "Come on in. I probably should have just told you this to begin with."

I took a seat on the same milky white couch where I'd sat before and waited for her to begin. She wrung her hands on her way over to sit across from me.

"Hank Robins is a vengeful man." She stared at me as if waiting for a reaction.

"Why do you say that?" I finally asked.

She twisted her hands again as if the motion echoed her inner turmoil. "Hank claimed that my Darnell paid off some judges so that he could win the ETA Competition in September."

"ETA?"

"Elvis tribute artist."

"Of course." I fought the urge to roll my eyes. "And you went to the concert so you could confront him about his accusations?"

She looked down at her fidgety hands. "No, not exactly." She rose, crossed the room, and pulled open a drawer atop a pine secretary. She slipped out a piece of white paper.

"My Darnell left an overnight bag at my house. I was going through it yesterday, and I found this." She handed the folded, letterlike sheet to me.

I glanced up at her, saw the grief on her face, and then carefully touched the note. If this was significant, I didn't want to ruin any fingerprints—if Lynette already hadn't. Trying to just touch the edges, I opened the letter and stared at the computer-printed words:

Pay $2000
or I'll tell the media what you did.

I glanced back up at Lynette. She stared at me, her expression pensive. "Do you know what this is about?"

She closed her eyes for what felt like hours before slowly opening them. "Darnell received two thousand dollars for winning the ETA competition. Hank thought he'd paid off the judges. Hank also thought that he was going to win the competition and it would thrust him into the spotlight. He wanted to give up his job as a delivery driver and perform full-time. Of course, so did my Darnell."

I leaned forward. "Then why not just ruin Darnell's reputation by taking this straight to the media?"

"He didn't have any evidence. And Hank's lazy. He figured if he could hold this over my Darnell, he'd ultimately come out on top."

Could this be a key piece of evidence? Excitement fluttered up my spine. "Did you confront Hank at the concert?"

"No, I saw you and decided to leave."

I stared at the note again, at the computer-generated words. "Why were you keeping this a secret?"

Lynette collapsed into the chair behind her and covered her face. "I didn't want my Darnell's reputation to be ruined. Dying sometimes serves to make a person more famous, more fondly remembered. If this gets out . . ."

"So you haven't even told the police?"

She shook her head.

"Are you going to?"

She stared at me. "I don't want to."

"You should."

I stood to leave, even more questions circling around in my brain. Not circling as in about to go down the drain. More like hungry vultures circling their prey—their prey being my peace of mind.

"His funeral is tomorrow at the Oak Grove Funeral Home. Three o'clock," she called, still wringing her hands.

"You planned his funeral, correct?"

"Yes, I did. His fan club wanted to make sure it was an event that would make him proud."

I paused by the front door. "Lynette, where were you on Thursday, October 28, when Darnell died?"

Her face went white. "I was planning a fundraising event that Darnell would take part in. It was for the fan club. You know, throwing in some community service never hurts one's reputation."

"So, other members of this fan club can verify you were with them at the time?"

She fidgeted. "No, I was planning it here at my house alone."

CHAPTER 16

I HAD a lot to chew on as I drove home. Lynette had no alibi—but did she have a motive? Hank was blackmailing Darnell. That might be a motive for killing Hank, but why Darnell? I'd uncovered some lies and had enough experience to know I needed to look closer at anyone lying. So the investigation was coming along, but not fast enough for my taste. I needed more answers. I needed to get down and dirty.

My cell phone rang. I popped it off my belt and stuck it to my ear.

"This is Gabby."

"So, have you found out anything?"

I pulled the phone away from my ear and stared at the unfamiliar phone number across the screen for a moment before responding. "Excuse me?"

"About my husband's death?"

"Jamie?"

"Yeah, who else is it gonna be?"

Uh, how about my boyfriend? Another client? My good-for-nothing dad? "No, I haven't found out anything substantial yet, but I have some good leads. Jamie, did you know that Hank Robins was blackmailing your husband?"

"What?" Her screech was so loud that I had to pull the phone away from my ear again. "Why would that man blackmail my husband?"

"Something about your husband paying off some judges at a competition."

"Oh, that. That's ridiculous. My husband won on his own right. Ask anybody."

"Don't worry, I will."

"You talk to his boss yet?"

"No, I haven't talked to him yet. He's next on my list, though."

"Good. I tell you—that man had blood in his eyes."

I hung up and glanced at the clock on my van's console. It was already eleven o'clock. No wonder my muscles ached and my eyelids felt heavy. It had been a long day, one filled with no answers and more questions.

When I reached my apartment, I saw a note taped to the door. I hesitated before pulling it off. Last time someone had left me something at the door, I'd nearly been blown up. A note seemed harmless.

Unless anthrax was inside.

I froze but only for a moment. The thought was ridiculous. I tore the envelope and opened a typed letter:

Gabby,

    Please help me. Whoever stole my identity has now racked up thousands of dollars of debt on my credit card. The police won't do anything. The credit bureau doesn't care. You're the only person who can help. You and Riley.

Mrs. Morgan

Wow, what was it with everyone wanting my help lately? You crack one case, and everyone thinks you're Sherlock Holmes. Not that I minded. But I didn't know anything about ID theft, so how would I even go about helping? Maybe I'd ask Parker. Surely the police could do something. Maybe Mrs. Mystery just hadn't talked to the right person.

Out of curiosity, I pounded on Riley's door. I heard his TV blaring from the other side, so I knew he was home. When he answered, I held up the letter. "I thought you'd helped her clear this up."

He did the eyebrow cock. "Excuse me?"

"I thought you'd taken care of Mrs. Mystery's ID theft."

He folded his arms across his chest, and I noted how comfortable he looked in an oversized San Diego sweatshirt and worn jeans. "I helped her call all of the credit card companies and cancel her cards. I closed the cell phone account opened in her name. What more can I do?"

"Well, she left me a note begging for assistance. She wants me to track down whoever is doing this. I don't get it—she's a mystery writer. Shouldn't she have some idea how to go about finding the bad guy?"

"You'd think. But she's so reclusive. Maybe she only knows how to do these things in her fictional world."

"Maybe."

"Are you going to help?"

I let out a breath. "I don't know. I have a lot on my plate right now."

"I noticed you haven't been here a lot lately."

"Neither have you."

"Yeah, the law firm is taking up a lot of time. Getting all of this preliminary stuff set up is time consuming."

"Is it going okay?"

He shrugged, looked in the distance, and nodded. "It's going great. There's nothing like helping those who can't help themselves. The fatherless and the widows, you know."

I tilted my head. "You're only helping the fatherless and the widows?"

A smile brushed his lips. "No, but in the Bible, God commands us to help them. I feel really fulfilled being able to defend people who don't otherwise have the money. I'm planning some fundraisers in order to pay for the services."

"That sounds great."

"I can't tell you how glad I am that I left my old life behind."

I smiled. "I'm glad you're happy. So you're telling me you don't ever miss the black-tie events, the TV cameras, the limelight?"

"Not one bit. That chapter of my life is closed."

His answer didn't surprise me. "Good."

He shifted, and his hands went to his hips. "So, Gabby St. Claire, what kind of trouble are you getting into lately?"

I glanced at my watch just for the dramatic effect. "Do you have a few hours?"

"For you, I do." He opened his door wider and extended his arm to invite me inside.

This is what I loved about Riley. He always made me feel like I was the only one in the room. Like I was important. I can't say anyone else ever made me feel that way.

I wandered into his familiar apartment, the place where we'd had numerous powwows and crime-solving brainstorming sessions. His bird, Lucky, chirped in the background. I smiled, remembering when Riley first found Lucky in a tree outside the apartment building. That day seemed so long ago, when it was really just a few months. I heard Riley shut the door behind me as I approached Lucky's cage.

"Hi, Lucky."

"Pretty girl."

I laughed. "I can see Lucky is learning some more phrases."

"I have to be careful what I say. That bird is like a tape recorder."

"Tape recorder," Lucky repeated.

Riley and I both laughed. In the back of my mind, I wondered who Riley had been talking about when Lucky learned to say, "Pretty girl." I hadn't seen any women visiting Riley at his apartment. In fact, he'd vowed not to date until he got settled in his new practice. He wanted to put space between any new relationship and his breakup with his ex-fiancée.

I settled on Riley's navy blue couch and began pouring out everything I'd learned about Darnell Evans's death. Riley listened, nodding when appropriate and asking all the right questions. Why couldn't Parker show this interest? That's all I wanted—for him to listen. It seemed to be asking too much.

"And how are your classes going?" Riley turned off the TV and leaned his elbows onto his knees.

I remembered the one I'd missed this week and shrugged. "Okay."

Riley seemed to pick up on all the undertones of that one word. "You can't ignore your education, Gabby."

I felt my shoulders tense. "I'm not. I'm going to get my degree."

"I'd feel a lot better if I knew you were doing this investigation into Elvis's death officially—with police support and backup. You'll have that when you have your degree and your job."

"I can take care of myself."

Riley didn't say anything. But I knew what he was thinking—that no one could truly take care of themselves. That we needed to depend on others, that it was healthy, that no man was an island, that we all need somebody to lean on. I could hear Bill Withers singing about it in my mind.

I stood. "Well, I should go to bed." I remembered the original reason I'd come over and smacked my forehead. "Mrs. Mystery! I forgot."

"I'll help Mrs. Mystery."

"Really?"

He shrugged. "Sure. It would be my pleasure."

"Thanks, Riley." I stretched. "Okay, I really do have to go. It's been a long day. And I have a funeral to attend tomorrow. I hate funerals."

"Need company?"

I jerked my head toward him, unsure if he was sincere. Of course, when was Riley ever not sincere? "You want to go to a funeral with me?"

"I know they're miserable to attend alone."

"But you said you have tons of work to do."

"People before projects, Gabby. People before projects."

Why did I still have the feeling that what he really wanted was to get his Sunday school badge? That I was his little project—and a person, which made it the best of both worlds for him. People were his projects. Would I ever really be able to trust this man again?

I knew I wanted to.

CHAPTER 17

BACK AT my apartment, I sat down at my computer. Fatigue dragged at me, but I had more to do before I could sleep. Time to do some more research. My computer screen flashed to life, and I typed in my name and password.

The computer informed me that the information was invalid.

Huh?

I'd used the same user name and password for months now.

I tried again and got the same response. What was I supposed to do? I was no techie. But my computer is where I kept track of all my business files, my tax information, my everything. I could not be locked out of it.

I knew Riley was still awake, so I hurried back across the hall and banged at his door. He pulled it open, and a look of alarm spread over his features. "Is everything okay?"

Hype down on the drama, Gabby. Simmer. I controlled my voice, making it as even as possible. "My computer seems to be acting up, and I was wondering if you could help me?" I fluttered my eyelashes. I never did the fake thing very well.

A flash of . . . something . . . lit his eyes. "I thought you could take care of yourself."

My fakeness disappeared faster than Beyoncé ditching Destiny's Child. "Ha ha, you got me."

I turned on my heel and marched back to my apartment. I didn't need Riley's self-righteous banter right now. Couldn't he see my over-the-top level of stress?

"Of course I'll help you, Gabby."

This was no time to hold a grudge. "Thank you." He walked across the hall and into my apartment where I nodded toward the computer as if he'd never been in my living room before. "It's right there."

He pulled the rolling desk chair under him and stared at my blue computer screen. "Your password didn't work?"

"You wouldn't be here if it did."

He patted his hands in the air as if to tell me to chill. "Easy, Gabby. I just have to ask a few questions."

I plopped onto a chair and sighed. "I know. I'm sorry."

"What's your password?"

My password? Blood rushed to my cheeks. No way was I telling him my password. What had I been thinking when I asked him to come here? Of course, he'd ask for my password. And I'd never, ever tell him what it was. Ever.

"Gabby?" He waved his hand in front of my face.

I came back to reality. "My password?"

"Yes, your password."

I needed to buy time. "You promise not to tell anyone?"

He threw me a look of total frustration. "Gabby, what am I going to do with your password? I'm a lawyer, not a web-savvy criminal."

"Okay, it's . . . nancydrew, all one word." I lied. Guilt washed through me, but I just couldn't tell him the truth.

He glanced back at me with what I'd call amusement. If he only knew.

He typed, then looked back at me when an error message occurred. "You sure you didn't accidentally change it?"

"How does one accidentally change their password?"

"It's happened before."

"I'm sure it has." I shook my head, trying to think of an excuse to get him off my computer without seeming suspicious. "No, I'm sure I didn't change it." I simply told you a made-up one.

He played some more on the screen, typing and bringing up foreign-looking pages. He was trying hard, and I was feeling guilty. I should confess. I should tell him. It was the right thing to do.

"Riley—"

"You realize your server isn't secure, don't you?"

I forgot about my confession. "Excuse me?"

"Your server. You have a wireless DSL, but it's not secure. So anyone who's wireless can get on to your computer."

"Repeat in English, please."

He leaned back in the chair and turned to face me. "When you don't have a secure server, anyone who has wireless can pick up on your signal and log into your account. That could be how your password got changed."

I let my head flop back until it hit the top of the couch. "Tell me you're joking."

"I wish I were."

I knew my real user name and password didn't work, so I went with my original line of questioning. "So, what do I do?"

"You hire someone who really knows about computers to come out and fix it. I don't know enough to correct the situation." He shrugged apologetically.

I thought of my dwindling checking account. Bills were coming due. How much would it cost to have someone come out? I didn't even want to think about it.

"There's a girl at my church who does stuff with computers. Would you like me to ask her if she can help?" Riley studied my face. I'd bet he knew exactly what I was thinking—financial stress! Financial stress! Why did he have to read me so well?

"Is she expensive?"

Riley grinned, confirming my initial thoughts. "She probably wouldn't charge unless she had to buy something."

Yes! "I'd love it if she came out. I'll offer her my services for free also, if she ever needs a crime-scene cleaner."

He cocked his eyebrow and shook his head while wearing a slightly amused grin. "I'll leave that part out. I'll call her in the morning, then."

I nodded. "Thanks."

CHAPTER 18

PEOPLE WERE mourning—and loudly. They wore shirts with Darnell's Elvis-ized face across it. "Love Me Tender" played in the background. And everyone had handkerchiefs instead of disposable tissues.

At least one hundred people had shown up at the funeral home for the service. I wondered how many were members of his fan club. How many people really knew him? Did they really love Darnell Evans, or did they love the man he imitated?

I adjusted my black dress and tried to look solemn. Maybe I should have taken Riley up on his offer to come with me. I hated funerals.

The last funeral I'd attended had been my mother's. I stood up front with Dad and a few aunts and uncles. My life had changed forever. We weren't a *Leave It to Beaver* family, but any hopes I had of warm and cozy Polaroid moments died with my mom. She'd kept us together.

"Hey," someone said beside me.

I glanced over and saw Chad, dressed respectably in a suit and tie. I almost didn't recognize the beach bum. "What are you doing here?"

"The same thing you are."

First he intruded on my business, and now he was intruding on my snooping? How dare he? "I'm paying my respects," I whispered quickly, jabbing a finger into my chest.

"You're snooping."

"Don't be ridiculous."

He grinned. "You know, you're cute when you're mad."

I felt my face turn to a very un-cute shade of red. "Very funny."

"I wasn't being funny."

Judging by the heat on my cheeks, my face was now bright crimson.

The minister walked on stage—wearing a jumpsuit and sporting side-burns. Give me a break. I rolled my eyes.

As the ceremony started, I glanced at the people gathered. I spotted Jamie in the first row, along with a few other people—brothers and sisters maybe? The next row back contained Lynette. I'm surprised she decided to show her face here, although she did plan the funeral.

How strange was that? Why had Jamie let Lynette plan the funeral? She'd probably say it was because Lynette was the president of his fan club. But still, the woman had been having an affair with her husband! Was I missing something? Or did these people live in an alternate reality?

The next row back held a large man with a round, full stomach. The sight of him triggered something in my memory. What had Jamie said? That Darnell's boss, Rodger Maloney, had a big, fat pregnant belly? I would bet my eyeteeth that the man in the third row was Rodger, solemn and rough hewn like someone who spent his life doing hard labor. What had Jamie said he was? A plumber?

I needed to talk to the man. Maybe I could grab him after the funeral. He might hold some answers for me.

A movement at the back of the chapel caught my attention. Someone slipped into the last pew. I did a double take. Mrs. Mystery? What was she doing here? I tried to get her attention, but my neighbor's gaze remained focused on the speaker up front. I'd catch her later and find out the scoop.

As the funeral continued, my thoughts drifted to my morning at Mr. Hermit's. I'd cleaned his place some more before coming to the funeral. With each box I unpacked, I found more sad evidence of how lonely he'd been. I couldn't get my mind off the man. Then on the way to the ceremony, the landlord called and told me that the state would bury Mr. Hermit.

I shifted in my seat as an idea struck. What if I had a funeral for him?

I could certainly organize something. I could try and contact those people I'd seen in the pictures with him. His body could leave this world with some dignity. If I understood correctly, the state would provide a coffin, something low-grade, but it would have to do. I couldn't afford much.

Even better, maybe we could use some of the money from selling his belongings to pay for the funeral. My brain whirled in full gear.

Before I realized it, everyone was standing so they could attend the graveside service. I stood also, and Chad beside me. I glanced back to where Mrs. Mystery had sat, but she had disappeared. Good thing I knew how to find her later.

"Figure out any leads during the ceremony?" Chad whispered as we walked outside.

I remembered Mrs. Mystery, and I shrugged. "Nothing of interest."

"What's next?"

"Next, I talk to Elvis's wife."

"At a funeral?"

"No better time than the present."

Chad smirked and shook his head. "I was just thinking no worse time than the present."

🐾

I waited for Jamie. I knew it was probably a total social faux pas to approach a grieving widow at her husband's funeral. But I did it anyway. Trying to gather some manners, I placed my hand on her bony shoulder.

"Gabby!" She smiled, and her face lit up like a police car that'd just clocked a speeder. "How are you? I'm so glad you could make it."

The woman made it sound like I'd made it to a dinner party. Not that I was surprised. The woman had a strange way of reacting to her husband's death.

I cleared my throat and tried, more for my sake than Jamie's, to appear sympathetic. "Glad I could come out and help support you during this time." I cringed at the fakeness of my words and decided to get to the point. "Jamie, do you know where Hank works?"

My lack of manners didn't seem to faze her. "Sure, he's a driver for Henderson's Delivery. Why?"

"I have a question for him."

She pursed her lips and grabbed my arm. Her sharp, two-inch nails dug into my flesh. "You gonna question Rodger still? I'm telling you, that man's full of vengeance."

I stored her response away for later evaluation and brushed her claws from my arm. "I'm going to. I just haven't yet."

She pointed a red-tipped fingernail at me. "I really need some answers, sweetheart. Darnell needs to rest in peace. I don't want his ghost coming back to haunt me."

"Of course not."

She smiled, and I wanted to buy the woman some whitening strips . . . and a nicotine patch . . . and a sandwich. "I knew you'd understand."

And that was that. I had no more work to do here. I walked halfway to my van before I noticed Chad trailing me. "What are you doing?"

He put a little skip in his step until he was at my side. "I'm going with you."

"Why?" I flipped my keys into the air.

"Because it's safer that way."

"Is it?"

"It's as the Beatles once said, 'We'll get by with a little help from our friends.'"

I stopped. Maybe this man wasn't my nemesis. Maybe this man was the male version of me. "Fine. You can come. Some company might be nice."

We climbed into my van, I cranked the engine, and we pulled away from the weed-infested cemetery. That cemetery itself was a crime, though I supposed its inhabitants weren't the wiser for it.

"So, how's business going?" Chad asked.

"It's going."

"What's that mean?"

Great, someone else who has a knack for asking questions. Now I knew how it felt for others to be around me. "It means whatever you want it to mean. It's going fine. I'm busy. I'm getting paid."

He flicked a piece of thread from his pants leg. "You're doing a bum job, huh? Sometimes you've got to pick those up in the downtimes."

Finally, someone who understood me.

Because he was my competition, I reminded myself. The man was trying to steal my business. Didn't he know I had college loans to pay? I didn't have a hefty bank account to hold me over during ski season.

Did I like this man or hate him? I couldn't decide.

"I'm packing up some things for a man who died without family, if you must know," I finally said.

"Interesting."

"Actually, it is interesting. Piecing together this man's life has been eye opening . . . and sad. I mean, he died without anyone, not even a dog to mourn him."

"I came across a few people like that in my days at the funeral home."

I drummed my fingers on the steering wheel, that Beatles song still going through my head, the one about someone needing me and feeding me when I was sixty-four. "I'm thinking of giving him a funeral," I blurted. I held my breath, waiting for a reprimand. Parker would try to put me in my place. Riley would try and counsel me. What would Chad do?

"That sounds like a great idea."

My head swerved toward him. "What did you say?"

"I said that's a great idea." He glanced back at the road, as if to remind me that I was driving and his life was in my hands. Scary, if I did say so myself. "I could help. I do know a few things about funerals."

Someone to help me. That would be nice. Not someone to scold me or someone to guide me. Just someone to be there right beside me. Why did my heart lift so much at the thought? And why was I suddenly starting to think in rhyme, like I was writing a cheesy campfire song? "I just might take you up on that offer."

"I hope you do."

CHAPTER 19

"DO YOU think he's at the office? I mean, he's a delivery man. He's probably on the road." Chad leaned back into the van seat like it had a built-in massaging mechanism. Totally relaxed, totally at ease, and totally in my business.

"I guess we'll find out."

"What exactly do you hope to find out?"

Argh. The questions again. I made a mental note that I needed to stop asking as many, lest I annoy people the way Chad Davis annoyed me. "Where Mr. Elvis was on the day Darnell Evans died—"

"And what day was that?"

"He was last seen on October 28, which the medical examiner's report confirms. And I'm going to ask him about the blackmail letter—"

"What?"

I sighed. Did I have to explain everything to the living, breathing book of questions sitting beside me? "Yes, Hank was blackmailing Darnell over some ETA competition."

"ETA?"

I sighed again. "Elvis tribute artist. Get with it." I snapped my fingers in his direction.

"Excuse me."

I looked over and saw him grinning. Good. He got my humor. The building where Hank worked appeared at the end of the road. "We're almost there."

I pulled the van into the parking lot of a metal-sided building. While the place wasn't run down, it wasn't particularly well-kept either. Gray sides, grass around the perimeter, glass door. The faded lines on the parking lot asphalt matched the building's dreariness. Henderson's was splayed across a white sign atop the space, and a few trucks with a matching logo were outside.

I turned the van off, tossed the keys in the air, caught them, and looked at Chad. "Let's do it."

A subtle smile inched across his lips but illuminated from his eyes. "Okay, boss."

Inside, a non-distinct receptionist sat at an elevated desk. And honestly, with all the oddballs I'd met on this case, non-distinct was almost freakish. Her back straight, her expression sane, she asked, "May I help you?"

I held my head high and laced my fingers. "I'm looking for Hank Robins. It's rather important. Is he here, by chance?"

She shook her head in a nondescript way. "No, he's doing a run."

I tilted my head. I heard that it makes people seem more approachable, something I'm trying to work on. "Does he have a regular route that he drives?"

"No, ma'am. We deliver all over. Some customers are regular. Some aren't. It just depends on the day."

"I see." I nodded. "Do you know when he'll be back?"

She glanced beyond me at what I assumed was a clock. "Hard to say. Could be soon. But you never know. He could have gotten held up." She looked back and forth between Chad and me. "Are you fans?"

"Fans?" Chad had his arms crossed and leaned against a gray wall as if he was enjoying the show.

"He's quite popular in the area. He's Elvis, you know." The receptionist's sane expression slipped a bit. Maybe she did fit in with this crowd.

I waved in the air as if owning up to her statement. "I have seen his show. He definitely leaves an impression."

Chad cut me a sharp glance.

"Speak of the devil. Or should I say 'the King'?" The receptionist nodded behind me.

I turned around and spotted the Hound Dog walking in through the front door. He stopped in his tracks when he spotted me. His shoulders slumped as if seeing me exhausted him. Gathering his gusto, he drew in a breath and swept past me.

"I'm busy."

I stuck close to his side. "I just have a few more questions."

"I never did find out what agency you're with."

"You tell me why you were blackmailing Darnell Evans, and I'll tell you who I'm with." Give me a microphone, and maybe I'd try ambush reporting for my local news station.

Hound Dog glanced at the receptionist, horror across his face at my accusation. Then his attention fell on me. "Let's take this outside."

I grinned at Chad as we followed the driver. He stuffed his hands deep into his pockets. This was a different man from the one I'd seen at the concert. He seemed dejected and beat down, like a hound dog that had been swatted with one too many rolled-up newspapers.

"Let's just get down to business. I know you blackmailed Darnell. I've seen the note. Where were you on October 28, the day Darnell was murdered, Mr. Robins?"

His eyes shifted between Chad and me. "I was working."

My lip twitched cynically. "A likely story. Do you have anyone who can verify this?"

"I work alone."

"That's a shame." I crossed my arms over my chest, trying to look tough.

Hank fidgeted, his eyes jerking back and forth between me and Chad. "Are you going to arrest me?"

Wow, he really thought I had that power? I wanted to blow on my fingernails and buff them against my shirt, I felt so impressed with myself. But I had to get back to the task at hand. "Arrest you for what? Blackmail or murder?"

"I didn't murder no one."

I tightened the cross of my arms. "Prove it."

"I can't."

My hand flew from where I had it so nicely tucked, and I pointed at Hank. "Because you did it. Darnell was going to be the end of your career. Without him around, you'd be the only shining star in the area. What I don't understand is, why did you kill him when he was so close to leaving for Vegas?"

Hank stepped back, his hands in the air. "You don't know what you're talking about. Blackmail is one thing. Murder is a whole different ballgame, girlie."

"Girlie?"

"You and your friend need to get out of here."

I stepped closer. "Did you just call me girlie?"

Chad pulled me back.

"You heard me. Beat it. I can't afford to lose my job."

"Yeah, it looks like you're really enjoying it." I motioned at his blah environment.

"It helps pay the bills, okay? And the ex-wife."

My hands went to my hips. "Of course, you'd have more money to pay the bills and your ex if you had more Elvis gigs. And you'd have more Elvis gigs if Darnell were out of the picture. You could give up this lousy job and do what you really love."

"You don't know what you're talking about. If you really want to investigate someone, talk to my ex-wife."

"Your ex-wife?" What was I missing?

"Yeah, she was having an affair with the man."

My eyes widened. "Lynette Lewis?"

"She's a money-hungry fool. I wouldn't be surprised if she was embezzling funds from the man's so-called fan club. Now get out!"

Once inside the van, Chad and I looked at each other.

"I wasn't expecting that one," I admitted.

Chad nodded. "Me neither. By the way, you were good."

I beamed. "Thank you." I liked Chad Davis, I decided. He was a nice guy after all.

"You have time for one more stop?" Chad asked.

My stomach rumbled. "Only if we can grab something to eat first."

"Sounds good to me. We'll grab something on the way. My treat."

"If you insist." Great. I was becoming a freeloader, just like my dad. I could not keep accepting free meals from people. "On second thought, it will be my treat."

"I hope the restaurant's expensive then."

On third thought, I hated the man. Must be nice not to have to live from paycheck to paycheck. Here I was, barely scraping by, yet I'm buying his lunch. What was wrong with the world?

I spotted some golden arches in the distance. "Well, you are in for a real treat."

● ●

"Have you heard anything else about the mold man?" Chad stuffed a bushel of fries into his mouth.

I pictured the mold man's dead body lying in the crawl space. I thought of Chad being there before me and again wondered if I could be sitting across from a killer. A killer who was trying to keep an eye on the investigation, so he was keeping me close. Made sense to me. I wondered if the man owned a gun.

Yet Chad had seemed truly shaken up by the incident. Or was he shaken up about taking another man's life? Of course, I didn't really know anything about Chad Davis. Maybe I should get to know him.

If essential to my investigation, I'd get to know the man. I'd spend time with him and find out about any secret hobbies, any bad taste in music, and any Elvis fetishes.

But every minute of it would be pure torture.

I pulled my thoughts back to Chad's question. If I'd heard anything about the mold man. I swallowed a bite of my hamburger. "Nope. Not a thing."

"Do the police think the same man is responsible?"

Was he trying to find out inside information so he could know if he was a suspect or not? "That's my understanding." I wiped my mouth, hoping none of my Big Mac's special sauce was slathered across my face. "So, tell me more about you. Where you're from, how you got here, yada, yada, yada."

"Well, since you put it that way." He laughed, a low chuckle that sounded mighty surferish. I pictured him on a surfboard, conquering a wave. I'll bet he looked good out under the sun's rays. "I grew up in the area, went to college out west, ended up starting my own funeral home. I made a lot of money, but the job was a real drag. It was starting to get to me. Luckily, I invested pretty wisely. Wisely enough that I can be comfortable for a while. So here I am." He smiled and leaned across the table. "Your turn."

"No, no, no. That was way too basic. I need more personal details. That was definitely the Cliff Notes version."

He laughed again. "Okay, how about this? I love Swedish fish—I never go surfing without eating some. I've been surfing since I was eight. I won a couple of small championships when I was in high school. I've never been married because I've never met the right one, and I have a bad habit of playing with my toes."

I pictured his sand-encrusted feet. "Yuck."

His eyes sparkled. "Yeah, I know." He leaned back into the molded-plastic booth. "Now it's your turn."

I shrugged. I had to get to know him, not vice versa. "Not much to say. Pretty boring, really."

"With a personality like yours, I seriously doubt that."

"What's that mean?"

"It means you've got spunk. You've also got a determination that probably didn't come from having a pampered life. You've got that sweet face but the tongue of a wiseacre—"

I paused mid-bite. "Who uses that word?"

"What word?"

I pointed my french fry at him. "Wiseacre."

"I do."

"Interesting." I ate the rest of my fry.

"Anyway, where was I? Oh yeah, your sweet face. And your eyes have a fire in them. And they're very lovely eyes, if I do say."

Yes, I could get used to Chad Davis as a friend, fake or not. "Thank you."

"And you're a crime-scene cleaner. How did you become a crime-scene cleaner?" Chad leaned closer. "Were all the jobs at Merry Maids taken?"

I crossed my arms across my chest and scowled. No, I did not under any circumstances want Chad Davis as a friend.

CHAPTER 20

THE NEIGHBOR living to the left of the house where Darnell Evans died appeared too high to answer any questions. The neighbor across the street wasn't home. But the neighbor to the right, an elderly lady, was both home *and* sober. Would wonders ever cease?

"Come in, come in," she insisted.

We stepped into her small home. The place smelled vaguely of collard greens. Their bitter stench could saturate a house, and I'd recognize them anywhere. They were one of my dad's favorites.

She seated us around a waxy, dining-room table overlaid with a crocheted tablecloth and offered us cookies and tea. I decided right then that I wanted her as my grandmother. She seemed the type, especially since she had pictures of her family plastering every available surface. I thought of Mr. Hermit and what a contrast this woman's house was to his.

"Have a cookie." She pushed a plate of warm, sugary treats toward us.

I couldn't resist taking one. Snickerdoodles. Absolutely heavenly, I thought as I bit into one. "These are delicious."

The woman glowed. "I make a batch every day."

I nearly choked. "Every day? What do you do with that many cookies every day?" She certainly didn't eat them. She was as skinny as my vacuum-cleaner hose.

"I share them with neighbors and friends and those who need a pick-me-up. Snickerdoodles, chocolate chip, peanut butter delight, macadamia nut. I just can't help myself."

I needed her as a neighbor. "If you ever want to move to Ghent, let me know. I'm sure I can find you a place close by."

"So, what can I do for you?" She looked at us with sharp, perceptive eyes hidden behind dainty bifocals.

"Have you seen anything suspicious going on at the house next door?" Chad asked. I scowled, remembering why I didn't want to be his friend. He was not only trying to steal my business, but he was also invading my snooping turf. The nerve.

"I'll tell you what I told the police. I hadn't seen anyone over there for years. I had to call the city several times trying to get the owner to even cut the grass. That house was an eyesore for the entire neighborhood. Then about three weeks ago, I started seeing little Bobby over there. Told me he was going to sell the place. Honestly, it's about time. His folks have been dead for years now, but I guess sometimes you just want to hold on. Anyway, I saw his car there several times." She blinked at us. "Is that what you wanted to know?"

"Did you see any other cars there?" I asked.

"I saw a white van there one day."

That would be mine.

"I also saw one of those . . . what do you call them? Those hippie vans."

Vanagons. That would be Chad's.

"And one day, I saw a black sedan. I think it was a Kia, but I couldn't get a good look at it. It was foreign, though. My husband used to work for the Ford plant, and I learned to spot those foreign cars a mile away."

It sounded like she got a good look at plenty of things. There was nothing like a nosy neighbor to keep a neighborhood safe.

"When was that?" I asked.

"On the day they say that Elvis man died."

I wondered what kind of car Darnell Evans had. I'd have to ask Jamie.

"Is there anything else unusual you've seen over there?" I'd grab onto any details she had to offer.

"I saw two young people who looked an awful lot like you over there a couple of days ago." The woman's eyes twinkled. "Who did you say you were again?"

"This is Gabby St. Claire," Chad said, extending his arms like I was the prize if you answered enough questions correctly. "She's been asked to in-vestigate Darnell Evans's death. She's one of the best in the area."

I really enjoyed being with Chad Davis. I was so glad we'd met.

"That's right." She nodded faster and faster. "I remember reading about you in the newspaper a few months back. You helped solve that crime involving that young politician, right?"

"That's me."

"Well, I hope you can figure out who killed Elvis. I saw him in concert once, you know."

I leaned toward her. "You saw Darnell Evans in concert?"

"No, I saw the real thing. Boy, did that man know how to make a girl's heart swoon." She placed a hand on her heart and closed her eyes as if reliving the event. I smiled at the sweet expression on her aged face.

"Thank you, ma'am, for your time."

"Catch the man who did this. This neighborhood used to be pretty spectacular, you know. People were proud to say they lived here. Now, it's crime ridden and run down. A murder is the last thing we need."

"Understood." I rose, and Chad followed my lead. "Have a great day."

"How long have the two of you been married?"

I skidded to a halt. "Married? Us?" My hand flung back and forth between Chad and me. "Oh, we're not married."

Chad grinned beside me. "But we will be soon." Before I knew what he was doing, he pulled me toward him and kissed my temple. "She's one special gal."

For one of the few times in life, I felt speechless. As soon as we stepped outside, I turned to Chad and saw the amusement in his eyes.

"I couldn't resist." He nudged my chin with his knuckle. "You're just so cute when you're mad. Your face turns all red and matches your hair."

No, Chad Davis would never be my friend.

i i

As soon as I climbed in my van, I ignored Chad by pulling my cell phone out and dialing Jamie's number. Her gum-smacking voice sounded over the line. She informed me that Darnell drove a black Hyundai. I'd guess that was the car the neighbor had spotted. I wondered if the police had found it.

She also informed me that everyone knew Lynette and Hank had been married at one time.

Of course. Because they were both so famous that the paparazzi couldn't get enough of them. Forget Bradgelina, tell us about Hankette. The world wanted details.

Before I hung up, I had one more question. "By the way Jamie, what was Darnell doing on October 28, the day he died? Was it work as usual?"

"He supposedly took off early to do a concert at a nursing home."

"Which one?"

She threw out the name of one about fifteen minutes away. As soon as I hung up, I started down the road toward it.

👣 👣

If the entrance to the crawl space had been like the opening to the underworld, walking into the nursing home was like entering Bizarro World.

Pictures of Darnell Evans were strung up and down the hallway. On my way to the front desk, I passed one woman inching down the hallway with her walker, wearing a T-shirt with his face plastered across it. This man had been an enterprise in himself. Who would have thought?

I paused by one of the posters and studied the man's face. The wrinkle creases around his eyes. His nose—too large and hooked to look like the King. His receding hairline. Yet something about his smile and the look in his eyes did ring of Elvis.

"Can I help you?"

I approached the petite woman at the front desk. I quickly sized her up. Long, poofy hair with big, hairspray-plastered bangs; tapered, stonewashed jeans; an oversized sweatshirt; and big hoop earrings. The girl was obviously stuck in the eighties. I glanced at her desk, cluttered with miniature Snickers wrappers. Obviously a chocolate nut.

"I was hoping to speak to someone about Darnell Evans."

"You mean Elvis?" She nodded too brightly and smiled.

Puh-lease, people. The man wasn't the real thing. I made sure to keep my tones even. "Yes, Elvis."

"What would you like to know?"

I nodded and smiled brightly. "About his last visit here."

"It was a lovely visit."

"Anything unusual about it?"

Her bright smile and sparkly eyes remained frozen in place. The perpetual cheerleader, I figured. Stuck in her prime of twenty years ago. You met them once in a while, the poor souls for whom the nightmarish teenage angst of high school really was the best years of their lives. "He couldn't linger afterwards like he usually does."

"Why not?"

"He just said he had an urgent appointment."

"I see." I leaned closer and lowered my voice. "Any hints about what kind of appointment it was?"

"Nope." She shrugged and popped a bubble. "I just know the residents were real disappointed. He usually stays afterwards, signing autographs, giving kisses."

I signaled at all the pictures hanging up of Darnell. "It looks like he's got a lot of fans around here."

"Oh yes. He's like a celebrity." Nonsensical nodding, blinking, smiling like she had Vaseline on her teeth. Maybe it didn't happen at every school in America, but at mine, the cheering coach made her cronies put Vaseline on their teeth to ensure they'd keep smiling. Of course, I was never a cheerleader, so don't get the wrong idea. I was the girl who stirred jalapeño juice into their Vaseline.

"I would have never guessed."

"He just brightened everyone's days." She tried to look sad, but with her smile still stretched across her face, the emotion didn't work. "We're really going to miss him. It's a shame. He was such a nice man."

I had to find out who that appointment was with. When I did, I'd find Darnell's killer.

CHAPTER 21

NO SOONER had I deposited my glittery purse in my bedroom than someone knocked at the door. A fresh-faced girl with caramel-colored, straight hair stood on the other side.

"Gabby?"

"The one and only."

"Riley said your computer is acting up?"

I swung the door wide. "Come on in."

She stuck out her hand with its unmanicured fingertips and stubby nails. I liked her already. "I'm Amy."

I noticed her confident grip. Not too sweaty, not bulldozer strong. The woman had a perfect handshake; I had to give her props for that.

"What's going on with your computer?" She readjusted the leather bag on her shoulder. If Sierra came over, I'd have to hide that lest we get an hour-long lecture on the mistreatment of cows.

"Apparently someone's locked me out of my own PC."

"That's a bummer, but I think I might be able to help."

I opened the door wider. "Then by all means, come inside."

She stepped inside, and I saw her gaze sweep my humble abode. "Cute place."

"I like it."

Her gaze swept me this time. "Riley's told me a lot about you, you know."

"Has he? All good, I assume."

She laughed, and I wasn't sure how to take it. "Of course. We all love hearing his Gabby stories."

Gabby stories? What did that mean? A quick picture of Riley sitting in Sunday school class, sharing a prayer request about his kooky neighbor who didn't know the Lord, flashed through my mind. The brat.

"So, where's that troublesome computer of yours?" She clapped her hands together and looked around.

I pointed to the corner, wondering about her keen observation skills.

"What a beast!"

I knew my computer was old and kind of big when compared to the flat, thin computer screens they had out nowadays. But that computer let me do what I needed. It had been one of my first big purchases. I felt a special connection with my "beast." I scowled at Amy, but she was already gliding across the room.

"Let me see what I can do."

She plopped at my computer desk, a nicked monstrosity that I'd picked up from someone's trash pile. It was a perfectly good desk. I don't know why anyone would want to throw it away. It was solid wood—so what if the wood was stained orange and the drawers had big, oversized wooden knobs.

Amy's fingers began flying over the keyboard. I paced, anxiety knotting in my stomach. A moment later, the computer guru looked back at me innocently.

"I need your user name and password."

I felt my face turn red. I'd desperately tried to change it last night, but I'd been too late. Now, the whole world would know my sad secret.

I briefly considered just letting the computer rot—or do whatever computers did. Rust, I supposed. I would buy a new one—a smaller one with a flat screen. No big deal. I'd just work a few extra jobs. Maybe even do some mold remediation.

But I had forms on there that I'm sure the IRS would like to see. I had to access the information in that computer.

When I admitted my password, would Amy share the information in prayer-request form with everyone at church? I could hear it now: Not only is Riley's neighbor kooky, she's also sad. Very, very sad.

She continued to stare at me.

I cleared my throat, feeling hot. "My password?"

"I promise not to tell anyone." She smiled as if trying to be reassuring.

"Well, it's . . ."

She nodded, leaning toward me.

"I changed it a few months ago, when . . ."

She continued nodding, her fingers poised to type.

I went with a last-ditch effort to avoid the unavoidable. "Do you just want me to type it?"

She shook her head. "It would be much easier if you just told me."

I laughed, weakly. Took a deep breath. Wondered how I could have ever been so stupid.

"My username is . . ." Dramatic pause. Closed my eyes, wanting to crawl under a rock. ". . . gabbythomas, one word."

I couldn't open my eyes to see the pity in her gaze. I heard computer keys pounding.

"And your password?"

I swallowed, wondering why she hadn't laughed, why her voice sounded the same. Obviously, she was a great actress who could conceal her pity/ amusement/curiosity with the best of them.

"One word, happyeverafter."

I continued to press my eyes closed and waited for the laughter. And waited. And waited.

"Yep, someone's hacked into your system. This is going to take a while."

I popped an eye open. How could she not react to the news that my user name was the junior high equivalent of writing "Gabby ♥ Riley" all over my notebook? It was sad, very sad. Yet she hadn't reacted. I wasn't sure how I felt about that.

I sat on the arm of the couch behind me and folded my arms over my chest.

"So, what do you do for a living, Amy?"

"I work for social services. I do all of their computer troubleshooting."

Social services. My mind jerked back to Mr. Hermit. Social services had to get involved with that case. I thought of the funeral I wanted to throw for him and wondered if Amy might have some information that could help.

"Do you know what happens if a person dies with no family?"

She glanced back at me. "Then the state handles it. They look for the next of kin. If no one claims the body, it's cremated. The state will hold onto any important papers for up to five years. After that, they're destroyed."

I thought of all of Mr. Hermit's pictures, of the smiling faces I'd seen posed next to him. Destroyed. A life ended like it was never even there. "It's kind of sad."

"Isn't it? I hate hearing about those cases." She stopped tapping away at my computer for a moment and looked up at me. "Is something on your mind?"

I shrugged, wondering if I should even go there. "I'm cleaning the apartment of a man who died without anyone. I'm thinking of planning a funeral for him."

"That's really nice of you." She nodded, her sincere-looking eyes focused on me.

"But I don't have a lot of money, so I'm trying to figure out how to go about doing so. Who I need to talk to, yada, yada, yada."

"Maybe the church could help out."

The church? I hadn't thought of that. Did I really want to get them involved? It would be much easier to have someone else—several someone elses—helping me. But then, I'd probably feel like I owed them something. At least a visit to church. "I wouldn't want to ask them for that."

"That's what we're here for—to help people. Besides, it can't hurt to ask, right?"

"I don't know . . ."

"Just think about it. It might be the solution you're looking for."

CHAPTER 22

I'M FINDING myself talking to God lately, yet I don't even believe in him.

What's up with that?

Take this evening, for instance. Long after Amy left and with my computer now working, I'd plopped down to check my e-mail. I got one from my dad. Since when did he have e-mail? Last I knew, he couldn't even pay his electric bill. In the note, Dad had actually admitted that he'd been a sorry father figure and that his life was spinning out of control. Even stranger, he ended the e-mail without asking me for anything. Not so much as a penny.

After I read it, I'd actually looked up to the ceiling and asked, "What's up with that?" In itself, the action wasn't strange. But I'd actually pictured a fatherly figure up in heaven when I asked the question. Then I'd actually imagined that fatherly figure listening to me.

I've been so accustomed to my real father being a hungover freeloader that I have no idea what to do with a dad who's actually making sense when he talks.

I stared at the screen for a long time, trying to figure out how to respond. Finally, I shut my computer down to pay Mrs. Mystery a visit. I needed to know her connection to Elvis. Maybe she could offer some insight on his murder.

I paused. Nah, that would be too easy.

Still, I wanted to know why she went to Darnell's funeral. Just call me nosy. I've been called worse.

I pounded on Mrs. Mystery's—aka Margaret Morgan's—door upstairs. A minute later, the door cracked open. One eye peered over the safety chain connecting the door to the wall. "Can I help you?"

"Ms. Morgan, it's me. Gabby. Your neighbor."

The door remained in place. "Yes, Gabby, I can see that it's you. I'm old, not blind."

I stiffened but continued. "I was wondering if we could chat."

"Sure, what would you like to chat about?"

I shifted, wishing she would open the door so we could communicate like normal people. Of course, normal wasn't a word that came up very often in reference to me. I cut to the chase. "About Darnell Evans."

I couldn't be sure, but I think her one eye lit up. "Darnell was a wonderful performer. I've been a member of his fan club for years now."

"Really?"

"Yes, I hardly ever missed his concerts."

"What do you know about him?"

"Not much, other than he can do a great rendition of 'Can't Help Falling in Love.'"

I shifted again, really wishing I could see more than her eye. "Ms. Morgan, could I come inside and talk? Is everything okay?" What if her peculiar behavior had been brought on by an intruder hiding in her house or something equally sinister?

"It's fine, just fine. I don't let anyone into my apartment, though."

"Why?"

"It messes with my feng shui."

Great, the woman knew about feng shui but had no clue about paper shredders. Did I unknowingly audition for an episode of *The Twilight Zone*? I focused my attention on her interest in Darnell Evans. Talking to her was just one more way of gaining insight on the man . . . hopefully.

"What does being a member of his fan club include?"

"Let's see, I got an autographed picture and a monthly newsletter. Plus, we had meet and greets every once in a while. He did a special concert just for us last September."

I couldn't be sure, but I think the woman swooned.

"Did you pay to be a part of the club?"

"Just twenty dollars a year. Very reasonable, don't you think?"

"Very. Thanks, Ms. Morgan." I told her goodnight and went back down to my apartment. That conversation got me nowhere—just like every conversation I seemed to be having about Darnell Evans. Why are any clues so elusive?

Back at my apartment, a place that set feng shui back a hundred years, I pulled out a piece of paper from my desk drawer. I needed to take my mind off my life. What was the best way to do that? By meddling into someone else's.

I wrote down my list of suspects, including Elvis's wife, lover, competition, and boss.

His boss. I still needed to talk to Rodger Maloney. Maybe he would have some answers for me. I flipped open my calendar. I could squeeze him in tomorrow morning.

And squeeze him, I would.

👣

Ace Plumbing was tucked into a strip of shops in an older section of Virginia Beach. And when I say older, I mean it was built in the '70s. The business sign was a white rectangle with *Ace* in blue and *Plumbing* beneath it in red. A van with a matching logo sat in the parking lot, taking up a prime parking space.

I pulled my pleather coat closer around me. I really wanted black leather, the sleek sophisticated kind, not a biker-tough one. But of course, being friends with Sierra, I'd never hear the end of it, so I wore a fake plastic version instead. Some things just weren't worth it. If there's one thing my mom taught me, it was to choose my battles wisely.

A girl at the front desk barely looked at me when I asked to see Rodger. Instead, she drearily pointed with a mechanical pencil to an office across the hall. Then she went back to her Sudoku puzzle.

I approached Rodger's office just in time to hear him saying, "Get your lawyers involved if you want! We did nothing wrong, and I stand behind my work." Then I heard a beep. Not quite the same effect as slamming a phone on its receiver.

I peeked my head in the doorway in time to see a red-faced Rodger staring with obvious hatred at the black piece of plastic with an antenna that lay lifeless on his desk calendar. My gaze swept the rest of the room, where I spotted miscellaneous pieces of equipment like computers, monitors, and telephones. It appeared his office also acted as storage for the rest of the building.

The man's eyes flickered to me and narrowed some more. Then he straightened his shoulders, and his jaw seemed to twitch as if he were unable to move and his lips were unable to find anything polite to say.

"Mr. Maloney?"

His fingers laced in front of him, and he leaned back into his chair. I couldn't tell what kind of chair it was because his girth covered the piece of furniture in its entirety.

"Yes?"

"I was hoping I could ask you a few questions."

"Concerning?"

I opened my mouth, but suddenly the man was on his feet.

"Did that woman send you?"

I stepped back, though I didn't mean to. "That woman?" Jamie?

"I told her to go through my lawyers." He let out some not-so-nice words, muttering them while looking at his phone again. "She had to send her lawyer over, didn't she?"

He thought I was a lawyer? That was a first.

"I'm not a lawyer, sir."

His eyes widened. He looked at me some more. Then his face turned red again.

"Then you're from the Better Business Bureau—"

"Sir, I'm investigating the death of Darnell Evans."

He stopped cold. Blinked. Sat down. Laced his fingers again. "What can I do for you then?"

"I heard there was a rift between the two of you."

"He was leaving Ace to start his own business. He wanted to take half of my customers. I would have been put out of business if that happened."

Something wasn't computing. I pushed my thoughts aside and continued asking questions. I'd deal with my doubts later.

"Do you know why he wanted to start his own business?"

He shrugged. "Better money, I assume. He wanted to be his own boss."

"Did the two of you get along?"

"Until he tried to take my customers."

I leaned closer. "What happened then?"

"Then I fired him."

Fired him? Why hadn't I heard anything about that? "When did you fire him?"

"The day he died."

He got fired the day he died? Did Jamie know that? "So he didn't have any appointments that day?" I needed to find out why he left the nursing home early.

"No appointments on my end. I told him to turn in his equipment and get out." He paused and rolled his eyes. "Only I didn't say it that nicely."

I had a feeling this man didn't say anything nicely.

"Where were you on the day he died?"

"I was right here in the office, taking care of these mountains of paperwork."

"Thanks."

I heard Rodger pick up the phone as I left. I stopped by the receptionist and closed her Sudoku book. She glared at me.

"Do you keep track of when Mr. Maloney is in the office?"

"Yeah, I have to know where he is when people call." She tapped her pencil on her puzzle book, clearly annoyed that I'd interrupted her "work."

"Can you check on the date of October 28?" From my calculations, which I'd figured and refigured, that was the day police believed Darnell died.

She shrugged and dropped her pencil. "I guess." She ran a finger across her desk calendar and stopped on the date. "He didn't come in that day. Says he was sick."

Another suspect without an alibi. Perfect.

Now I just had to figure out why Darnell wanted to start his own business here when he was scheduled to headline his own show in Vegas.

CHAPTER 23

I LEFT Ace Plumbing and made it to my afternoon criminal justice class just in time. I soaked in information about laws and justice and crime. Usually, nothing could tear me away from paying attention in class. I loved learning this stuff.

But not today. Today, I couldn't wait to get home. I had a to-do list a mile long. I had houses to clean, a funeral to plan, a murderer to accuse.

Of course, as soon as I walked into my apartment building, Sierra flew into the hallway. Her eyes were wide and sparkling with excitement.

"Guess what?" Sierra asked.

I gripped the front door handle, bracing myself for another animal cruelty horror story. "You've single-handedly managed to save all the whales in the world?"

"No, the news isn't quite that good." Her momentary frown disappeared. "I've been promoted to project manager! The director has been so impressed with my work that she's put me in charge of an entire team. An entire team." She positively beamed.

I released the door and felt strangely like I should give her a hug. I didn't. Instead, I patted her shoulder. "That's great, Sierra."

"I was hoping you might want to go out to eat tonight and celebrate."

Celebrating something sounded like a great distraction. "Name the place."

"There's this new seafood restaurant down on the beach I was hoping to try."

Unusual, since Sierra didn't eat seafood, but what did I know? Maybe they had a special vegan menu. "I'll see if I can round up Riley or anyone else to go. Sound good?"

"Wonderful."

Right before we were supposed to leave, Chad showed up, no doubt to pester me about something. Before I could shoo him away, Riley invited him along to our celebration and promptly received a scowl from me. He'd shrugged innocently.

We piled in two cars to go to the restaurant. I ended up with Chad and Bill McCormick, the right-wing talk-show host in our building who'd just gotten back from his mini-tour. He went on and on about his ex-wife being pregnant with her second husband's child when she never wanted kids with poor Bill. I actually felt sorry for the guy. I really did. But all he ever did was complain. It was enough to make me pull my hair out.

Finally, we arrived at the Virginia Beach oceanfront. Since tourist season was over, the strip was relatively quiet. We parked on the street in front of the restaurant.

"Is this weird to you that Sierra wanted to eat here?" Riley whispered as he pulled the glass door open and held it for me.

"Yeah, a little."

We were seated right away. Small talk ensued, broken up only by the waitress taking our orders.

Rather abruptly, Sierra placed her napkin on the table and stood. I feared she was going to give a long, drawn-out speech on what her new position would mean to all the animals on the planet. Instead, she announced, "I'm going to run to the restroom."

She disappeared between a maze of tables. I stared out the window at the ocean and the sunset smeared behind it. Gray waves swelled, then crashed and receded. The process repeated itself over and over. Some things would seem like a broken record doing so, but not the waves. Watching them felt therapeutic.

"Beautiful, isn't it?" Chad said across from me.

"Yeah, it really is. It's mesmerizing."

"Maybe in the summer I could teach you to surf. There's nothing like being one with the waves."

So Chad planned on sticking around through the summer, huh? But I had no desire to surf. It brought back too many thoughts of Dad. Surfing had been his demise, his idol. I didn't answer and continued to stare out the wall of windows in front of me.

Poor Sharon, the owner of the Grounds, was listening to Bill talk about how huge his ex looked now that she was pregnant. I even think I heard him say that he hoped she didn't lose the weight after the baby was born. Love could turn pretty ugly, couldn't it?

"You're being quiet," Riley said beside me.

"Just thinking."

Chad rubbed the scruff around his mouth. "About what?"

"Life. Dying. Relationships."

"You know what I say?" Chad started. "Life's a Dance You Learn as You Go."

I smiled at the song reference. "Or as my favorite redhead said, 'It's a Hard Knock Life.'"

Riley's gaze darted between the two of us as if he'd just entered a new world where people understood me. Gabby's world. I liked the sound of that.

Chad and I smiled at each other across the table.

In the distance, I saw the waitress appear with a tray of food balanced above her head. I could taste my grilled salmon now, and my mouth began to water. I loved a good seafood dish.

The waitress placed a salad at Sierra's empty seat. What was taking the girl so long? Should I go check on her? It seemed like such a motherly thing to do, checking on someone in the bathroom. The girl could take care of herself.

I'd give her five minutes before I got up.

I glanced behind me, just in time to see Sierra duck behind the crab aquarium. Most restaurants had lobsters in aquariums, but this one had decided to try something new. You could pick your own crabs to boil. Just lovely.

"Oh no," I muttered. Suddenly, everything made sense.

"Free the crabs!" I heard my friend shout on the other side of the restaurant.

The next thing I knew, the aquarium fell over. Water gushed all over the restaurant's new carpet. And little red crustaceans with gigantic claws surfed toward me. I screamed and jumped on my chair.

Riley muttered, "Sierra."

Bill laughed hysterically, probably glad for the fodder for his talk show tomorrow.

Chad said, "Dude," and watched with obvious fascination as the crabs drifted our way.

And a very angry, managerial-looking man ran from the kitchen area, screaming, "What have you done? What have you done, you ignorant little fool!"

"Run little crabs! Run! You can make it to the ocean, to freedom!" Sierra shouted, all the while urging the beasts toward me. Okay, actually toward the door behind me. Semantics.

"Do you know how much I paid for those per pound?" the managerial-looking man asked. "You're going to repay every dime and then some." He picked up a crab and promptly yelped and flung it across the room.

The crabs looked a little confused, like they didn't know where to go once the wave of aquarium water left them washed up on the plush carpet.

"You can't put a price tag on a life, you sick little puppy." Sierra stood on a chair and began preaching. "These crabs deserve to live, not to be sentenced to death in a hot tub and then eaten by sad carnivores who don't know the meaning of moderation." She ran toward the crabs, which sent them clucking our way. I screamed again and continued standing on the chair, imagining what it would feel like if one of those suckers got ahold of my toe.

I looked over just in time to see Chad opening the door that led to the beach. "This way, little guys." He waved his hand in a come-hither motion.

The crabs clucked toward him as if they understood.

"I'm calling the cops!" Manager Man shouted. "This is insanity! Do you realize what you've done?"

"Put me in jail! It's worth it to save a life. Your method of cooking these creatures is beyond cruel and unusual punishment. You boil them to death while they try desperately to escape the pot of death . . ."

She continued, but I tuned her out.

Please, tell me this was a nightmare. What would Parker say if one of his comrades in arms showed up to this scene and spotted me here? Wouldn't that just be the icing on the cake? I could hear him lecturing me now.

"Look what you've done! I had them shipped in from Maryland. Maryland, I tell you. Have you lost your mind?"

"Crabs have feelings too! How would you like to be boiled alive?"

Customers ran to the front door as if next Sierra might pull out a pipe bomb. I almost ran out the door myself.

"Everybody calm down."

I looked over as Riley took control of the situation. The logical lawyer in him emerged.

"Sierra, I advise you to have a seat and not say another word until the police get here," Riley said. Then he turned to Manager Man. "And sir, your yelling is doing nothing to calm down your patrons, so I suggest you keep your voice down so that you can try and resolve this situation in a mature manner."

"I'll show you mature." The manager came toward Riley swinging. My eyes widened as I realized the man was trying to punch Riley. Riley ducked, and when he came up, I could see the frustration on his face. Manager Man wasn't the most athletic-looking man, so I had no doubt Riley could take him. But Riley wasn't the type to take anybody in a fistfight—only in the courtroom.

I looked up at the door just as Parker, two uniformed cops, and a woman wearing a suit entered. Parker's gaze zeroed in on me as if he had some kind of trouble radar and could always manage to find me in the midst of it. I couldn't read his expression, but I'm pretty sure there was some embarrassment there.

His attention turned to Manager Man as he tried to take another swing at Riley, who again managed to duck the punch with graceful precision. In three steps, Parker was across the room and grabbing Manager Man's arm.

"What do you think you're doing?" he asked, his voice authoritative and . . . a little scary, if I were to be honest. It made me cringe.

"That woman turned over my crabs! She's insane!"

By now, the restaurant had cleared of everyone except for our table, the staff, and the cops. I looked down and saw a lone crab bobbing toward my chair. I glanced at Chad and nodded toward the gourmet meal at my feet. While everyone else's attention was distracted, Chad scooped the creature up in an oversized linen napkin and shooed him outside.

"Someone tell me what's going on here!"

Everyone quieted at Parker's instruction. My boyfriend's gaze fell on me. "Gabby, would you like to start?"

I cringed. "Not really."

"I'll tell you what happened," Sierra started. She hopped down from her chair and pointed an accusing finger at the manager and his wait staff. "These people were keeping these crabs in captivity."

"Crabs? This is all about blue crabs?" Parker ran a hand over his face, and then he turned to Sierra. "You're behind this, right?"

"People applauded Martin Luther King Jr. when he stood up for the rights of the living."

Parker shook his head. "He stood up for people's rights, not crabs."

"And he was a hero."

He grabbed her arm, not hard though. "I'm going to have to take you in, Sierra."

"But I'm your girlfriend's best friend. You can't arrest me."

Parker's face turned red. I knew Riley saw it too, because he glanced over at me.

"Why don't you take her in, Parker, and I'll get statements from all these witnesses," the woman said.

He nodded at her and led Sierra outside. She was still talking incessantly about Susan B. Anthony, Rosa Brown, and Abraham Lincoln.

The woman approached our table, and I wondered if she was a trainee or something. I'd never seen her before. And where was Parker's new partner? I'd yet to meet him.

The suited woman looked at me before pulling out a pad and pen. "I'm Detective Charlie Henderson. Who'd like to start?"

CHAPTER 24

MY JAW fell to the floor. This was Charlie? No wonder Parker looked so happy to have a new partner. She had legs a mile long, a flat stomach, and an anything-but-flat chest.

"Are you okay, ma'am?" Charlie asked. I realized the woman was looking directly at me. I nodded, in a daze. "Would you like to start?"

This was his partner? I couldn't believe it.

"Ma'am?"

I tried to focus on her face, her perfect, pretty little face. "Yes?"

"Would you like to start?"

Had Parker led me to believe Charlie was a he, or had I assumed the fact? "Not really."

"I'll start." I looked up and saw Riley approaching. He glanced at me as if he understood every single thought going through my mind. Impossible. Wasn't it? He filled Charlie in on everything that had transpired. I continued to stare.

The woman was a redhead also. But it wasn't curly and red like mine. Hers was sleek and perfectly styled and had a bronzed finish to it. She was tall and slender. Her complexion was flawless.

I'd bet she never embarrassed Parker.

Insecurities hit me faster than that aquarium had hit the ground. Flashbacks of Riley's fiancée showing up paraded through my mind. Was there something about me that just said, "Please, cheat on me"? Of course, Riley and I hadn't been officially dating, so it wasn't officially cheating. And I had no proof that Parker was cheating on me, only a crab pot full of insecurities that told me I wasn't good enough.

I'm a scientist. I'm supposed to be unemotional and base my theories on facts. Was I doomed to fail in my career of choice?

◦ ◦

Chad drove me back to my apartment, while Riley went down to the jail to see about getting Sierra out. I wanted to go, but Riley seemed to think it best if he went alone. So I let him.

But I was still thinking about Charlie.

Of all people, why did a beautiful woman have to be assigned to partner with my boyfriend? Didn't. Seem. Fair.

"That was a riot, huh?" Chad shut off the ignition and looked at me with those sparkling eyes of his. Sparkling eyes were my downfall, but I wouldn't go there. Not. In. The. Mood.

"Yeah, a riot."

He walked me up to my apartment, seemingly oblivious to my inner turmoil. Either that, or he ignored it. Then again, did he even know I dated Parker? I glanced at Chad with his hands stuffed deep into the pockets of his jeans, his tousled hair, and his oversized, cable-knit sweater. Clueless would be my best guess when it came to Chad.

"Hey, do you mind if I check out your Web site?"

I stopped and leaned against my apartment door with my arms across my chest. "Why?" Did he want to one-up me when he designed his own Web site?

"I'm just curious to see what you've done."

"Am I supposed to believe that?"

He grinned that lazy grin of his. "Okay, fine. I've already seen your site."

"And you want to see it again, why?"

"I had some ideas I wanted to subtly bring up. I thought being subtle wouldn't hurt your feelings as much as the harsh truth."

I ignored that last comment. "You want to give me some Web site ideas. I'm your competition."

"I thought you were my friend."

Oh, he was smooth. Real smooth.

And was he my friend? I mean, sure, we'd been talking quite a bit lately. But friends? I'd have to ponder that one later. Right now, I pondered my Web site. "What's wrong with my site?"

He leaned against the wall beside me. "I really think if you add some before-and-after pictures of your cleaning scenes that it will give people a better idea of what you do."

I hadn't thought of that before, but the feature could be productive. I already had a stack of before-and-after pictures that I'd taken for insurance purposes. If I did use Chad's idea, I wouldn't post the really gruesome photos. I'd like to say that people wouldn't want to see them, but I know there are a lot of crazies who would.

I already had listed on my Web site all of my certifications, the services I offered, even a couple of testimonials. Pictures could do the trick though.

I pushed myself from the door and unlocked it. I motioned for Chad to follow me inside, where I went immediately to my computer. Thanks to Amy, I logged on. I smiled this time when my user name and password worked. Note to self: change user name and password in case anything like that ever happens again.

I typed in my Web site and waited for the pages to appear. As I waited, I stared out the window at the dark, nighttime sky. I couldn't see any stars, not here in Ghent. But a streetlight did reflect on some tree branches and look rather lovely.

My computer was running especially slow today. What had Amy said? I should get a new modem or something. Maybe I'd buy myself one for Christmas.

I tapped my fingers on the keys as I waited for my brilliant business, Trauma Care, to flash onto my computer screen. I'd paid some big bucks to have this Web site done a few months back. I needed to think of an effective marketing ploy to get the word out about my business. I'd done the Yellow Pages ad. I often went to fresh crime scenes to leave my card. But this way, people could be directed to my Web site to get an idea of my prices and what I did.

"Come on, come on." Maybe that new modem wouldn't wait until Christmas.

Finally, my page popped on the screen. "Here it is."

Chad came up behind me and peered over my shoulder at my Web page. I got a whiff of . . . well, he smelled like salty ocean air, actually. And I liked it. I needed to have my head examined, good and hard.

I blinked at what I saw on my computer screen. It wasn't my page.

I checked the Web address. Nothing wrong there. So what had happened?

Chad leaned in closer. "Did you update it since yesterday?"

I scrolled down on the page and drew in a quick breath. Someone had hacked into my site. Gone were all of my beautiful pages. In their place was the outline of a body and the words, "The only crime scene you need to worry about is your own."

CHAPTER 25

"WHOA."

I stared at the page, imagining all too clearly the outline of my own body on the floor. "Whoa is right. That's a threat."

Chad's arm draped the back of my computer chair. And though I was in crisis mode, I not only noticed the action, I liked it. Head examined, Gabby. Put it on your to-do list.

"Someone knows you're on to them."

"You think?" Calm down on the sarcasm, Gabby. Calm down. "How did they do this? And how do I get my Web site back?"

"People experienced with computers can do amazing things."

A new thought popped into my mind, and I swerved my head around to face Chad. "How good are you with computers? Did you want to come up here under the guise of helping me when in fact you just wanted to see my reaction to the catastrophe you created?"

Chad backed up. "Whoa."

I stood and glared. "Did you?"

"Gabby, I wouldn't do that to you."

I stepped closer and stared into those hazel eyes of his. "Are you trying to ruin my business by ruining my Web site and disguising it as a threat?"

Chad caught my finger, which at some moment had started to point at him, and jerked it to a halt. His hands covered mine with surprising strength. "No, Gabby. I didn't do that to you. You need to chill."

"Chill? Chill?" I wanted to flail my arms, but Chad still held my hands for some reason unbeknownst to me. "How can I chill when someone is intent on ruining me? Why can't anything in my life go right?"

129

I wanted to collapse in tears and feel sorry for myself because my boyfriend, whom I loathed, had a beautiful partner. Because my business, which was really just a temporary job on my way to being a forensic investigator, had been tampered with. Because my life, which when compared to the people I cleaned up after wasn't that bad, felt empty.

But I didn't collapse. I didn't believe in feeling sorry for myself. At least not in front of other people.

After I fell silent for a moment, Chad lowered his hands while still holding mine. "Are you okay now?"

"Define okay."

"This isn't the end of the world."

I took my voice down a couple of notches. "But it could be the end of my life. What's the difference?"

Chad locked gazes with me. His look told me he silently pleaded for my logic to return. "You know I didn't do this, right?"

Deep inside I did. "Maybe."

"You should call the police."

"They can't do anything."

"Call them anyway."

"Fine." I would if I got around to it—which I most likely wouldn't. I'd blame it on my growing to-do list. A girl's gotta have priorities.

"And you should be careful. Really careful. You're on someone's list."

I pictured the dead mold man. Yeah, I was on someone's list for sure. In fact, my name was probably highlighted and moved to the top.

So whoever had changed my password earlier had done it on purpose. The action hadn't been a random prank. When would I ever be that lucky? No, they'd hacked into my site and threatened me.

Which of my suspects was capable of doing this? Did Lynette have some hidden tech genius inside? Doubted it. Jamie? Doubted it even more. Rodger Maloney might be capable of it. I remembered all that computer equipment scattered around in his office.

I shivered. I didn't want to think about my own personal crime scene.

The next day, after a fitful night of sleep, I cleaned Mr. Hermit's house. I was almost finished with the project, but I had to stop early in order to clean up after an accidental death-by-power-tool. Surprisingly, the scene wasn't too messy, but the family wanted me to remove any reminders of what had happened. The job probably took two hours altogether, and that's only because I threw in some extra services, things like adding some sanitizer to the air and wiping down surfaces around the scene. I take my job seriously and want to leave the houses sparkling and families comforted.

At home that afternoon—after checking on Sierra, who'd been released on bond with a temporary restraining order—I had to make some phone calls, starting with the man who designed my Web site. He said he had a backup of my site and would get my space live again in a couple of days. I didn't bother to ask how much he would charge. I didn't want to know.

Afterward, I briefly considered calling my dad to acknowledge his e-mail. I decided not to. I'd wait first and see if he'd walk the talk. Anyone could claim to change. The hard part was actually doing it.

I cast thoughts of my dad aside, realizing they were getting me nowhere. Instead, I found the number of the Las Vegas hotel where Darnell was supposed to headline. I called and asked to speak to the event coordinator. I was then directed to someone in marketing, who directed me to someone else whose title I instantly forgot.

A fast-talking man came on the line. "What can I do for you?"

I stared at the picture of the glitzy hotel on my computer screen and visualized Darnell Evans standing outside of it. The images just didn't mesh in my mind. "I'm wondering about an act you had lined up to come in. I can't find it listed on your Web site, though. It's for an Elvis tribute artist named Darnell Evans. He's supposed to be headlining a show at your hotel."

The man laughed. And continued laughing. An all-out laugh. Not just a chuckle.

What was going on?

"Lady, we don't have any Elvis impersonators do shows here. You must be thinking of a hotel somewhere on the other side of the strip. We're a classy joint. You know, we have people like Celine and Barry, even Mariah. But no Elvis."

I tapped my finger against my mouse. "I guess I don't need to ask you if you're sure about that."

He hung up, still laughing.

I put the phone down and leaned back in my computer chair. So Darnell had lied about getting his own show. Why would he do that? What exactly was he planning? And when did he plan on telling people?

While I was on the net, I decided to search for Mr. Hermit's family. I'd found some photos in his closet, and one of them had a name on the back. I liked to imagine that the boy in the photo was Mr. Hermit's son, that they'd lost touch, but that the son would be exceedingly happy to find out his father still loved him. That he'd be saddened by his death and grateful that I was thinking about throwing a funeral for the man he called Dad.

I typed in the man's first name with Mr. Hermit's last name. Twelve entries appeared. I ruled out five of them just based on the birth date that came up. I decided to start calling the rest of them.

The first two numbers had no answers. The third was an answering machine with a different name on it. The fourth rang and rang. I was about to hang up when a man came on the line.

"Hi, I'm trying to find the family of Richard Spruce."

Silence reigned a moment, and I held my breath. Finally, he said, "This is his son."

I stood and paced my way into the kitchen. "Just to confirm we're speaking of the same Richard Spruce, did your father live in Virginia Beach?"

"Yes, he did."

Wow, I'd actually found the man's son. With the phone under my chin, I propelled myself onto the kitchen counter, one of my favorite places to sit and think. I gripped the phone and tried to think of the right words.

"Sir, I'm sorry to tell you that your father has passed away." My eyes locked on the parking lot outside as I awaited his response.

"Yeah, I know." The man's voice sounded icy. I continued anyway, determined to do my good deed.

"I'm in the process of going through your father's things and—"

"I don't care what you do with them. Same thing I told my father's landlord. I hadn't spoken to my father in fifteen years. I didn't want anything to do with him while he was living, and I sure don't want anything to do with him in dying."

The sadness I felt surprised even me. "I see."

He grunted, and I feared he might hang up.

"Sir?"

"Yeah?"

"Are there any other family members who might care?"

"Just me. And I don't give a—" The man hung up the phone before I could hear the rest of his sentence.

I put the phone down and looked out the window some more at the sunny day outside. What had happened between the man and his son? How could it have been so bad that not even death could mend the hurt?

It looked like I'd be planning that funeral after all.

I picked up the phone and called Amy to see if the church would help out. I'd planned one funeral in my life, and I didn't really desire to plan another one by myself. Amy didn't answer—probably at work—so I left a message. Between the church and Chad, I should be able to plan something.

As soon as I hung up, the phone rang. Maybe Amy was monitoring her calls. I snatched the phone up and said, "Thanks for calling back."

"Gabby?"

The voice didn't sound like Amy's.

"Yes?"

"This is Charlie."

Of course. Charlie. I didn't have time to commiserate. Her voice sounded strained.

"Gabby, Parker's been shot. You need to come to the hospital now."

CHAPTER 26

"GABBY?"

I looked up to see Riley sliding his key into the door to his apartment. A wrinkle formed between his eyes, and he stepped toward me.

I bypassed my friend and started downstairs, holding tight to the railing so I wouldn't stumble. "I can't talk."

"What's wrong?"

I heard footsteps behind me.

"I have to get to the hospital."

"Why?"

I stopped on the first floor, and Riley collided into me. I turned around and wanted to crumple into my friend's arms. "Parker was shot. By a bank robber. In his chest. They don't know if he'll make it."

Suddenly, Riley had my keys. "I'm driving."

Riley was probably just home for lunch break. He had important cases to work on, people to help, appointments to keep. He was a busy lawyer. "You don't have to. You're working." I reached for my keys.

His hand grasped my elbow, guiding me outside. "I insist."

A moment later, I sat in the passenger seat of his well-used Toyota Corolla. It sputtered to life, and I stared at the world around me as Riley drove to Norfolk General. I closed my eyes, picturing a bullet entering Parker's chest, close to his heart. I imagined the pain on his face, the grimace. The tough guy giving in to a gut-wrenching cry.

The last time I'd spoken to Parker, our conversation had been tense. I didn't even tell him that I was being aloof because I felt insecure about Charlie. I just left it a mystery for him to figure out. He'd sighed and left.

134

What if that was our last conversation?

The hospital was only a couple of blocks away. Riley parked and then slipped his arm around me as we hurried into the emergency room. It was as if he knew I might turn to gel at any moment—and yes, the human body really could turn into gel. I'd seen it with my own eyes.

I spotted Charlie sitting with a few other uniforms. Our eyes connected, and she stood. I rushed to her. "How is he?"

Her eyes were red, as if she'd been crying. "He's in surgery."

"And?"

She remained stiff. "And that's all we know."

"Did you catch the person who did this?"

She nodded once. "We did."

"I hope he rots in jail."

I sat in an uncomfortable chair across from Charlie, Riley beside me, leaning on his knees and his eyes closed. Praying maybe?

Please God, let him be okay.

There I was praying again. But none of my usual cynical thoughts emerged with the prayer. This time I wanted to believe. I wanted there to be a God who cared about whether Parker made it or not. I wanted to have a hope that a higher being was in charge.

Hours ticked by. Someone brought me some coffee, a doughnut. No doubt it was a police officer. They liked stuff like coffee and doughnuts apparently. And here I was thinking my sarcastic thoughts even in the midst of possibly losing my boyfriend. What was wrong with me? Couldn't I turn my sarcasm off even for a minute?

I might lose my boyfriend. I mean sure, we didn't always get along. But I didn't want things to end this way. He was still Parker. My Parker. He was the one who called me names and made fun of me for investigating cases I wasn't supposed to investigate. If something happened to him . . .

Finally, a man in scrubs came through the doors. Charlie perked, so I figured this must be the surgeon. Parker's surgeon.

I held my breath. I didn't want to hear what he had to say. I wanted to hear it.

Charlie and I both approached.

The surgeon's wrinkled face looked exhausted. "He's okay."

I let out the breath I held. Thank you, Jesus.

"The bullet missed his heart by less than a centimeter," the surgeon continued. "He must have had someone watching over him."

"Can we see him?" Charlie beat me to the question.

"He's resting now. It's probably better if you just come back tomorrow and give him tonight to recover."

"But he shouldn't be alone." No one should be alone during hard times.

"His sister is with him."

Parker had a sister? I think I vaguely remembered hearing about her. Still, it was weird that she was here and in the room with Parker, and I didn't even know it.

What did I really know about that man? Our conversations had never been particularly deep, but . . . Parker had a sister?

Riley led me again to his car. It was dark outside. I didn't have any words, only exhaustion.

Back at home, I fell into bed, something in my heart feeling unsettled.

CHAPTER 27

I NEEDED to put the finishing touches on Mr. Hermit's house the next morning. But first I had to visit Parker. Maybe meet his sister. Then I had another job to do in the evening.

I parked at the hospital, went inside, and was directed to the ICU. I buzzed in to the nurses, and they unlocked the door to the unit. Once inside, I passed patients wearing blah hospital gowns, hooked up to beeping machines, and surrounded by family members with red, tired eyes. The nurse had said that Parker's bed would be the fifth on the right.

I stopped when I heard familiar voices. Charlie was already here. Go figure.

I peered around the corner, unnoticed.

What I saw muted the world to me.

Parker and Charlie stared at each other, smiling, murmuring.

The thing is, I'd never seen Parker look at me like that. Never.

And I can't say that I'd ever looked at Parker the way Charlie gazed at him. Ever.

Parker spotted me. A different kind of grin spread across his face. He held out his arm. "Gabby."

I forced a smile, though inwardly reeling over the realization that my boyfriend was in love with someone else. I wasn't even sure if he knew it.

"Hey, you." I grabbed his hand on the opposite side of the bed from Charlie.

I'd never seen Parker look like this. Circles under his eyes. Perfectly styled hair out of place. Skin pale. Wearing an outfit that cost less than two hundred dollars. His eyes looked doped up still, and I had no doubt that some type of painkiller was dripping in through that IV.

He kissed my hand and then patted the bed beside him.

I carefully lowered myself there. "You gave us a scare."

"Yeah, I gave myself a scare."

Charlie cleared her throat. "I'll be back later. I'll give you two some privacy."

Parker nodded. Watched her walk away. Turned back to me.

"You okay?"

I nodded, feeling like I should be the one asking him that question. "Yeah. Now that I know you're okay."

"I owe my life to that woman, you know."

"What woman?"

He smiled, though weakly. "Charlie."

"How so?"

"She was about to take the bullet for me. Pushed me out of the way. That bullet could have hit my heart, I hear. Then she called for backup and tracked down the guy who shot me."

"Wow, she sounds like some kind of woman."

"I guess she's been all over the news this morning."

I hadn't watched. No time. I had to break my normal routine because I was running out of hours.

"Where's your sister?" I looked around the area for evidence that she'd been here.

"She had to go home to take care of her kids. She'll be back later."

She lived that close? Why didn't I know that? It seemed like something you'd tell your girlfriend.

Parker's eyelids drooped. This wasn't the time to ask him about his family. Instead, I squeezed his hand. "Get some rest."

"Come back later?"

I smiled, though I knew it didn't touch my eyes. "Of course."

Before I stood, he was asleep.

◦ ◦

I had to call Amy back again. She'd left a message on my machine. Said there was a small group meeting tonight at Riley's. That I should attend and talk about the funeral. It would be casual. There'd be free food.

Free food, the key to every single's heart.

Before I could dial her number, Chad called.

"What are you up to today?" he asked.

Did I even want to mention Parker? Not really. I'd keep to the basics. "Just doing a few jobs. And you?"

"Trying to figure out what I'm going to do."

"You could help me." What had I just said? Chad Davis was my competition. I wanted to retract my hasty words.

"I'd love to."

I paused. "Really?" I considered my options. It would be really nice to have someone helping me. My day would go by faster, the work would be halved.

"Of course. Apparently you've got the market on crime-scene cleaning in the area. I'm finding it hard to break in."

Pride swelled in me. Ha! Take that Chad Davis.

"Fine then. Since you're desperate." I waited for a reaction, but when I heard none I continued. "Meet me at the job site." I rattled off the address.

I continued, not believing what had just transpired. I hoped I wouldn't regret this.

I was packing up the last of Mr. Hermit's things when I heard a knock at the door. I found Chad standing on the front steps with a dopey grin on his face. "I'm here to serve."

"Just what I like to hear." I started walking back down the hallway. "The man's son gave the landlord permission to sell all of Mr. Hermit's possessions. The furniture has already been taken away, and I'm just going through the small stuff now, deciding what can be thrown away and what can be donated."

"Did you say Mr. Hermit? Is that the man's name?"

"Not really. Sometimes I give people names like that because it makes them seem less real. Then I get less emotionally involved."

"Why do I have a feeling that's not true?"

"Okay, it's in an effort to get less emotionally involved."

"There's nothing wrong with showing some emotions."

"I want to be a scientist."

"You are a scientist. Even scientists have feelings."

"No, feelings cripple me. They don't allow me to be objective."

"Is anyone really objective?"

"I don't know." I turned on my heel and headed back down the hallway. "Right now I'm down to the nitty-gritty of receipts and past tax returns. Nothing too compelling. I'm thinking I should be able to finish up here today. Then I have another job to go to. If I still like you by the end of this job, you're welcome to join me on the next."

"How kind of you."

I pointed to the largest box in the corner. "You take that one. I'll finish here." I picked up a shoebox.

"Again, your kindness is astounding." He knelt beside the box. "So what am I doing again?"

"Just make sure he doesn't have any diamond rings or insurance policies hidden in those papers."

I'm sure his son would be more than happy to collect on those, though he wanted nothing to do with his father's death.

"So, how did you get started in doing this, Gabby?"

"My mom died; I had to drop out of college because of mounting bills. I wanted to do something that made me feel like I wasn't a total and complete failure in the life department."

"Giving up your dreams for your family is noble."

"Is it noble if it's driven by guilt?"

He didn't say anything. And for some reason, I continued.

"My brother was kidnapped on my watch when I was ten years old. It turned my family upside down. My father started drinking again. Stopped working. My mother had to get a part-time job on top of her forty-hour-a-week job. I think my father's always blamed me. That's why he doesn't feel guilty collecting money from my paycheck. It's retribution."

"What happened with your brother?"

"He was never found." In my best nightmare, I imagined him growing up with another family and thinking everything was normal. That he had a mother and father that showed him some kind of twisted love and that they'd kidnapped him to fill an empty void in their life. In my worst nightmares . . . well, I never went there. I couldn't.

"Did you find it hard to get started in this business?"

I shrugged, remembering those early days of feeling totally out of my zone. I'd kept my chin up and pretended like I knew what I was doing. "I started cold. Big mistake. I didn't think I needed any training to clean houses. I mean, I knew enough about hazmat materials to know you just didn't stick them in the Dumpster. But I quickly discovered that I needed more. I got certified, and I still take courses on occasion so I can be the best crime-scene cleaner possible. I keep adding equipment to the business." I left out the fact that a few months ago much of my equipment had been burned when a house I was cleaning was set on fire. Thankfully, I was insured.

I plunked the shoebox down with a thud, crossed my legs, and leaned against the wall. "Your turn."

He rested his arms against the top of the oversized box. "What do you want to know?"

"Why a crime-scene cleaner? Why give up a job as a funeral home director?"

He shrugged. "It gets to you after a while. I couldn't do it anymore. I'd trained for all those years to do the job. Did it for two years. Then I woke up and realized how miserable I was. The job had robbed my joy. Some people can do that job and go on with their lives, like it doesn't affect them. Not me. So I sold my house, my car, and my plasma TV. Decided I wanted something simpler. Now I'm renting an apartment in Ocean View. Driving a beat-up Vanagon. Doing odd jobs on the side. Surfing. Skiing. And I'll keep doing that until the money runs out and I realize I have to grow up."

Hearing his story made Chad Davis seem much more human.

"And that's how two weirdos got to be crime-scene cleaners," I said.

"Amen and amen."

We both began to work silently again. After a few minutes, Chad looked up. "This is the guy whose funeral you're planning, isn't it?"

"Supposedly. I haven't done very much planning lately. Plus, none of his family wants anything to do with him."

"I wonder what happened."

"Yeah, me too."

Chad plucked a letter from the box. "Maybe this has something to do with it."

"What's it say?" I leaned forward.

As Chad opened the letter, the paper crinkled in protest. His eyes scanned the words before he cleared his throat and began reading. "I can't believe you actually married that woman, Dad. I tried to warn you that she was no good, but you didn't listen. Now, I don't want anything to do with you. As far as I'm concerned you made your choice: her over me."

Chad lowered the letter and our gazes met.

"They had a rift because his father got married?" I asked. If my father got remarried, I'd be jumping for joy. Finally, he'd have someone else to take care of him.

"Maybe the woman was out for his money."

I looked around the house, which was nothing to brag about. "Doubt it." I pointed at the box. "Are there more letters?"

Chad dug around inside before emerging with a handful of envelopes. "Some that have been returned, addressed to his son."

I leaned forward, itching to get my fingers on those papers. "Can we open them?"

"Who's here to stop us?"

I eyeballed them when guilt hit me. "It somehow feels wrong."

"His son left all of the man's stuff to you, did he not?"

I remembered our conversation. "In a manner of speaking."

Chad ripped open an envelope. "Then there's nothing illegal."

"How about on a moral level?"

He paused. "We don't have to read them if you don't want to."

I grabbed another letter. "No, I really want to."

Chad began reading aloud the letter he invaded. "I've thought about what you said. You're right. I shouldn't be with Susan. You're more impor-tant to me. Please come back home."

"When's it postmarked?"

He flipped the envelope over. "Ten years ago."

I didn't expect the weight that pressed on my chest. "Sad."

"Very."

We cleaned the rest of the house in silence.

CHAPTER 28

"SO, DID I pass your test?" Chad wound the vacuum cleaner cord around the cylinder designed to hold it in place.

I collected various cleaning supplies and placed them in the container I used to cart them around. "I suppose I'll allow you to come to my next job with me."

Chad paused from his winding. "You'll allow me?"

I, on the other hand, didn't miss a beat as I gathered things to leave. "That's correct. I'll allow it."

His hands went to his hips. "Maybe I don't want to."

"Okay, fine. Then don't."

"Maybe I do want to."

I stopped working long enough to give him a dirty look. "Make up your mind, snail! You are half inside your house and halfway out!"

"What?" His voice rose in pitch as if I were a total mystery to him.

"It's my favorite haiku."

"O . . . okay." He continued to put the vacuum cleaner together.

"So anyway, I have to go clean up a house that an SUV drove through. They're supposed to be releasing the scene"—I glanced at my watch—"in eleven minutes."

"What can you even clean up? Isn't it going to just be bricks and wood?"

"Two people were killed. I doubt the family will want to live there again, if the place doesn't end up being condemned. But I'm going to assess the damage, see if I can contract some work out for patching the hole where a bay window used to be. Then I'll get rid of some furniture, have the carpet cleaned, put out an AirScrub or two."

"Of course."

"So, what do you say?" I really wanted him to come with me. Being with Chad was much better than being alone with my thoughts.

"I'm in."

"Great, we can drop your car at your apartment, and then you can ride with me." I remembered his Vanagon. "It will look more professional than both of us driving separately."

As I closed the door to Mr. Hermit's house, I realized I would miss this place. I felt like I'd gotten to know the man during my days cleaning here. Sadness pressed in on me as I remembered the way the man had died alone, with no one there to mourn his death. I'd stuck the rest of the letters into my pocket when Chad wasn't looking. I had to know if there was more information. Who was the woman? What had happened to make the son dislike her so much? What had happened to end their marriage?

I called the landlord on the way out to let him know I'd finished. He said he'd stick the check in the mail. I told him I'd stop by tomorrow to pick it up. I couldn't rely on other people's timetables for payment.

I glanced at the clock in the van. It was almost three. I had to go to this job and still stop by to visit Parker again. My heart panged at the thought of him. Parker and I had been through a lot together. I mean, sure, he got on my nerves. And I think I embarrassed him. And we had little in common other than investigating—him on an official level, and mine on a not-so-official level.

And I'd never looked at him like Charlie did.

The weight on my chest began to crumble. I even laughed. Out loud. Which caused Chad to give me a strange look.

Why was I mourning over this new realization? Parker and I weren't meant to be together. Charlie had helped me to realize that. I knew I could finally close this chapter in my life.

If I'd really been in love with Parker, would I have left his bedside? No. I'd have stayed with him all day. I would have cried all night when the hospital made me leave.

"Should I be driving?" Chad asked.

"Why do you ask?"

"Maybe some of those fumes are getting to you. You know, you have to be careful working with chemicals . . ."

"No, I'm fine. I'm great actually."

• •

Chad and I stayed at the hit-and-run house for four hours. I would have been there until the wee hours of the morning had Chad not been with me. He was helpful. Very helpful. His muscles came in handy. Plus, he had a great manner with the family, easing them and speaking in comforting tones. The father and daughter hadn't been there. An aunt was taking care of cleaning up the mess while the immediate family mourned.

And this is why I'd never touch alcohol.

My father had succumbed to its evil lure early on in my life. And I'd seen way too many other stupid things that people did as a result of alcohol.

A drunk driver had run off the road and crashed into this family's house while they were watching Saturday morning cartoons together. I squeezed the image out of my mind as I drove back.

I had to go visit Parker.

The clock told me it was almost eight.

I bet visiting hours ended at nine, if not earlier. I sucked in a breath.

"Everything okay?" Chad asked.

"I need to go to the hospital."

"Are you hurt?"

"No." I paused, contemplating what to say next. "Parker was shot last night. I need to go visit him before visiting hours end."

"Parker? Isn't he your boyfriend?" Chad straightened and stared at me.

"Yeah, I guess you could say that." Not for long, though.

"Why do you seem so blasé about it?"

"I seem blasé?" I pointed to myself for effect. Did I really seem like I didn't care? Last night, I felt like I might break in two.

"You're not going to make it in time if you stop to get my van."

I bit my lip. "I know."

"I'll go with you. But I'll wait in the waiting room, of course. You can drop me off afterward."

"Really?"

"Sure. I don't have any plans."

"Thanks, Chad."

"No problem. That's what friends are for."

▮ ▮

Charlie sat beside Parker when I walked into his hospital room. She stood to leave when I arrived, but I put my hand on her shoulder and gently pushed her back down into the plastic seat beside Parker's bed.

Her face looked full of questions.

"Stay. Please," I insisted.

She looked postured to spring. "Are you sure?"

"Positive." I sat on the other side of Parker and took his hand. He smiled weakly, not the million-dollar smile I'm used to seeing. "How are you?"

"I'm okay. Ready to get back to work." He glanced at Charlie, and the two exchanged a look.

"The doctor said you'll be staying home for at least a couple of weeks." I patted his hand and wondered how this gorgeous man had ever taken notice of me. "Then you'll have desk duty for a while to make sure you've fully recovered."

"That's going to be a beast." He groaned and pushed his head into the pillow behind him.

Charlie waved a finger at him. "You have to take care of yourself, or you're not going to be healthy enough to do your job. I don't want to lose you . . . as a partner."

I watched the two of them interact, stunned by how perfect they were for each other. Why had I ever thought Parker and I were right for each other? Or had I just been reeling over being dumped by Riley for his fiancée?

Or maybe I was—I hated to even think it—lonely and desperate. Maybe that's why I felt so deeply for Mr. Hermit. Because I could relate to him.

I didn't want to live my life alone.

Impulsively, I asked, "Do you both want to come to my place for Thanksgiving dinner?"

Parker and Charlie both jerked their heads toward me and stared as if I'd just offered the two law enforcement officers a puff from a crack pipe.

Parker squeezed my hand, as if concerned about my mental well-being. "Gabby, you don't cook."

I shrugged. "Minor detail. So what do you say? Do you have plans, Charlie?"

She threw a worried glance at Parker before connecting with my gaze. "No, my family all lives up in New York. I won't be able to make it home."

I looked at Parker. "And you?"

"Gabby, are you sure you're not biting off more than you can chew?" Great. Even when my boyfriend is close to death, he can still muster the energy to doubt me.

"Yeah, I've thought this through." Okay, not really. But I'd thought it through about as much as I needed.

Parker and Charlie looked at each other. They looked a little scared. Finally, they both shrugged and nodded.

"I'll be there," Parker said.

"Me too," Charlie said.

I grinned. "Come together."

Parker's eyebrows collided together on his forehead. "What do you mean?"

"I mean, I want the two of you to show up together. As a couple."

"Gabby—"

"We're not—"

I held up my hands. "I know, I know. You're not together." I let go of Parker's hand. "But you should be. The two of you are perfect together. I don't know why I didn't see it before."

"Gabby—" Parker tried to speak again.

I kissed his forehead. "I have to go. But I know she'll take good care of you." I nodded to Charlie on my way out. My step felt lighter as I walked away.

CHAPTER 29

"HOW'D IT go?" Chad asked as we exited the hospital.

I swung my arms to the side, snapped my fingers, and clapped. It was a Chad move I'd copied. It looked so lighthearted when he did it that I couldn't resist trying it myself. "Great."

"Great?"

"Yeah. We broke up." I smiled at the stars shining on us outside. Granted, there were only a few stars. The rest were blocked because of smog and city lights. But the few that were brave enough to shine through were appreciated.

"You like broke up, broke up?" He ran a hand through his already messy hair.

"Yep." I'm free! Free as a bird. Free as a man wrongly accused being released from jail. Free as a—

"Shouldn't you be sad?"

I shrugged. "No, I was the one who called things off."

"You broke up with a man who was just shot in the chest?" Chad's voice rose. "That's harsh."

"No, not harsh. I did it out of love." I hit the clicker on my key ring and heard my van unlock a few feet away.

"You're weird. Do you know that?"

"People have mentioned it a time or two. By the way, what are you doing for Thanksgiving? I'm having some people over. Would you like to join us?"

He continued to eye me suspiciously until I disappeared out of sight and climbed into my van.

"I guess," he called from the opposite side.

"Great. I'll add you to the guest list."

I drummed my fingers on the steering wheel as I backed out of the parking space. My industrial-strength vacuum cleaner shifted in the back, and I made a mental note to secure the device when I got home. I couldn't have equipment flying around in the back of my van, especially when I considered where that equipment had been.

"I was thinking about something while at the hospital." Chad's voice drew me out of my state of delirium.

"Oh?"

"What do you think about going into business together?"

I practically slammed on the brakes. Thankfully, we were still in the parking lot. I eased off the brake and crept through the lot. "Say again?"

"We work well together. I can do the stuff that you're not that great at."

"There's stuff I'm not great at?"

"You know, lifting heavy stuff."

Okay, I guess I could concede that. "Continue."

"We could take more jobs, make more money. Split it fifty-fifty."

"Fifty-fifty?"

"Sixty-forty?"

"That's better."

"Think about it. I know you don't like working alone."

I didn't like working alone, but how did he know that? Had I mentioned it earlier?

"You want to be partners? Or would you be my employee?"

"If I were partner, then I would share the load."

Someone to share the load with. Now that was a tempting offer.

∙ ∙

I dropped Chad off at his place, which was, of course, right on the beach. He asked if I wanted to hang out for a while but I declined. I both loathed and felt fascinated by the man, which basically equaled the same thing as Mentos mixed with Diet Dr. Pepper—fun, explosive, and a very bad idea. Besides, Parker and I had just broken up. I needed to clear my head.

I watched Chad climb the wooden stairs to his oceanside abode. He unlocked his door and waved before disappearing inside. I wondered what the inside of his apartment looked like. I pictured a surfboard in the corner and various beach pictures decorating the walls. For some reason, I smiled. Against my better judgment.

I hummed "Don't Worry, Be Happy" as I pulled away. Chad was a "don't worry, be happy" kind of guy.

Of course, my dad had been that kind of guy also. They weren't the marrying type.

Not that I wanted to get married anytime soon. And definitely not to Chad Davis.

I wasn't the type of girl who dreamed about a big princess wedding. No, I was the type who dreamed about going to Vegas . . . where Elvis could officiate. Of course, I would never look at Elvis the same way again, so that dream had to die.

I leaned back in my seat and turned onto the highway. I couldn't wait to get home and unwind and listen to the new U2 CD I'd just purchased.

"Listen, and listen closely," someone whispered.

I bristled as I felt someone's breath tickle my cheek.

CHAPTER 30

THE MAN'S breath felt warm and sticky and . . . smelt like he'd just eaten a tub of popcorn. "I've got a gun, and I'm not afraid to use it."

Panic alarms wailed and whined in my head as I felt a barrel pressed into my side. The weapon of choice might have been a magic marker, but it could be a gun, and that was all I needed to know.

"Are you listening?" The voice was a harsh whisper, gruff.

I gripped the steering wheel so hard that my knuckles bulged like a snowcapped mountain range. "Yes."

"Leave the dead Elvis alone, got it?" The man's voice—and I was 99 percent sure the intruder was a man—sounded shaky. Great, I had a nervous criminal in my van. I just hoped he didn't accidentally pull the trigger if I hit a pothole. My eyes scanned the road briefly.

The gun poked harder. "Got it?"

"Got it." I glanced into my rearview mirror. Maybe I could get a look at the intruder, a clue to who the murderer was. Which could be useful . . . if the man didn't kill me first.

"Don't do that!" The barrel pressed harder.

My rib cage cried for a time out. "Do what?"

"Keep your eyes on the road."

I licked my lips and stared at the taillights and traffic light ahead of me. "Okay." What street was I on? I needed to remember details, just in case I lived to tell the police about this. Great, no street signs. U2 would be proud that I was wandering where the streets have no name.

"I don't want to hurt you."

"I don't want you to hurt me." Keep your voice calm, Gabby. Calm. I had to resist the urge to freak out. Maybe I should throw on the brakes like I saw Sandra Bullock do in a movie one time. The gunman would be thrown forward, knocked out, and I could run away.

It sounded like a plan. I eased my left foot over to the brake and did a mental rehash of making sure my seatbelt was still fastened. I wanted to press the brakes but couldn't. Something mental stopped me. Something about the man accidentally pulling that trigger if I jostled him.

"If you don't ease up on your little investigation, you're going to end up like Elvis. Got it?"

"Absolutely. Drop the investigation. I'm on it. Or off it, depending on how you look at it." Stop talking, Gabby. Incessant babbling will only annoy him. Sweat poured down my forehead, and my heart pounded in my ears.

"I don't want to hurt anyone. I'm not that type of person. But it's too late now. I'm in too deep. I've killed two people. A third won't hurt my record much more."

"Of course."

"Don't patronize me." The man raised his voice, and the gun dug harder into my side.

I shrank. "Okay."

"Pull over."

I sucked in a breath and did as he said. While traffic zoomed by on the highway, I went right into a turn lane and threw on the brakes.

"If you look back at me, I'll shoot you."

The door opened, and the man jumped out. I counted to ten and looked back. The man had disappeared. Drat.

I pulled into the parking lot and called my dear old friend Detective Adams.

◆ ◆

"So since I've been through all of this pain and suffering, the least you can do is tell me something new about the case." I smiled wide and blinked my eyes, trying to appear sweet as I stood in the grocery-store parking lot with police cars flashing their red and blue lights around me.

Detective Adams gave me one of his looks before tapping his pen against the pad of paper in his hand. He clicked the top of his writing instrument and put away his notebook before stuffing his hands deep into his trouser pockets. "There is something new I can tell you."

My smile disappeared as shock took over. I resisted the urge to lunge forward in surprise. "Really?"

He raised his chin in a brief, no-nonsense nod. "Darnell Evans didn't die from a gunshot wound."

"Really?" I know I'd seen one of those while I was under that house. The image had stayed with me for days now.

"He died from a peanut allergy."

I stepped back. "Really?" I had to think of a more original response.

"He'd been dead a couple of days before he was shot. It appears he was shot with his own gun, which is missing."

Was it the gun that had been pressed into me tonight?

I shook my head. "This case is getting weirder and weirder."

"If he'd just died of an allergy, we may not have a murder case. But the gunshot wound makes this a whole different investigation. On top of that is the fact that Ryan Hoffman—"

"Who?"

"The mold remediation man."

"Oh, right." I forgot that some people actually remembered others by their real names.

"Ryan was shot with the same gun."

My hands went to my temples. But when I noticed they were still trembling, I jerked them down. I didn't want the detective to know how scared I'd been. Instead, I focused on guns and peanuts and mold. "That just doesn't make sense. Why would someone shoot a dead person?"

"There are a lot of sickos out there."

I leaned closer and glanced around for any listening ears before asking, "Any suspects?"

I saw the detective tap his foot against the asphalt. "I can't tell you that. I'd say you have to figure it out yourself, but given the circumstances, I don't think that's such a great idea."

"But if someone hadn't threatened me, then it would be okay to stick my nose into your investigation?" Maybe the detective was finally coming around.

"I wouldn't say that. But I know I can't stop you from being as curious as a cat."

I smiled, somehow feeling proud.

"But Gabby, remember this: Cats have nine lives. You don't. Please stay out of trouble."

"Always."

I thought I heard him groan as I walked away.

CHAPTER 31

BACK AT my apartment, I could hear a crowd inside Riley's place. I wondered who he had over. It sounded like they were having a good time between the rolling laughter, loud exclamations, and enthusiastic cheering that reverberated outside.

I stared at his door with its chipped red paint for a moment, before sticking my key in the lock and starting inside my apartment.

Riley must have internal radar for whenever my door opens. And to be honest, I kind of liked his freakish intuition. No sooner had I deposited my sequined purse onto the floor beside my couch than Riley's door flew open.

"Gabby, we were waiting for you. Amy's over, and we want to help plan the funeral."

I perked. I'd totally forgotten about our meeting tonight.

"We just finished our Bible study and were goofing around." He took a couple of steps toward me and touched my arm. "How are you, by the way? Is Parker doing okay?" His voice sounded low and sincere, like he really cared. He made my knees feel weak.

I swallowed, wondering when I had become so boy crazy that all the men in my life were suddenly targets. Watch out Bill McCormick. You just might be next on my list. "Parker's fine. We broke up."

Riley gave me the same look as Chad earlier. His grip on my arm tightened, and his blue eyes narrowed in confusion. "Broke up?"

I blew his concern off with a wave and grin. "It's all good, believe me. I'll tell you more about it sometime."

"Okay then." His fingers loosened, and he stepped back, still appearing uncertain.

"Oh, and I was just carjacked. But I'm fine now." I waved a hand in the air to blow it off also. Why be a drama queen?

"Carjacked?"

"Yeah. By a man with a gun. Probably the same one who warned me that the next crime scene I encountered would be my own." I shrugged. "It's all in a day's work."

"Gabby, are you okay?" With one gentle movement, Riley pulled me into an embrace. My head went into his chest, and I pressed it there until I heard his heart beating.

Man, did I like being in his arms, smelling his aftershave, feeling cherished—

"Gabby?" He must have taken my silence for distress. He hugged me tighter.

"I'm okay."

"It's okay to admit that you're not okay, you know."

"I know," I muttered into his chest. "But as long as I'm still breathing, I guess I'm okay. In my line of work, breathing isn't taken for granted."

The door opened behind us. "Is everything—"

Riley pulled out of the hug—darn it!—and I saw Amy standing there with wide eyes and red cheeks, like she'd just interrupted something intimate.

"Sorry . . ." She fumbled backward into the apartment.

"You're fine, Amy. Gabby was just telling me about her night." Riley stepped away from me and toward Amy. "She's going to come on over. Right, Gabby?"

I nodded. "Right. Let me just grab a notebook." And I did just that. Grabbed my yellow legal pad before walking into the lion's den at Riley's.

I recognized Amy, of course. But I also recognized the pastor, or Shaggy, as I liked to call him. He waved hello. A few other friendly faces congregated, all of them appearing to be close to my age.

"Gabby, we'd love to help you plan the funeral." Shaggy took a sip of his coffee, raising his pinky in the air as he did so. "We think it's a very noble undertaking, your idea. We want to do whatever we can to help."

"Excellent, because I need all the help I can get." In more ways than one.

For the next hour, we discussed burial options. Cremation seemed to be the best, we decided. Pastor Shaggy suggested we scatter his ashes somewhere meaningful. Did I have any ideas? I thought of the man's pink flamingo collection. He obviously had a taste for the cheesy.

"How about Mt. Trashmore?" Mt. Trashmore was a real place in Virginia Beach. A park built on top of an old garbage dump. Today, people flew kites off the landmark, one of the only hills in the otherwise flat tidewater region. The landmark also boasted a skater park, playground, and lake. Just label me proud.

Everyone nodded in agreement. Mt. Trashmore it would be. This way we wouldn't have to rent any kind of facility. Pastor Shaggy would do the eulogy. Amy would find an urn and clear up any legalities as far as releasing the body. She had connections through her work at the social services office. Then everyone opened their calendars or BlackBerries or PDAs, and we set a date for early next week, provided no snags tore into our plan.

The process had been much easier than I'd expected.

If only I could get Mr. Hermit's son to come.

But the funeral was in three days. Would I have enough time to convince anyone that this man's life was worth honoring?

CHAPTER 32

THE NEXT day, I had more investigating to do.

I wasn't going to let some crazy guy with a gun who just happened to sneak into my van and threaten to kill my sorry soul throw me off the case. If anything, that gunman had convinced me to pursue this case.

I paced my sticky kitchen floor as I tried to sort through the facts.

I needed to narrow my suspect list down to the one person who was strong enough to move a two-hundred-pound body, smart enough to hack into my computer, savvy enough to cover up the crime, and deranged enough to shoot a dead man.

Since I knew, based on the carjacking, that the person responsible was male, I ruled out Jamie and Lynette.

That left Rodger and Hank.

Hank had motive: fame, fortune, and blackmail. But did he have the means? He looked strong enough to manhandle Darnell's body. But Hank didn't seem like the type to learn computer code and hack into my Web site.

That left Rodger Maloney.

I remembered the computer equipment I'd seen in Rodger's office. Maybe he knew enough about technology to hack into my computer. Had he designed his company's Web site? I'd have to check into that. Being a business owner, he had to be savvy and have a certain amount of common sense. Despite his bulging belly, he appeared strong enough to drag Darnell's body under the house and deranged enough to shoot a dead man.

Rodger had to be the killer. He was the only suspect who made sense.

I picked up my pace, walking from one side of the kitchen to the next, tagging the countertop and then the refrigerator, over and over again. Who needed a treadmill when you had a kitchen?

I pictured the crawl space beneath the house. How had anyone, regardless of their strength, dragged someone into such a small space? I could hardly maneuver my own body down there. There was no leverage room to drag a body into the confined area.

I rubbed my temples, hoping the action would somehow help me see more clearly.

I drew in a quick breath. What if there was another way to get a body under a house? I tore up subfloors all the time, and what's underneath a subfloor? A crawl space.

What if someone—Rodger Maloney—had torn up the floor inside and deposited Darnell's body under the house?

I stopped pacing.

Bingo! That had to be what happened.

Now I just needed to get inside that house so I could check out the possibility for myself. If my theory proved true, then I'd simply need to nail down a few other details to seal my case before I turned Rodger in to the police. I could focus my investigation.

I already knew Rodger's motive: money. The man couldn't stand the thought that Darnell might take away his business that he'd worked so hard to build and establish. The idea had made him desperate enough to kill. I'd seen the man angry and knew he'd be a foe to cross on the wrong day.

I also knew that to kill someone by peanut would be a premeditated crime. Had Rodger Maloney lured Darnell to that house only to secretly slip him a deadly dose of legume? And why did he choose Bob Bowling's house, of all places?

I needed to investigate for myself. But how would I get inside that house without getting arrested?

Someone who just might be able to give me some guidance of the soft and chewy variety popped into my mind.

◌ ◌

I found Bob Bowling's address and decided to pay him a visit. I'd been trying to perfect my sweet eyelash flutter lately, and maybe if I played nice enough, Doughboy would let me inside his parents' place for a little look-see.

Bob's real home rested in a nice older neighborhood in Norfolk, one not too far from Ghent. His current house with its white wood exterior and matching picket fence appeared much nicer than his parents' old place. And I'd bet a million dollars that Elvis didn't rest in peace under this one. I pulled into his U-shaped driveway, parked, and pounded up the brick sidewalk to his door. I carefully avoided the ivy-covered wreath and knocked.

Doughboy answered a moment later. He blinked, as if trying to place me.

I handed him a business card. "You hired me to give you an estimate on cleaning some mold under your parents' old house." I exaggerated some innocent blinking until he could place me, the poor, helpless girl he'd pulled out from underneath a worm-and-dead-body-infested house.

"Oh, right. The crime-scene cleaner." He pushed his oversized glasses up on his nose. "What can I do for you?"

"I was wondering if I could ask you a few questions."

He leaned in the doorframe, not in a sexy way. More like he was expanding out the door like a marshmallow under heat. He wasn't necessarily a big guy, just kind of soft-looking. "I've given up on selling the place. No one will want to buy a home where two people have been murdered. There's no need to clean up the crawl space now."

"I'm not here about cleaning up the crawl space."

He stared at me a moment, and I wondered what was going through his head. Finally, he pulled open the door. "You've got me curious. Come in."

I stepped through his doorway and noted that his house could use a good cleaning, from the crumpled newspaper littering the glossy wooden floor to the boxes filling the room to my left. Was the man moving?

"I have an eBay business." He shoved a box out of the way with his foot.

"Mr. Bowling . . ." My mind worked quickly. "I've been thinking about investing in some property, and I think your house might be just what I want. I'm interested in taking a look inside."

"Inside? The place is a mess. You don't want to buy that old house."

I shrugged, trying not to appear overly eager. "I'm pretty handy. I think I could fix it up. Plus, it doesn't bother me that dead people were found there. I'm around stuff like that all the time."

"Ma'am, I just have to be honest with you." He leaned closer, as if about to tell me a secret. "It's a dangerous neighborhood. I hadn't been inside the house for several years, up until a few weeks ago. I couldn't believe the damage that vandals had done to the interior. It's nowhere for a single young lady to live."

I ignored his sexist comment for the sake of sleuthing. "Damage? What kind of damage?"

"Graffiti all over the walls. Drug paraphernalia everywhere. Syringes stuck into a mattress in the spare bedroom, and broken bongs in the living room. Need I go on? Someone obviously made themselves at home. I can't help but wonder if Darnell Evans was associated with that whole drug scene and if that's what got him in trouble."

Could drugs be the motivator behind this murder? Had I been looking in the wrong direction entirely? No one that I'd talked to had mentioned Darnell doing drugs.

Regardless, I still wanted to see that floor, to see if my theory was correct. Rodger Maloney still remained my number-one suspect.

"I'm still interested."

He balked. "You're serious?"

"Very."

"Why?"

I searched for a quick answer. "Because I think Ocean View is going to be revitalized one day, and I want to be there when it happens. I want to get in early."

He stared at me a moment. "Okay, fine. But view at your own risk. I definitely don't need another crime happening at the place." He reached up on the wall and pulled down a key from a hook. "Here you go."

"You're just giving me a key?"

"Lady, once you see the inside of the place, you'll realize that it can't be damaged much more than it already is."

ⓘ ⓘ

I'd learned a few things since I started this amateur investigation stuff. For starters, don't go into potentially dangerous houses alone.

For that reason, I called Riley. At work. Yes, it was Sunday, but apparently he was really busy and trying to cram in some extra hours. I explained the situation, and he said if it meant spending some time with me, he could take a break from his heavy caseload.

Okay, not really.

He'd remained quiet for several moments before finally agreeing. Sheesh, he'd fuss at me if I went without him, yet he was grumpy when I asked him to go. What's a sleuth to do?

As I cruised down the road toward Riley's office, I called Jamie. Lately, I could be mistaken as someone trying to win the title of Multitasker of the Year. I was becoming rather good at talking on the phone while doing . . . well, everything. Next, maybe I'd try brushing my teeth while driving, or showering as I ate breakfast.

"Gabby! You figure out who killed my Darnell yet?" The Priscilla Presley wannabe smacked her gum as she answered.

I rolled my eyes as I pulled up to a stoplight. "I'm still working on it. I have a few good leads."

"I thought you'd work faster than this."

I scowled out the window, causing the driver beside me to respond with a very un-nice motion. I looked back toward the stoplight hanging above me, thankful it finally turned green. I charged ahead, both on the road and in my conversation. "Listen, Jamie, did you know that your husband didn't have a show lined up in Vegas?"

"Of course he did. It's all he talked about for weeks."

"He was going to start his own plumbing business."

"Hogwash. My Darnell hated plumbing. He only talked about starting his own business to get under Phony Maloney's skin."

He got under his skin all right.

I had a feeling that all other career options had sunk like the Titanic for Darnell and starting his own business seemed his only option. Sure, he'd made some money as Elvis, but not enough to support himself and his wife and his lover.

And maybe his drug habit?

"What about drugs? Did your husband do drugs?"

She gasped. "How could you ask that? He was Elvis."

I rolled my eyes. "And the real Elvis did drugs. Your husband did want to be just like Elvis, right?"

She paused. I couldn't even hear her Hubba Bubba in the background. "He only did drugs on occasion and only then for recreational fun. He wasn't addicted or anything crazy like that."

No, never—because drugs were never, ever addicting. "What kind of drugs did he do?"

"Pot. Weed. Whatever the kids are calling it nowadays. Nothing major."

I'm sure the police couldn't agree less. "Who did he get his drugs from?"

"Beats me."

I hung up just as I pulled in front of Riley's law practice. The heavy, ornate wooden door opened a minute later, and Riley appeared, tugging at his sky blue tie. He climbed in the van and slammed the door.

"This isn't a good idea," he announced.

Hello to you too, Riley. "Then why are you coming? I didn't twist your arm."

He looked over and gave me a half grin. "Because I know you, Gabby St. Claire, and I knew you'd go with or without me."

I couldn't argue as I pulled away and took off toward Ocean View. I gave him a rundown of everything that had happened as I drove. He listened and nodded and held on for dear life until we pulled up to dear old Bob Bowling's house.

Once in the driveway, I hopped out, anxious to prove my theory.

"This place is a dump," Riley muttered behind me as I unlocked the door. Nothing got past him.

Inside, everything appeared just as Bob Bowling had said. I'd seen worse before—I'd cleaned worse before. Still, judging by the garbage left inside, drug users, maybe even dealers, had taken over the place at some point.

I visualized the crawl space of the house and the location where I'd found Elvis. Then I waded through broken furniture, old magazines, and broken beer bottles until I reached the back bedroom. I stepped through the crime-scene tape and stood in the dingy room with its upturned mattress and broken mirror. The police had been in here. Fingerprint dust bruised most of the visible surfaces.

A musty smell filled the room and reminded me of the stench from the crawl space.

"What now, boss?" Riley asked.

I liked the sound of that. And I loved the way his tie looked draped around his unbuttoned collar.

Focus, Gabby. "Over there." I pointed to some wrinkled carpet. "I think the police beat me to it."

Riley helped me shove a nasty mattress against the wall, and then we tugged at the carpet. The layers felt loose, like they'd been disturbed recently. Sure enough, a gaping hole opened in the subfloor.

Riley stepped back with his hands on his hips and stared at the opening in front of us. "What do you think?"

I pointed at the space. "I think this is how the killer got Elvis under the house. It's the only way that makes sense, given the cramped quarters in the crawl space. I don't care how strong a person is—it would be near impossible to drag a man's body under there."

"So someone pulled up the floorboards, dumped his body, and then nailed the floor back down?" With each explanation, Riley motioned with his hands to emphasize his points. I wondered if he learned the technique in law school. Maybe they had a class on Advanced Talking-with-Your-Hands Techniques 101.

"Yep. It's what any smart killer would have done."

And I had a feeling that smart killer's name was Rodger Maloney. Now I just needed to place him at the scene.

CHAPTER 33

CHAD RAPPED at my door the next morning. We were going to the next job site together. I was still considering his proposal—job proposal, that is.

The offer tempted me. Working with Chad would open up possibilities. With his background at the funeral home, he had certifications that I didn't. He could teach me a thing or two, and I could show him a few tricks.

And when we got along, we had fun.

When we didn't get along, I wanted to smear crime-scene sludge across his smug little face.

We started down the road together, heading off toward a suicide cleanup in Chesapeake, Norfolk's neighboring city and an all-around thriving bedroom community. While neighborhoods and strip malls composed most of the city, a very rural part still existed as well. That's where we headed.

As I drove, Chad turned to me and in all seriousness said, "I think I've found a solution to our dilemma."

I gripped the steering wheel, wondering what important, life-changing choice I'd forgotten about. "Dilemma?"

"As to whether or not we should become partners."

Oh, *that* dilemma. I braced myself for whatever his solution might be. "Okay, and what is that?" I hoped that maybe he would add some interesting insight that would make my decision easier.

He propped his feet up on my dashboard. "Here's the deal, Gabby. I think we should like, thumb wrestle for it. If I win, we become partners. If you win, we don't."

I stared at the road, feeling dumbfounded. He could not be serious. Of all the bad ideas I've heard in my life, that one ranked up among the most outrageous. "That's the dumbest idea I've ever heard."

I glanced at him for just long enough to see a sparkle in his eyes.

"You're afraid you'll lose, aren't you?" he said.

"You're crazy."

"You're afraid."

"I'm not afraid."

"Then what are you waiting for?"

I sighed. "You don't make big decisions like that based on who wins a silly little child's game." I rolled my eyes and continued to watch the road. The nerve of some people. The nerve of Chad Davis. Who did he think he was? Were we in elementary school or something?

We arrived at the little farmhouse and worked mostly in silence, me still fuming over Chad's nerve and Chad probably trying to think of some other juvenile way to convince me to be his business partner. We opened the windows, though it was cold outside, in order to let the house air out. I also placed some AirScrubs around the room where the man had shot himself. They were loud. Good. That way I couldn't hear Chad if he tried to talk to me.

"What are you thinking about?" Chad shouted.

I glared at him, amazed at the strength of his voice. "I'm thinking it's loud in here."

"It's a good thing I'm loud too, huh?"

Yeah, just great.

I worked in silence for a while longer and then my mind drifted back to one of the first times I'd met Chad: when we found the dead mold man under the house. I wondered about the man, whose name I knew was Ryan Hoffman. I wondered how his death tied in with the first murder. I shuddered again, thinking that it could have been me.

"What are you thinking about now?" Chad yelled.

Why fight the inevitable? I should just talk to the man. "I'm thinking about the two men who were murdered."

"Do the police have any leads?"

I shrugged in my Tyvek suit. "I don't know."

"Maybe the question should be, do you have any leads?" Chad stopped scrubbing for long enough to get his question out.

I didn't miss a beat in my floor-cleaning routine. Time was money, right? "I do have a few, but I'm zeroing in on one man in particular."

"Do you have any evidence to back up your theory?"

"Nope, just suspicions and possible motives." I eyed his inactive hands. "You know it is possible to work and talk at the same time."

He scowled—I could see it beneath his mask—and got back to work.

I rocked back on my heels and looked at the progress we'd made. This job would take longer than I'd thought. I licked my lips and noticed that they were dry, probably because I'd been biting on them, deep in thought.

Against my better instincts, I asked Chad, "Do you have any Chap-Stick?"

He grabbed his book bag, pulled a tube out, and tossed it to me. Then he pulled his mask up, and I saw those sparkling eyes again. I knew I was in for trouble.

"You know what will happen if you use that ChapStick, don't you?"

"What?" Did he have a strange lip disease that wasn't detectable to the human eye?

He grinned. "It will be just like kissing me."

I tossed the ChapStick back at him, a little too hard because he flinched when it hit him. "Grow up."

"You like it."

"Whatever, Chad."

As my eyes scanned the house, my stomach let out a rumble. Dinner sounded really good right about now. So did getting away from Chad Davis.

"You mind running down the street to get us something to eat?" I seemed to remember that we passed a Burger King on the way, in between some trees, a gas station, and a rundown farmhouse.

"Why don't we both take a break? It beats you staying at this place alone."

"Nah, I'll keep working until you get back. It's best if only one of us goes. Besides, I'm used to working alone. It's what I do best." I cringed at my own words. Truth was, I hated working alone and found tremendous comfort in Chad's presence.

He shrugged. "Fine. What do you want?"

I gave him my order, and a minute later, he left. Thank goodness.

Thumb wrestling? Sharing ChapStick like kissing? Who was this man? And did I really want him as a partner? Or would I kick myself if I said yes?

I pulled my mask back on and continued scrubbing the hardwood floor. The stuff on the floor rarely affected me anymore. I'd seen too much of it.

The other students in my class still balked when they saw crime-scene photos. Not me. I was used to them. At least I could use that to my advantage. I remembered the paper due in a couple of days, the one I kept putting off. I needed to get busy. I planned on writing it on—

Something whizzed past my head.

I froze mid-scrub. My internal alarms screamed as an acidic odor filled my nostrils.

Another whiz sizzled my hairs.

Get down!

I hit the ground.

But before I did, something white hot burned into my shoulder.

CHAPTER 34

PAIN OOZED from my shoulder. On the hardwood floor beneath my crouched body, my blood blended with that of the man who'd committed suicide.

It's one thing to see someone else's blood on the floor. Seeing your own is an entirely different story.

As I saw the red liquid dripping from my shoulder, panic flashed through my mind. My heart pounded to the drumbeat from an imaginary approaching army.

An army from the opposing side.

Someone was trying to kill me.

Out of fear and pain, I gasped. I grabbed my throbbing shoulder and looked for an escape. The shooter could strike again. I had to hide.

But what if he came inside and found me? What would I do then? With my injury, I'd be no match against an opponent. I had to find a weapon, a way to protect myself.

I eyed my spray-bottle cleaners, wondering if one of them could work. I had a razor on my belt and a hammer in the tool box.

I'd work with what I had.

I had to move fast. The house's open windows seemed way too inviting, and I doubted that Chad had locked up on his way out. Just call me Sitting Duck.

Chad!

Had the shooter got him on his way out? The man obviously used a silencer. I hadn't heard any gunfire, just a whiz.

Lord, please let Chad be okay.

169

I glanced beyond the window to the driveway. The van was gone. Chad had to be safe. Now, I had to worry about me.

I had my cell phone with me. I could call for help.

I moved my hand from the wound and saw the blood again. My head floated, and I feared passing out.

Focus, Gabby. Be strong. Block out the pain.

I reached inside my hazmat suit and grabbed the phone. My bloody fingers felt sticky against the metal. My shoulder throbbed.

I couldn't pass out.

Wouldn't.

I dialed 911.

"9-1-1. What's your emergency?"

"I've been shot. I'm located at . . ."

I glanced at the window. I only saw trees. Where was I located? I had to remember the address. My pathetic life depended on it.

"I'm in Chesapeake, off of South Battlefield Boulevard. On a country lane down the street from Burger King." Good job, Gabby. Real detailed. How many Burger Kings were there in the area? Uncountable.

"Can you give me something more specific?"

My shoulder throbbed. How much more blood could I lose before I went into shock?

What was the name of this street? It had reminded me of something . . . what was it?

The street name had made me think of the Beatles. But before the Beatles, I thought of water bugs because the street name was . . . "Waterloo Way! I'm on Waterloo Way. I've been shot by someone outside the house. I don't know if the shooter is still there or not." My words all crashed into one another as I rushed to get them out.

"Okay, ma'am, remain calm."

Wood splintered on the far wall. "Another shot has been fired!"

My mental soundtrack reached a frantic crescendo.

"We've got someone on the way there now."

I snapped my cell phone shut. I had to find shelter. If the shooter came inside, I'd be a goner for sure, out here in the middle of the floor. I had to hide.

SUSPICIOUS MINDS   171

I put my fingers back on the hole in my shoulder. Pain jolted through my body. I had to ignore it, to push ahead. I was too young to die. There were still more songs to memorize and torture people with. I still hadn't made it into Guinness World Records and . . . and I never break a promise, which meant I had to go to church with Riley still. Funny how these things always come back to me when my life is on the line.

Shelter, Gabby. Shelter.

I grabbed the hammer and some disinfectant, then jerked open a closet. I could bunker there, between a vacuum and some bulky coats. The crowded space beat being out in the open with a madman outside.

Once wedged between a fake fur and an AC filter, I flipped my phone open again and found Chad's number. My heart pounded in my ears.

I didn't know how much longer I'd be conscious. I had to work quickly.

"You change your mind?" I could hear the smile in Chad's voice. "You want to use my ChapStick after all?"

"Chad, I've been shot."

"Are you kidding, because that's, like, not even funny."

"Do I sound like I'm kidding? Someone's firing at me. They hit my shoulder, and I'm bleeding—a lot."

"I'm turning around right now, Gabby."

"Be careful. The shooter's still out there."

"Stay put, Gabby. I'm on my way."

Blackness filled my world.

CHAPTER 35

WAKING UP in hospital rooms was becoming a common occurrence for me.

I was pretty sure that wasn't a good thing.

But when I came to, doctors were bending over me like I was a strange, three-eyed being who'd dropped from the skies.

"Hello, young lady."

Great, a perky doctor who looked like Dick Van Dyke. Just what I needed.

"How's my shoulder?" I tried to sit up, but a terrible pain shot through my right side.

"You're going to be fine. The bullet did quite a number on you, but it's nothing you won't recover from. We're going to keep you overnight so we can keep an eye on you, though." He looked at me with the same big, friendly eyes as Dr. Mark Sloan on *Diagnosis Murder*. How appropriate.

I forced a semi-friendly smile. "Of course."

Staying overnight in a hospital is one of my favorite things to do, and I had been thinking about a vacation lately. What better location than Chesapeake General? Unlike a hotel, insurance covered this visit. While enjoying the lovely accommodations, I had nurses waiting on me hand and foot, hot meals served to me three times a day, and if I was lucky, I'd even get a sponge bath. What more could I ask for?

The doctors left me with my bandaged arm and groggy head.

I'd been shot.

It still seemed surreal.

You know what that meant, right? It meant I was getting close enough to finding the right answer that someone—the killer—had to get desperate.

A detective came in. Lately, I'd been getting to know detectives from all the area cities. How fortunate. I ran through my spiel, detail by detail, starting with finding Elvis dead.

When the detective snapped his pad of paper shut and left, Chad came in the room. I felt a little sorry for him. I mean, I assumed he found me bloody and passed out in a closet. It was my worst fear: finding someone I loved near death.

Not that Chad loved me or anything. But you know what I'm trying to say?

Chad looked pretty near death himself as he stood by my bed with pale skin and twinkleless eyes. Very un-Chad.

His hands went to his waist, like he was trying to be casual. He licked his lips, and I almost made a comment about him using some of that lip balm he'd offered me earlier. But the strain in his voice when he asked, "How are you?" made me keep quiet.

"Considering my cleaning scene has now become a crime scene . . . I wonder if this means the homeowner's not going to pay me."

He looked at me in silence for a moment before chuckling slowly and shaking his head. "You're crazy, you know that?"

"I've been called worse." I glanced at the phone on the table beside my hospital bed. "Speaking of being called, I need to call my friend Sierra. Maybe she'll bring some clean clothes out for me."

"You must be on medication." Chad shook his head. "You were really reaching with that wordplay."

I scowled and started to reach for the phone but stopped as pain coursed through me. I winced and grabbed for my bandaged shoulder.

"Let me get that for you." Chad walked to the other side of the bed and picked up the receiver. "Tell me the number."

I did, and he handed me the phone. A moment later, I heard whales singing in the background and a perky little, "Hello?" That's Sierra for you. I wouldn't change a thing about her.

However, I did make the mistake of starting the conversation by trying to be friendly and asking what she'd been up to.

"I'm preparing for a big save-the-lobster demonstration I'm going to do Thursday down at the oceanfront. Did you know that—"

"Actually, Sierra, I'm in the hospital." This is why I liked to cut out those polite formalities that people seemed so fond of. "I wondered if you could bring me some stuff."

"Hospital?" Her voice rose a few decibels. "Why are you at the hospital?"

"It's a long story, but I really need to work on a paper that's due soon. Plus, some clean clothes would be nice. Do you mind?"

"Of course not."

I twirled the phone cord, contemplating my next question. Should I let Riley know what had happened? I really needed to separate myself from the man if I was ever going to get over him. The last thing I wanted to do was to become clingy and needy. I cringed at the mere thought. Logic and desire collided inside me.

No, I wouldn't involve Riley. He'd already done enough for me.

I quickly told Sierra goodbye before my mouth took on a mind of its own and the R-word popped out.

With the phone dangling in my hand, I glanced up at Chad. He looked distracted and slightly intrigued by the instructions posted on the bathroom door. I cleared my throat, and Chad rescued the phone from me before I flung it across the room. Then he looked at me again with his hands on his hips.

"So . . . uh, can I get you something to eat?"

Something about his raspy voice comforted me. It must have been the painkillers. They did funny things with my mind.

"I'd love that burger and fries you were on your way to get."

"Yeah, sure, I can totally do that." When Chad reached the door, he stopped and turned back toward me. "Gabby?"

"Yeah?"

"I'm really sorry I left you alone. This might not have happened if—"

"I told you to leave, Chad. You have nothing to feel bad about. Besides, if I'd been the one to leave, the gunman would have probably shot you."

He didn't say anything else as he walked away. Nor did I.

: :

Sierra showed up before Chad returned. She made me explain what had happened, detail by detail. If I were a wild animal, she'd probably stage a protest to end violence against me. I could hear it now: "Save Gabby St. Claire! Honk your horn to show you care!"

I twisted my lips when, even in my imagination, the sound of car horns were nowhere to be heard.

Great, even in my daydreams I was unlovable and alone.

I really wanted to ask about Riley. But I restrained myself. Instead, I asked about Sierra's court date over the incident at the seafood restaurant. She told me, but I didn't listen. Shame on me.

When a moment of silence fell, I cleared my throat and asked what I'd vowed not to ask. "So, was Riley home when you left?"

She shook her head, and her sleek, bobbed hair swished back and forth. "His car wasn't there."

"Oh." The statement shouldn't have disappointed me. The man didn't have to rush to my side every time I needed him. Besides, Chad had been here for me. I could hear Rod Stewart singing "That's What Friends Are For" as the soundtrack to my life over the past couple of days. Chad had been a great friend during my stay here at the hospital. I hadn't been totally alone. Chad would honk for me if Sierra ever staged a demonstration.

Besides, Riley would be here at the hospital if he knew I'd been shot.

I eased my head back into the pillow. I had to get over that man. If I didn't, the next step would be obsession and then stalkerdom. Before I'd know it, I'd be setting up a little Riley shrine in my bedroom. I'd secretly collect paper cups and tissues he discarded. I'd start my own Riley Thomas fan club, and it would rival that of Darnell Evans.

Except I'd be the only member.

Yep, if I didn't get over Riley, those would be the roads I'd go down.

Couldn't. Let. That. Happen.

"One burger and some greasy, salty fries!" Chad popped into the room again, proudly holding up a stained paper bag. His gaze fell on Sierra. "Hey, Gabby's friend. How are you?"

"I'd be better if my friend would stay out of trouble. Doesn't she know I already have the overwhelming task on my shoulders of saving all the innocent, helpless animals in the world? To add my best friend to that list just isn't right."

"I wouldn't say I was helpless." I suddenly felt small and incapable.

"Did she tell you about her last hospital visit? She has a knack for trouble, I tell you. She's like a dolphin to tuna fisherman. She always seems to get caught in other people's nets." Sierra continued on and on about the evils of the fishing enterprise.

Chad glanced at me and smiled for the first time since I'd been in the hospital. Sierra had that affect on people.

My cell phone—which a nurse had brought to me an hour or so ago— beeped from the table where all my clothes were heaped. Sierra retrieved it for me. I saw that Detective Adams had left me a message. Out of curiosity, I excused myself from the conversation to find out what he wanted.

"Gabby, I thought you might want to know that we just found the gun used to shoot you. From the initial tests, it appears to be the same one used to kill Darnell Evans and Ryan Hoffman."

CHAPTER 36

THE PAPER I'm doing for class is on suicides and crime scenes.

I closed my eyes to give them a break from reading some research material. A girl's got to do something to pass her time at the hospital. Sierra had left a couple of hours ago, and Chad had gone to find a magazine to read. There was no better time to start working on my paper than while here in the comfort of my adjustable hospital bed.

If only my shoulder didn't pulsate, my head didn't throb, and my eyelids didn't feel like they had lead weights attached to them.

This paper was due on Thursday. The ten-pager couldn't be late. So even though I really wanted to take a nap, I opened one of my books again and continued reading.

Of all the crime scenes that I clean, the suicides affect me the most. I mean, why would a person want to take their own life? I'd been through some hard times, and I'd never been tempted to end it all. I wanted to give life a chance to get better.

But that was just me.

While doing my research, I'd discovered that suicide is the number-eight cause of death in the U.S. The books I read also said that most people who try to end their life are simply crying out for help.

Did the tragedy boil down to the same struggle I'd been wrestling with lately? Did our society today make it too easy for people to become isolated? A person could form friendships on the Internet without ever leaving home. Order groceries online to be delivered to their front steps. Use the computer to work from the comfort of their living room. Criminals, even, could hop onto the net and steal someone's identity, all while wearing pajamas and sipping java. Today, society's members could avoid ever inter-acting face-to-face. The result: loneliness.

Faces roamed through my mind.

Mr. Hermit, who died without anyone to miss him.

Mrs. Mystery, who seemed to prefer solitude.

The dead Elvis, who was loved for imitating someone else.

And how about me? I'd been distancing myself from people so much lately that I refused to even think of my neighbors or clients by their real names. Was I reluctant to get too close to people for fear of . . . what? That they'd get to know the real me and run away? That I might actually care about them and let them down somehow? That I might be abandoned by them, like I'd felt abandoned by my own parents, first when my mother died and then when my dad's life crashed downhill at breakneck speed?

I couldn't examine loneliness without questioning my own under-standing of the issue. I'd been assuming that loneliness was caused by ex-ternal situations—like isolation—but I myself was an example of the fact that one could be surrounded by people and still feel empty.

People did strange things to combat loneliness. Some tried to draw attention in positive ways and others in negative venues. Some filled their lives up by doing good deeds to get noticed and to be loved. Other people turned to crime and drugs or hurting themselves. What did I do to try and fill up my life?

"Surf's up!"

I winced at the interruption and turned to face Chad Davis. He stood in the doorway holding a surfing magazine, and I could tell by his wide smile that he was pleased with himself for tracking down the publication.

"How's it going, Gab?"

I took in his long-sleeved surfing T-shirt and faded jeans, along with his sun-kissed tan that really popped against his white shirt. I wondered if he went to a tanning booth or did the spray-on route.

Nah, I couldn't see him doing either, though how he got that tan at this time of the year perplexed me.

I closed my book and rested it on my chest. "I'm okay. Been better. Been worse. What more can I say?"

He perched himself on the edge of my bed, looking comfortable in the position, like he'd done this a million times before. "Did they catch the guy who did this to you yet?"

In the two hours since he'd been gone? How optimistic of him.

"That would be way too easy." I rolled my tired, bloodshot eyes. I knew what they looked like because I had made the mistake of looking in a mirror earlier. Not. A. Pretty. Sight.

"Any suspects?"

"Who knows? Not me." I wish I knew because then I'd track down whoever did this and . . . well, I don't know what I'd do. But they would regret the day they messed with Gabby St. Claire.

The title of number-one suspect was still held by Rodger Maloney in my book. I needed more evidence before I singled him out, though.

"I keep thinking about it, and I still can't figure out how someone knew you were at that farmhouse."

"They would have had to have been following me and waiting for the right opportunity." The thought frightened me. How could I have not noticed? I considered myself to be observant. Yet someone had trailed me all the way out to the boondocks and I hadn't even had the slightest suspicion? Between the man stowing away in my van and someone following me to a crime scene, maybe I needed to get a clue and rethink the detective thing.

Chad rested his hand on my leg, which seemed a little odd, but I'd never been good at deciphering the actions of someone trying to comfort me. I decided he was doing just that and kept my mouth shut.

A woman I didn't recognize appeared at the door. She wasn't a nurse, and my gut told me she wasn't on the hospital's welcoming committee.

She pushed her red plastic-framed glasses higher on her thin nose and swiped a curly hair behind her ear. "Gabby St. Claire?"

I fluttered my fingers. "That would be me."

She stepped closer, and her high heels clanked against the sterile floor. "I'm Dr. Killgore."

"Ear, nose, and throat?"

"Excuse me?"

"I thought I'd already seen every possible kind of doctor there is here— except I haven't seen an ENT yet, so I presume . . ."

"I'm the hospital psychologist."

Psychologist? The doctors must have thought the gunshot wound traumatized me or something. With the number of lawsuits going around nowadays, doctors always want to play it safe. The hospital was in no danger of having me sue them. I just wanted to put this experience behind me and get out of this place.

"Ma'am, I really don't think this, this . . . incident . . . has had any huge effect on me. I mean, sure, I know all about post-traumatic stress, but—"

Her icy hand landed on my arm, and even through her glasses, I could see her sharp eyes sizing me up. My hackles rose.

"Gabby, I'm here to let you know that ending your life is never the answer."

CHAPTER 37

I SAT up straight in my bed, causing pain to slice through my shoulder. I grimaced but pushed ahead. "Suicide? You think I'm suicidal?"

Killgore's small little chin bounced up and down like a bobble-head doll on a bumpy road. She gripped her clipboard and continued to assess me with beady little eyes. "That's what the nurses fear."

"What would ever give the nurses that idea? I thought I'd been in rather good spirits during my visit here, considering everything." I gestured rather roughly with my fingers toward my shoulder injury.

Chad cleared his throat and nodded toward my chest. I looked down at the book that rested there. *Suicide: A User's Guide.*

I held the book in the air like a preacher holding up the Bible at a revival. "This isn't what it looks like. I'm doing a paper on the subject so I can get my degree in forensics. I wouldn't have to read a book to figure out how to end my life. I get ideas every week when I go to work and clean up after dead people!"

She scrutinized me like . . . she felt sorry for me and my pitiful little life. I hated it when people felt sorry for me. "You don't have to be ashamed, Gabby. Many people who are in your position—"

"My position? What would that be?"

"Single and working a dead-end job aren't reasons to want to end it all. Things will get better."

"Better?" I screeched.

Her chin bobbed again. I imagined that bobble-head doll again. This time, I pictured jerking its annoying head off and flushing it down the toilet.

"The nurses overheard that your boyfriend just broke up with you. I know that can be hard. I'm single myself, you know."

"I broke up with him." If those nurses were going to eavesdrop, they needed to learn to do it properly.

"And you work cleaning up crime scenes? I know a very nice lady who can get you some temp jobs as an administrative assistant—" Her condescending voice grated on my ears like techno music at a symphony.

"I like my job! Maybe I won't even get my degree in forensics, and I'll just do this for the rest of my life!" I paused and tried to think of something wise to end with, and ended up with, "So take that!"

Her head tilted compassionately. "I'm going to recommend some counseling for you."

Chad gripped her arm and led the woman to the door. "Ma'am, she doesn't need counseling. Not anymore than anyone else does, at least." He nudged her out. "Have a great day."

As soon as she disappeared from sight, I erupted. "Can you believe the nerve of that lady? Coming in here and making all of those assumptions. How dare she?"

"You are hugging a book with 'Suicide' splashed across the cover."

"It's for a paper—"

Chad shushed me. "I know, I know. But just think about how it looks."

"My life isn't that awful. I know people who have it far worse." Mr. Hermit, for starters.

"You're right."

"And I like being single. It's better to be single than to marry the wrong person."

"Absolutely."

"Is this why they've been keeping me here all day? Because the nurses thought I was suicidal?" I threw my legs off the side of the bed. "I'm going to give them a piece of my mind."

Chad urged me back into bed. "They were just trying to do their job."

"I'll show them a thing or two about doing their job." I turned toward the door. "Eavesdrop on this, you good-for-nothing—"

"Gabby, now they're going to recommend you for anger management. Calm down."

I slumped back into the mattress. "Fine." I really wished I could cross my arms because it would go perfectly with my immature sigh and lower lip thrust.

"Let me find the doctor and see about getting you discharged."

"Please do."

🙙 🙙

An hour later, Chad wheeled me out—to my van. I'd forgotten that we'd ridden together to the job site. So it made sense that he'd taken my vehicle home last night and then brought it back this morning. And who was I to complain? I needed a ride home. And Chad was there for me.

As soon as I settled into the passenger seat with my seatbelt secured across my tender shoulder, I made up my mind. "I need to go clean up the site we started yesterday."

Chad cranked the engine and gave me a sideways glance. "No."

I felt myself straighten at his defiant response. "No what?"

He shook his head and began backing the van out. "No, you're not going back there."

Was Chad Davis telling me what to do? I guess he didn't have me all figured out yet. If he did, he'd know that I hated being told me what to do! "I promised the homeowner that I would clean up there, and I need to finish the job."

"I'll finish it up as soon as the police release the scene." His hands gripped the steering wheel and his eyes focused on the road.

I wanted him to look me square in the eye so he could see my determination. He seemed to sense my laser-vision gaze and refused to return it. "I'm sure the homeowners want to get back into their house, though."

"I'm sure they don't. A man committed suicide between those four walls, and you were almost killed there. I can't imagine they'd be in a big hurry to come back to home, sweet home!"

Chad could be so infuriating. And he still wasn't looking my way. The nerve.

"You need to go to your apartment and rest," he continued, as if he were my guardian or something. What is it with people trying to tell me what to do? After my last hospital visit, Riley had acted like a prison guard, making sure I didn't leave my apartment. Parker had constantly tried to boss me around. And now Chad thought he knew what was best for my life. Didn't these people know that I didn't need anyone watching over me? I was a woman. W-o-m-a-n, and I'd say it again. Thank you, Peggy Lee.

I continued to stare at Chad, daring him to look my way. "Resting is overrated."

Chad ran his hand through his sun-bleached hair and sighed. Finally, he turned his head and connected with my eyes. Frustration screamed from his weary-looking pupils. "Why don't you just let me take care of you?"

I leaned back into my seat, confused. "Why would you want to take care of me?"

He looked away and sighed again, then continued driving. Why was everything so complicated? Silence reigned for the rest of the ride. We pulled up to my apartment building, and Chad raced to the other side of the van to help me out. I let him, against my better judgment. I knew he just wanted to be useful, so why not let him feel good about himself?

Then he helped me up the steps like I was a little old lady or something. And I let him.

Then he helped me into my apartment as if I were a fragile piece of glass or something.

And I let him.

What was wrong with me?

Once inside my apartment, he patted the sofa cushions and motioned for me to come hither. "Why don't you, like, sit down and let me get you something to drink?"

I scowled, knowing I was acting like a spoiled brat but not caring. "I'm not thirsty."

"Why don't you just sit down then?"

I stared at the couch. "Because I don't want to."

"Why not?"

"Because I just don't!"

He sighed and did the hand-through-the-hair move again. "What do you want then, you cantankerous woman?"

"I wish I knew." I sat on the couch, and Chad immediately growled his irritation at my complacency. I glanced back at him. "I'm sorry. I don't know why I'm being difficult. I'm . . . I'm frustrated at circumstances beyond my control." There, I'd said it. I'd admitted my insecurities.

He plopped down beside me. "The Elvis thing getting to you?"

"It's got me all shook up."

He groaned, and I smiled before turning serious.

"I like being good at things, Chad. I like being in control and confident, and I don't feel like I'm going anywhere with this case. What does that say about my future in police work?"

"You'll figure out the case."

I cut a sharp glance at him. "How do you know?"

"I just do." He lowered his voice. "You're Gabby St. Claire. Why would I doubt you?"

I searched his face for a sign of sincerity . . . or a clue that he goaded me. He at least had the audacity not to smile or let his eyes twinkle for once.

Chad Davis was a great guy, I decided. I underestimated him too often.

I took note of the intensity of his eyes, the indention in his ear that told me he probably had had an earring at one time. My gaze swept the scruff on his face. Before I even thought of doing so, I reached forward and touched his cheek, felt the prickles there. "Are you growing a beard?"

"What do you think?" He rubbed his chin and winked. "Is it a good look?"

If he wanted to look like a homeless man, maybe. "Not really."

Our gazes caught. I should have realized what was happening and run away as fast as possible. But I stayed put with my gaze locked on Chad and his gaze locked on me.

Then we kissed, a slow, electrifying, yet urgent kiss.

I kissed Chad as if I hadn't kissed someone in months, when in fact it had been mere days. As easily as switching off a televangelist, I shut down my inner alarms. Gabby On-the-Rebound St. Claire again sought comfort in the arms of a man. And was thoroughly enjoying it.

Someone knocked at my door. Of course. I probably should have rejoiced at the interruption. I felt my cheeks flush as I pulled back and glanced at Chad. "I should get that."

The heat of his fingers on my arm matched the heat in his eyes. "Just because you should doesn't mean you have to."

I felt myself wanting to go down a path I shouldn't. "Oh, but I do."

I pushed myself from the couch—by all means fleeing temptation—and pulled the door open. Riley. He always seemed to be my conscience when I needed one. Why would right now be an exception?

"I heard you were in the hospital." My neighbor stepped inside and rubbed my uninjured arm. The worried wrinkle I'd come to expect knotted his forehead. "What happened? Are you okay?"

"Just a little gunshot wound. Nothing that time and some painkillers won't get me through."

"What can I do for you? I would have gone to the hospital, but I was out of town doing research and—" He stopped when Chad appeared behind me. His gaze darted back and forth between the two of us. "Am I . . . interrupting something?"

I felt myself blush again and averted my eyes to the floor. I'm not sure what came over me because the reaction was so unlike me. I nodded toward the man I'd just been making out with and cleared my throat. "Chad just brought me home from the hospital."

Chad reached his hand forward, as laid-back and carefree as ever. "Good to see you again, Riley."

Riley seemed to hesitate before extending his hand. "Chad. I'm glad you could be here for Gabby. Good to see you, also." He took a step back from me. "Do you need anything? Chad, I'd be happy to sit with her for a while if you need to get home."

I waved my hand in the air. "Hello? I'm right here. No need to make decisions about me as if I'm invisible." I felt like an eight-year-old in the middle of a custody battle.

"Nah, it's all good." Chad waved Riley off. "I don't mind staying."

"Actually, I need to be alone in order to rest." I shooed them both toward the door. "Thanks for your kind offers, but I'll be fine."

"You shouldn't be alone—"

"How do I know you're going to rest—"

"You're just going to have to trust me on this one." Once they were both outside my apartment, I stuck my head out the door. "But thank you both. I'll call you if I need you."

I shut the door before I heard any more protests. Right now, I just needed to be away from everyone in the male species.

CHAPTER 38

I LOOKED at the grass atop Mt. Trashmore, green and bright as it should be since the world's largest compost pile rotted beneath it. In honor of Mr. Hermit, I'd brought one of his pink flamingos. Taking a breath, I stuck it deep into the earth. Pastor Shaggy stood beside it, wearing a rock band T-shirt, faded jeans, and a gray blazer. He held a small Bible in his hands. Beside him stood Amy, holding a dollar-store vase with Mr. Hermit's ashes inside. A few members of Riley's church were there, including Riley. Chad and Sierra had also shown up. We formed a circle around the flamingo.

Pastor Shaggy cleared his throat. "We're gathered here to honor the life of Richard Spruce. Not much is known about Richard. He seemed to prefer living a life of solitude."

Did he really prefer it? Had he a choice in the matter? Or maybe no one had liked him, including his family.

He continued. "I firmly believe that every life should be honored, and I applaud Ms. Gabby for caring enough to organize this ceremony for Richard Spruce."

A few strangers paused from flying kites to come join us. I don't think they realized we were in the middle of a funeral. I mean, how many funerals included pink flamingos and an eclectic group of outcasts? Strangely enough, I could hear the song "Super Freak" playing from somewhere below—near the skateboard park, I think.

I glanced around again, searching the crowd. I'd mailed the letters to Richard's son, and I held on to this irrational hope that he'd received them and changed his mind about coming today. Apparently he hadn't. None of the faces gathered around registered any deep, personal loss. Sadness bit down on my spirit.

"The Bible describes heaven as a place where there will be no more pain or suffering," said Pastor Shaggy. "Believers will walk on the streets of gold. Heaven is a glorious place that's promised to those who believe in Jesus and accept him into their lives."

I tuned Pastor Shaggy out for a minute and thought of my mom. Was she in heaven? She was a believer. I mean, she didn't attend church every Sunday or anything. Did a person have to be a faithful church attender to get to heaven? Maybe I'd ask Riley about it later.

Next, Pastor Shaggy offered a prayer where he talked about God loving his children. But if God loved his children, why was hell even a possibility? It didn't make sense to me.

I couldn't ponder it too long. Sierra was up. She'd been perfecting her bird calls for quite a while now, and since Mr. Hermit had liked flamingos, she'd decided to do a sort of special music using bird calls.

She solemnly stood beside Pastor Shaggy and, like a well-trained soldier, brought her hands to her mouth. Drew in a deep breath. Looked at the sky. Then she began letting out the most hideous sounds I'd ever heard. The random guests who had wandered over had been polite and stayed up until then. They slowly slipped away.

Riley made eye contact with me, and we shared a hidden grin before turning serious again and giving Sierra our full attention. She had a good heart.

I glanced at the birds flying overhead and wondered if they understood what Sierra said to them. At that moment, one dropped a present onto the flamingo. It splattered right down the plastic bird's face.

Chad snickered, and I elbowed him. I hadn't done this to mock Mr. Hermit. I truly wanted to honor him, so I wasn't about to make this a laughing matter.

Though I wanted to laugh myself.

Sierra finished. One person applauded. No one else did because I don't think you're supposed to applaud at funerals. Or wakes. Or whatever they're called.

Amy stepped forward. She said a prayer and then began spreading the ashes over the side of Mt. Trashmore. Except the same wind that had enticed kite flyers out today also blew Mr. Hermit's remains back at those mourning him.

I felt a flake hit me in the face and jumped. Cleaning up after dead people is one thing. Being hit in the face with their remains constituted an entirely different story.

I noticed everyone else began jumping out of the way as if attacked by bees. Panic began to rear its ugly head when Pastor Shaggy stepped forward.

"I know Richard Spruce would be honored that you all came here today to celebrate his life. Let's have a moment of silence to reflect on his life."

Reflect on his life? That was the last thing I wanted to do. I feared too much that I'd end up like him.

People began to disperse after the ceremony. Chad and Sierra chatted with Pastor Shaggy. Riley nudged me.

"You okay?"

I shrugged. "I guess."

"What's on your mind?"

I saw an ash on my shoe and quickly shook my foot until the piece fluttered to the ground. "I don't want to end up like Richard."

"No one does."

I glanced up at my friend, the wise one who seemed to have all the answers. "How do you stop it?"

"Being alone is a choice, Gabby. You can either invest in people's lives—and I'm talking quality not quantity—or you can seclude yourself both physically and emotionally. Just because a person is surrounded by people doesn't mean they feel loved and that their life has meaning. And just because a person is physically alone doesn't mean they feel isolated and depressed."

I forfeited getting a ride home with anyone. Instead, I borrowed Sierra's car (she got a ride with Riley), and started down the interstate. I hadn't taken my painkillers this morning, just in case I needed to drive. Though each throb in my shoulder felt like a hammer smashed into my bone, at least I could take advantage of the freedom of the road. Life's about trade-offs, right?

I traveled from Virginia Beach into Norfolk. Went through the tunnel and into Portsmouth. Exited the interstate and drove through Portsmouth until I reached Portsmouth City Park. Found a parking space.

Then I wove my way between headstones in the cemetery adjoining the park. The grand cemetery nestled up against the Elizabeth River. Mom would have been proud to know she'd been buried in such a lovely place. I'd insisted on it. It didn't matter that it took the rest of my savings account to pay for the plot.

Strangely, I knew Mom would never know she was buried here. But I would. And when I came to visit her, I wanted this lovely cemetery to remind me of just how lovely she had been.

I'd seen pictures of her young and vibrant, before life had worn her down. Working two jobs, being married to an alcoholic, and having your son kidnapped could really age a person. I pushed the image out of my mind of my mom with dark circles beneath her eyes, frizzy hair, worn clothing. I liked to think of her as being happy.

Was my mom happy?

I couldn't be sure. There were times I remembered her smiling. I rarely remembered her laughing. Maybe a chuckle now and then, but it never seemed to come as a reflex. It always sounded forced.

I finally found the simple gravestone that marked the place where her body lay buried. I knelt there. Beside her name was Dad's. And under his name read 1954– until blank. One day, Dad would be buried here. Would I mourn his death?

Love shouldn't have to feel forced, yet I felt I loved my dad out of obligation. Sometimes I even wished I had someone else's dad. I wished I had a dad who loved me, who took care of me, who hugged me when I suffered through bad days and delighted in my accomplishments.

Instead, my father had red eyes, slurred speech, and alcohol-drenched clothing.

"I miss you, Mom. I keep my chin up and try to pretend that everything is okay, but it's not. Dad's miserable. I don't know how to help him, so I just keep giving him money." My chin trembled, though I tried to stop it. "Why'd you have to leave us, Mom?"

I let myself cry. I hardly ever let myself cry. Thought I was too strong for it.

My fingers dug at the grass. I ripped blades from the ground. Dirt invaded the space under my nails, stinging. Tears collided with the earth.

I wondered if my tears would eventually make their way to my mom. I imagined them seeping through the ground to reach her.

Was what Pastor Shaggy had said true? Did God love me? Did he really love all of his children?

I stayed on my mom's grave until the sun began to set.

CHAPTER 39

THE NEXT morning, I finished my paper and e-mailed the work of genius to my professor. As soon as I hit Send, the phone rang. I didn't recognize the voice on the other end.

Of course.

"Is this Gabby St. Claire?" The man sounded gruff and unkempt, like someone more accustomed to speaking in grunts than words. I figured the call concerned a cleaning job, which would be perfect because I needed some business—preferably something that I could do with my injured arm.

I leaned back in my desk chair. "This is Gabby. What can I do for you?"

"I need to talk. It's important."

Would he pay me if I listened? If I helped him clear the clutter in his head? To get rid of his mental crime scene of past mistakes?

Those painkillers I took last night when I got home must be doing things to my sense of humor. I had to stop before I started booing myself. "And to whom am I speaking?"

"Hank Robins. I know something that you need to know."

He had my full attention. "Go ahead."

"I know who killed Darnell. Can I meet you somewhere to explain?"

Twenty minutes later, I waited in a booth at a downtown Irish tavern. Hank, still wearing his delivery uniform, slid into the seat across from me. I waited for him to confirm to me that Rodger Maloney had killed Darnell. At the same time, I wasn't completely ready to rule out Hank as a suspect.

I liked to keep an open mind . . . about possible killers, at least.

The hunka, hunka burnin' love nodded toward my shoulder. "Accident?"

In case he'd been the shooter, I wouldn't pleasure him with an answer. "What can I do for you, Hank?"

I tapped my pen on the table and right into a puddle, courtesy of my water glass. I scooted my beverage to the side but reached too far. Pain shot through my arm. I should have taken another painkiller this morning. No time to think about that now. I got down to business.

Hank placed his dirty hands squarely on the table between us. "Darnell was going to leave Lynette."

I'd pondered that possibility earlier in my investigation but hadn't devoted much time to the thought. "Why was he leaving your ex-wife?"

"He didn't love her."

"Was she coming back to you?"

His lip twitched as if the thought disgusted him. "I wouldn't take that woman back if she were the last female on earth."

"Alrighty then," I said in a subdued Ace Ventura impression. "What does Darnell not loving Lynette anymore have to do with his murder?"

"I think she killed him."

The key words being *I think*. "You think she killed him because you think he was going to leave her? I don't think your objective opinion would hold up in a court of law."

"It would give Lynette motive."

"You're a fine one to talk about motive." I paused. "Besides, maybe you just have so much contempt for your ex-wife that you're eager to place the blame on her. Maybe it's to cover up your own guilt. For all I know, maybe the two of you went in on his murder together."

"I may not have liked the man, but I'm no killer."

"But at one time in life, you fell in love with and married someone who is? It still doesn't say much about your judgment."

He smacked his hand against the table. "Listen lady, I didn't come here so you could point the finger at me. I'm trying to help."

"Why?"

"Because it's my moral duty."

"Then go to the police."

"Lynette dedicated her whole life and existence to that man. She set up shows for him, laundered his costumes, worked tirelessly on his fan club, and even grew the list to over three thousand."

"He had over three thousand people in his fan club?" Three thousand at twenty dollars a head could add up to a big chunk of change.

Hank's shoulders slumped. "That's what I heard."

I leaned closer. "Do you have a fan club?"

The man's eyes darkened. He was jealous, but I didn't have to meddle to figure that out. Anyone could see the competitive nature between the two men.

"I have many dedicated fans," he snapped.

"Of course."

He lowered his gaze and practically growled, "Listen, Lynette was torn up that Darnell was leaving her. She's not used to being the one who's dumped."

"Why was he leaving her?"

The stormy expression disappeared, and I thought I saw a hint of a smile. "They'd been having some problems."

I leaned back and waved my hands in the air. Nobody was going to take me for a ride. "Wait a minute, wait a minute. How do you know all of this? It's not like you were on good terms with either of them."

"I have my ways."

"I need more of an explanation, or I'm moving you up on my list of suspects." Not that my list of suspects meant anything to law enforcement, but Hank didn't need to know that. I seemed to have convinced him that I had more power than I actually did.

He wagged his head in the air. I could see his internal struggle from the strained expression gripping his face. He ran a gruff hand over his face.

"Fine, it's not like I was doing anything illegal. I had a mole in the fan club. Are you happy now?"

"A mole?"

"Yeah, I paid someone to get close to Lynette, to find out what Darnell was up to so I could beat him to the punch line, if you know what I mean."

"And the mole told you all of this?"

"Basically."

"Does Lynette know about your mole?"

He sighed. "Yeah, she confronted me a few days ago."

From what he'd just told me, the only one with a motive for murder was Lynette—and that was for the murder of Hank, who was still alive, not Darnell. Man, were these people messed up. They actually made me feel a little better about my own family.

Did I even want to hear any more of his sordid, twisted tale?

Sure I did. It made for an entertaining story, if nothing else. "Okay, fine. I'll bite. What kind of problems were Darnell and Lynette having— according to your mole?"

"Multiple issues, one of them being finances." His head dipped closer. "All of that money from the fan club . . . nobody seems to know what happened to it."

Now that was interesting. "Do you have any ideas?"

"Lynette sure has been buying a lot of stuff lately. I've been wondering where she's getting the money."

"You sure seem anxious for your wife to be guilty, Hank."

"My ex-wife seems sweet and innocent, but on the inside she's the devil in disguise. She's a fate I wouldn't wish on my worst enemy. That's probably why Darnell was leaving her—he'd found a new girlfriend who'd treat him right."

"A new girlfriend?"

"Yeah, the woman I hired as my mole."

Could people even make up stuff like this? "Darnell, where can I find this spy woman?"

"She works at a nursing home where Darnell liked to perform."

CHAPTER 40

"WHY DIDN'T you tell me you were having an affair with Darnell Evans?"

The Vaseline-coated-teeth smile disappeared from the big-haired blond in front of me. "Excuse me?"

"Don't pretend like you don't know what I'm talking about. Darnell was not only going to leave his wife for you, he was going to leave his lover. How did you manage that?"

The receptionist glanced from side to side, as if making sure none of the residents were paying attention. "I don't know what you're talking about."

"I have a feeling you were the last person to see Darnell Evans alive. Explain that. Did you feed him some nutty Thai chicken? Some french fries cooked in peanut oil? Did you kiss him after eating a Snickers bar?" I pointed at her candy dish and all the empty wrappers littering her desk.

"I would never!" She shoved the glass dish under the desk where I wouldn't see it. "Never!"

"That's what they all say, lady."

She stood and began whispering, "Listen, I would never hurt Darnell. Never."

"No, really, that's what they've all said. All three of his women. Who knows how many more of you there are. You're really a disgrace to self-respecting women everywhere, you know." Like I had any room to talk, but still.

The woman pouted. "We weren't like that. We weren't."

"You weren't having an affair?"

"We were. But it wasn't cheap and based solely on emotions. Darnell and I had the real thing. Realer than you'll ever know."

Ouch. "So, why don't you tell me about the last time you saw him. The last time you saw him, I say?" If she could repeat everything at the end of her sentences, so could I.

"I told you the truth when you came in before. He said he had to leave the nursing home early for some appointment. He wouldn't tell me what. He just said he had some business to deal with."

Or did he mean he had some pot to "deal" with? "Did you know your sweet Darnell did drugs?"

She shrugged and fluffed her hair using those long, jewel-tipped fingernails. "I told him not to. He said they helped him to relax. He'd been under some stress lately, with all his business issues and dealing with that mean Hank Robins and trying to get over the headache of that ID theft."

"Was he suicidal?"

Her head swung back and forth, her large hoop earrings hitting her cheeks with each motion. "Definitely not. He had everything to live for. Everything."

"Did you know he wasn't going to Vegas to be the next big thing?"

"Yeah, he turned it down to be here with me. He was going to start his own plumbing business here. We already had a location and name set up and everything. We were going to call it Down the Drain. Down the Drain. Isn't that clever?"

How appropriate.

"And how did you go from being a mole for Hank Robins to falling in love with Darnell, the man you were spying on?"

"Lynette was no good for Darnell, no good at all. He deserved better."

How about Jamie? What did she deserve? "Do you think Lynette killed him?"

"I know she did."

I leaned against the counter. "How do you know?"

"Because I was with Darnell on the day he left her. She screamed at us as we pulled away, screamed that she hoped Darnell dropped dead, dropped dead."

"It's just an expression. It doesn't make her a killer."

"Yeah, well the next day is when he disappeared."

I stored the facts away for later review.

"Ma'am, is there anything else you want to tell me before I go to the police with this information?"

"Yeah, Darnell loved me." She patted her stomach. "And he loved our baby. He would have never purposely ended his life, not with everything in store for him in the future."

CHAPTER 41

AN HOUR later, after humming "I Still Haven't Found What I'm Looking For" for thirty minutes straight, I realized I needed my conscience to come over. I called Riley. Maybe he had some answers on murder, men, or his supposed Maker. Maybe he could help me find what I was looking for.

Riley's hair was still shower wet when he showed up at my apartment. He leaned in the doorway, but unlike Bob Bowling, Riley looked every bit the confident, handsome man. I noted that his grin appeared serious today.

"What's going on, Gabby?"

I urged him inside, where he sat on the couch. I plopped in the chair across from him and pulled my knees to my chest. Here goes nothing. "I'm confused."

"About?"

Where did I even start? I doubted he knew anything about Darnell Evans's murder, so I jumped to the next item on my list. "Everything, starting with my messed-up love life."

"You mean Chad? Why does he confuse you?" Riley should look into being a personal counselor if this lawyer thing doesn't work out. He had the questions down pat.

"I don't know. I don't know anything anymore." I rested my head in my good hand, which perched on my knee. "Here's the thing: I don't want to be alone. I'm so afraid of ending up like Mr. Hermit one day, afraid that I'll die and no one will want to plan my funeral."

"But someone did want to plan his funeral—you."

"But no one who actually knew him wanted to come." I locked gazes with Riley. "I've been thinking a lot about what you said at Richard's funeral. I know that being in a relationship doesn't equate to feeling complete. I mean, I have good friends—great friends. But people have come in and out of my life since I can remember. None of my relationships feel secure."

"I'll always be there for you, Gabby."

My throat went dry. I couldn't stop now, though, and ponder the implications of what he said. I had more questions. "I've been thinking about this whole God thing lately. I've reached some conclusions."

"Such as?"

I drew in a deep breath before blurting, "I want to help dead people. You want to help spiritually empty people. Bill McCormick wants to reform Democrats. And Sierra, she wants to save animals. Are any of us really that different? We all just want to make a difference."

Riley nodded slowly and thoughtfully. "Those are good points."

"But?" I just knew there was a but in there.

His unwavering gaze met mine. "I want to help people by giving them the one true hope—Jesus. All other pursuits are empty."

I shifted positions, tucking my legs under me. "Isn't that rather intolerant of you to say?"

"It's not intolerant. I believe in absolute truth. Truth isn't relative—everyone doesn't get to decide their own personal right and wrong. Can you imagine how chaotic the world would be if they did?"

"Pretty chaotic."

"There can't be many roads of worshipping many gods that will take us to the same heaven. If my God is true, then other people's gods aren't."

I studied that etched face of his, searching for the truth. "But Riley, why are you a Christian? Is it because your parents taught you to be? Is it because you're afraid of hell? Is it because you're desperate for hope?"

"It's because I believe that Jesus is truth, that he really walked on this earth and died for our sins. Why wouldn't I want to live for him?"

Food for thought. I'd have to chew on his words. I didn't want to believe in Jesus because I feared being alone or because the other alternatives didn't seem relevant. I wanted to explore the possibility of believing in a personal God for the right reasons.

Pounding sounded in the distance.

"Can someone open this door for me?"

Sierra.

Riley and I started toward the door. I grabbed his arm before he left my apartment. My throat burned as I looked up into his eyes. I had to look away before saying, "I'm not finished with this conversation."

"Good, I hope you're not." He placed his hand on my back and led me into the hallway. Downstairs, I spotted Sierra's face overtop an armful of groceries. She peered through the glass alongside the front door.

Riley helped her inside, and I slipped outside. The brisk wind cut through my long-sleeved T-shirt, but I didn't care. A few minutes later, Riley and Sierra joined me on the steps. Sierra shared her adventure in organic grocery shopping when Bill arrived home.

The meaningless conversation would have normally been okay. But not today. I couldn't get the haunting questions out of my head.

"I've been thinking more about this church thing," I announced.

Everyone got quiet.

Riley's gaze flicked up. "Okay."

I rubbed my arms to ward off the chill. "If I were to 'become a Christian,' would I have to wear cheesy Jesus T-shirts?"

He chuckled. "No."

"Put silly bumper stickers on my car?"

"Of course not."

"Memorize all the Christian clichés?"

"I'll knock you in the head if you do."

"Do I have to vote Republican?"

The chuckles disappeared, and heavy silence fell. I stared at the three people around me. Then, all together, they erupted.

"I wouldn't say that."

"Republicans aren't green. They're killing the earth."

"There are Republicans, and then there are idiots."

Can you guess who said what?

I thanked everyone and excused myself back up to my apartment. At my desk, I sighed, as confused as ever, and began to absentmindedly flip through some papers stuffed to the side of my computer. I came across the list of phone numbers that Jamie Evans had given me on that first day I met her. I stared at the names, at my possible suspects. Which one of these people had killed Darnell Evans? And why?

I flipped the paper over and over, trying to make sense of things, to get this case out of my head so that I could get on with life. As if.

Finally, I tossed the paper beside me on the couch and went to make some coffee. I stopped as soon as I'd risen from my seat. Carefully, I picked up the paper again. It was just junk mail Jamie had jotted the names on. I plucked apart the white tab that kept the paper closed and opened a brochure for a local computer servicing company. Why did its name sound familiar? I scanned the text. The company offered the standard services to computer users, both in the home and in the office. Networking setup, Internet help, security, upgrades.

Maybe I should have called them when I had all my computer problems.

Nah, Amy had done it for free.

When I went to bed, something nagged at the back of my mind.

CHAPTER 42

THE NEXT morning, a fast-paced knocking drew me to my door. With a rap like that, it had to be an emergency. I yanked the door open, only to find Mrs. Mystery standing there with an antique, oversized typewriter bundled in her arms.

"Do you want to buy a typewriter?"

I cocked my head to one side, trying to restrain a snide remark. "Excuse me?"

She thrust her armload forward. "A typewriter. I'm selling one of mine."

"You have more than one?"

"Every good writer does."

I shook my head as Bizarro World thoughts began twirling again. "Thanks, but I have a computer." I leaned against the doorway, taking note of the way she hugged the ancient machine like a long-lost love. "Why are you selling your typewriter, anyway?"

Her voice went high-pitched. "Because if I don't, I won't be able to pay my bills."

I tried to understand. Really. "Are you not getting any new book contracts?"

Her head swung back and forth, not unlike a pendulum. "No, someone keeps taking all of my money."

I let my head fall against the wall. "Please tell me you've had the identity theft resolved."

"No, someone keeps taking my money. Now they've opened a credit card in my name, and I keep getting the bills!"

"Have you gone to the police?"

"They say they can't do anything."

I couldn't stop myself—I sighed. Then I led her inside. I would have taken the typewriter from her hands first, but my injured shoulder put the kibosh on that.

"We've got to get this issue figured out. Did you call the credit card company and explain the situation to them? They're usually very good at resolving these things."

As she heaved the typewriter onto my dinette, the whole room shook. How had someone as fragile as Mrs. Mystery gotten downstairs with that beast of a machine? I'm surprised the weight hadn't dragged her down like an anchor.

"Can I see the credit card statement?"

"Of course. Let me run upstairs and get it."

I couldn't imagine her running anywhere. Twenty minutes later, she appeared back at my apartment, waving a sheet of paper like a surrender flag.

The bill was for more than six hundred dollars. Yikes. Someone had had a shopping field day in her name.

I looked the bill over. The charges were listed, as well as the stores and the dates. "These are local businesses."

"But I didn't go to any of them." Her face wrinkled as if I'd just accused her of murder.

"I know. But we can check them out. See if the clerk remembers anything about it. Maybe they even have a security video." I looked at the bill. "This last purchase was only a few days ago."

"When do we go?"

I glanced at my watch. Did this mean she was going with me? "How about now?"

"Let's roll."

◦ ◦

Mrs. Mystery wrung her hands together as we stood outside the seedy video game store. "Are you sure you know what you're doing?"

"I'm just going to ask a few questions." I put my hand on her bony shoulder, trying to reassure her. But the woman kind of felt like a corpse, which made me wince. So much for the reassurance.

"I have a lot of good years left, you know. I don't want my life to end . . . tragically." She shuddered.

"No one was ever killed for asking questions." I remembered several attempts on my life and questioned the validity of my statement. No need to share that with Mrs. Mystery, though. She was nervous enough already.

I pulled the glass door open and ushered her inside. A kid with thick glasses and a trucker hat stood behind the counter, reading the back of a game box. He raised his chin to acknowledge us.

"'Sup?"

"Not much, dawg." I cringed as I heard myself trying to be hip. I was way too old and neurotic for that. I tried a new approach: helpless and confused. "We desperately need your assistance."

He straightened and flashed a mouthful of braces. "Looking for a game for your little brother?" He glanced at Mrs. Mystery. "Grandson?"

"No, not quite." I plopped down the credit card statement on the peeling, sparkle-top counter. "I'm looking for any information on the person who made this purchase."

His eyes darted from me to Mrs. Mystery, then down to the paper I shoved at him. Dealing with people like me wasn't something you learned by playing Halo. Poor kid had a lot to learn. Glad he's the one working at the store tonight.

"Is this your statement?"

"Officially, it's hers." I nodded toward my neighbor. "But it's not hers, if you know what I mean."

His top lip arched. "Huh?"

"Someone stole my identity!" Every visible inch of skin on Mrs. Mystery seemed to vibrate as her arms flew through the air in wide gestures. "And we're here to find out whom."

Great, everyone wanted to be an amateur sleuth. Why couldn't they just leave that to me? I was about to step in, when the boy spoke.

"How can I help?"

"Who was working on"—I grabbed the paper from his hands and found the right line—"November 8?"

"I'd have to check the schedule."

"Great, we'll wait." Mrs. Mystery put her fragile hands on the counter with more force than I thought possible.

The boy disappeared through a door labeled "Employees Only."

I leaned toward my neighbor and lowered my voice. "You're better at this than you let on."

"I'm just pretending I'm the heroine in my latest novel." She said the words as if her thought progression was the most normal thing in the world.

I had no idea how to respond to that, so I tapped my toe against the vinyl floor instead and waited for the employee to return. A few minutes later, he emerged, squinting at a paper in his hands as if his glasses needed a redo.

"I was working on that date."

I shoved Mrs. Mystery's statement toward him again. "Can you check this credit card number and find out what the purchase was?"

He looked like I'd just asked him to give up his Wii for a year. "Really?"

I nodded. "Really."

He threw his head back and closed his eyes, as if with that one question I'd ruined his day. Then he brought his head forward and frowned, long and hard. I wanted to tell him that if I couldn't be deterred by a bullet wound, then his pout had no chance.

He rolled his eyes to the ceiling. "I can check an itemized list of the day's totals, I guess. It's going to take a while."

"It's a good thing no other customers are in the store then," Mrs. Mystery said.

I remembered my investigative techniques class and all the extra lab work I was scheduled to do—I checked my watch—in forty minutes. Yet I was here, and Mrs. Mystery was here, and she was being forceful. Plus, I didn't want the woman to have to sell her typewriters. Heaven forbid she ever upgrade to a computer.

The sales boy stomped to the back again. Thirty minutes later, he came back out with a stack of papers in his hands. "It looks like you purchased a new Xbox."

"I would never—"

I placed my hand on Mrs. Mystery's arm, urging her to remain calm and quiet.

"Is there a time listed?" I asked.

He flipped some sheets of paper. "Yep, 2:15."

I glanced up. Saw a ceiling tile that wasn't really a ceiling tile. I bet a camera recorded each moment underneath. "How long do you keep your security videos?"

"Two weeks. Why?" Realization appeared to strike the employee, and he slowly shook his head. "I'd have to get manager clearance for that."

I nodded. "Okay. We have time. In fact, why don't you just send the manager out, and we'll talk to him ourselves."

"He doesn't like to be disturbed. One employee got fired for bothering him." The teen shrugged. "He's a really busy man."

"So is the person who's opened a false credit card account in this woman's name."

He sighed. "If I get fired, you're finding me a new job."

I knew of some portable potties that needed cleaning. I'd be more than happy to put his name in for the position.

He returned with a man who could be his father. The old grump sighed and grumbled and mumbled excuses about why he couldn't show us the video. Finally, I leaned forward and put on my best stern expression.

"Do you know who this woman is?"

His eyes widened sarcastically—if that's possible. "Your grand-mother?"

I put my arm around Mrs. Mystery's shoulders—without flinching this time. "This is a famous mystery writer. She knows forty-three different ways to kill someone without the police ever finding out."

Mrs. Mystery stepped forward and jabbed me in the chest with a pointy finger. "And she's a crime-scene cleaner, so she'll get the evidence cleaned up before the police ever know what happened."

So Mrs. Mystery did know a little about me. Imagine that.

I flashed a devious smile at the manager.

"Plus, I'd hate for the police to find out about your little habit." I waved my hand in front of my nose. "Possession of marijuana could send you to prison, you know. I can smell the stuff a mile away."

"Yeah, and she's dating the police." Mrs. Mystery nudged me and smiled.

I lowered my voice, hating to break the news. "Actually, Parker and I broke up."

"I'm sorry to hear that." Her voice took on a grandmotherly tone.

"It's all good." I cut my gaze back to the manager and ditched the Chatty Cathy act. "So, how about it?"

"Will you two leave me alone if I show you the security video?"

We both nodded.

"And you'll keep your mouth shut about the pot?"

I didn't break eye contact. "As long as you cooperate."

He harrumphed toward the back, motioning the two of us to follow with one wide sweep of his arm. Once in the office, he pointed to the TV/VCR combo in the corner.

"Have at it."

I stared at the stack of unmarked tapes that formed a tower next to the TV. "Which tape is it?"

"You'll have to figure it out. The date and time will be at the bottom of the screen."

I sighed. I definitely wouldn't be making it to class tonight.

Maybe not even tomorrow.

CHAPTER 43

"OKAY, THIS is the date. It looks like we just need to fast forward it a few hours." I hit the Forward button on the VCR and leaned back. This would take a while. It already had.

This place had a bad vibe. Marijuana plant stickers covered almost every surface. I could still smell the pot the manager had been smoking, and a mask in the opposite corner had a bong sticking out from it.

I found an odd comfort in having Mrs. Mystery with me.

Like she'd be any help should trouble arise.

Maybe she really did know forty-three ways to kill someone.

"I didn't know that you and the handsome detective had broken up."

I glanced at the elderly woman, sitting so pretty in the chair, and shrugged. "Yeah, it's not a big deal. Not really. We weren't meant to be together."

She nodded. "Because you're meant to be with Riley."

I straightened. "I am?"

"Everyone can see it."

I shook my head. "No, Riley needs someone cultured and classy."

She leaned so close that I could smell the plaque on her breath. "You don't even realize the treasure you are, do you?"

Blood rushed to my face, and I pulled away from my neighbor—mostly to get away from the fumes. I didn't know what else to say, so I laughed. Chuckled, you'd probably say. Tried desperately to think of a response, preferably something sarcastic and witty.

Nothing.

"I'm serious, Gabby. You're a special girl. And I think you've yet to realize your potential." She patted my hand. Her eyes bored into mine so intensely that I had to look away.

"Wow. Thanks," I mumbled.

She sat primly on a metal folding chair with a Metallica sticker on the back, her purse resting securely in her lap and her ankles crossed daintily. "I was in love once, you know."

I perked. Hearing her story could be a good way to spend the time. "What happened?"

"I picked work over him."

I stared at my neighbor, trying to imagine her as a young, dewy-eyed woman. The picture just wouldn't materialize, and I usually had a great imagination.

"Tell me more. Please."

"I was at the height of my career. I thought he was slowing me down. I thought if I married him, I'd have to give up my writing in order to have children and keep house. I couldn't bear the thought."

"Couldn't you do both?"

She shrugged. I could see sadness in her eyes. "Maybe. But I was prideful. I wanted people to recognize my name."

Had people ever recognized her name? I'd yet to see one of her books in print, and I'd even checked Barnes and Noble once.

"So you decided to keep writing mysteries?"

She smiled, light returning to her eyes. "Romances."

"I thought you wrote mysteries."

"I do now. But I didn't then."

I continued fast forwarding, watching as a blur of video swept the black-and-white screen. "Why'd you switch genres?"

"All the romance in me died when Peter married someone else."

My heart panged, and I paused from my video search for a minute. "I'm sorry."

"I had some best-sellers, you know."

I studied her face, realizing that I didn't have Mrs. Mystery figured out, after all. "I didn't. I'd love to see a copy of your books sometime."

"I'm sure you've seen them before."

"I don't think so."

She smirked. "I write under a pen name."

"Why?"

"Because I like to live in anonymity."

"Why?"

"People might use me if they know who I am."

I let the conversation sink in. Or I tried to let it. Really, her admission was too much to comprehend. Was she some kind of best-selling novelist? If so, why was she having money troubles? And she was afraid of her success buying her friends who were only using her position to climb some kind of ladder themselves?

"Are you lonely, Mrs. Morgan?"

"I have my characters to keep me company."

"But they can't really keep you company."

"I'm happy, Gabby. I've never preferred being around crowds of people. I like the simple life."

So maybe her isolation wasn't isolation at all—maybe her aloneness was the solitude she needed in order to create her stories. Maybe the time helped her to recharge.

She patted my hand. "Besides, I've got a great neighbor like you, don't I?"

The blush came again. I looked at the screen, only to realize that I'd gone an hour and twenty minutes past the time I needed. I hit rewind and tried not to get caught up in replaying Mrs. Mystery's compliment.

Or her proclamation that Riley and I were meant to be together.

Or that I was special.

I'd always wanted someone to tell me that.

"You passed it again." She pointed to the TV.

I went six minutes too far this time. I sighed. I had to pay attention.

I hit play and began watching the video, waiting for the man or woman to check out.

"I wonder if that's him." Mrs. Mystery pointed to a man in the corner of the screen. The manager appeared to be helping the man. I saw a big sign that said Xbox on the wall above.

"I'd bet my bottom dollar."

I could only see the man's back. I leaned in closer. The grainy picture reminded me of those cheap gas-station videos they played on the news when trying to find robbery suspects. No one could tell anything from the images. Invest some money and protect your business, people!

"Turn around. Turn around!" Riley hated it when I talked to TV screens. Sometimes I did it just to get on his nerves. What did that say about me as a friend?

I stared at the TV again. What would I do when I saw this man's face? Burn the image in my memory and search desperately throughout the area for the suspect? That would be like finding an animal by-product in Sierra's house. Impossible.

I could inform the police, and maybe they would recognize the man. Doubtful, but it could be worth a try.

The man on the screen bent down to tie his shoe, looked up at the manager, and then picked up the box. But he still hadn't shown his face. Only one minute until checkout time.

Of course, the time on the camera and the time on the cash register differed by a couple of minutes. So I continued to stare at the man's back. At his not skinny and not fat build. At the T-shirt and jeans he wore. I got a glimpse of some glasses every once in a while. Finally, with the box in hand, he turned toward the register.

I squinted. Leaned closer. Tried to get a better look.

The man almost looked like . . .

I shook my head. It couldn't be.

My face nearly touched the TV screen.

Then I propelled myself back in my chair and shut my eyes.

It couldn't be.

I opened my eyes again.

It was.

* *

"Are you okay?" Mrs. Mystery waved her hand in front of my face.

I nodded. "I'm fine. I just need to get home and sort a few things out."

"You're not telling me something."

I hit stop on the VCR and ejected the tape. Then I shoved the evidence in my purse and motioned my neighbor to follow me. "I'll explain later. Let's get out of here."

No one said anything to us as we walked out of the store. I'd show the tape to the police. Then I'd tell them who they needed to arrest.

Inside the van, my cell phone rang. I saw Chad's number and answered.

"Hey, I have a job for us. I'm there right now and hoping you can join me."

"I might be able to get there tonight. I have to do something first."

"Alright. But I'll object to the sixty-forty split if I do all the work myself."

"Rightfully so." I tucked the phone between my head and shoulder, trying to concentrate on the traffic around me. "So, where are you?"

He told me the address.

I got off at the next exit and turned around. I had to go to this job pronto.

CHAPTER 44

MY VAN screeched to a halt in front of the familiar Ocean View house. I threw the vehicle into park and turned swiftly toward my prim passenger, who gripped her purse with bulging knuckles.

"Wait here," I instructed, keeping my voice firm.

I didn't hear her response as I jumped from the van and hurried toward the house. I rounded the corner to the back yard and nearly collided with Chad.

"Whoa! Where's the fire?"

I sucked in a breath, glad to see my new business partner in one piece. I grabbed his arm with enough force to tear it off. "Are you okay?"

He shrugged as if I'd lost my mind. "Yeah. Are you?"

"Something's not right."

"Is that what someone told you? Because I think you're, like, completely normal, Gabby." He grinned mischievously and nudged my chin with his knuckles.

I scowled. "That's not what I meant. I mean, this house, the homeowner, the dead bodies."

"If it will make you feel better, you can guard the crawl-space opening while I go in." He thrust a hose used for the mold-killing chemicals into my hands. "Use this to protect yourself."

"This isn't funny. Do I need to remind you of the two dead people who've been found under there? I don't know why I didn't see the connection earlier." It couldn't all be a coincidence. It couldn't.

"See what earlier?"

I stomped my foot to emphasize my words. "This home is the link to the murders."

Chad rubbed his goatee. Or maybe he hid another smile. I didn't care at the moment.

"This abandoned home is the dumping site," he finally said slowly.

"But what if it's not?"

"You're totally not making sense." Exasperation crept into his voice, and his smile disappeared.

"I just think we should go to the police."

"That's not a good idea." The whiny voice belonged to neither Chad nor me.

We both jerked our heads toward the sound.

Bob Bowling appeared from the side of the house.

With a gun.

I couldn't pull my gaze away from the steely weapon. I'd felt what a bullet could do to a human body. I didn't want the same fate to rip through my muscles and bones again.

"What's up with the gun?" Chad took a step back and held his hands in the air. In the process, he dropped the tank full of chemicals that could have potentially been used to protect us. Einstein.

Bob pointed the weapon at me again, and I drew in a sharp breath. Please don't let him be clumsy. Please don't let the Doughboy be clumsy. One slip of the finger and . . . I gulped. Couldn't think about it. Couldn't stop thinking about the feeling of a bullet ripping through my flesh again.

"Why don't you ask your friend?" The sweat covering Bob's pasty face reminded me of pastry glaze.

I shrugged, trying to play nonchalant. "I don't know what you're talking about. I just came here to do a job."

"Don't feign stupidity. I heard your earlier conversation. I thought you might figure things out eventually." His hands trembled.

The good news was that this man wasn't inherently evil. But the bad news was that he still was evil.

"Figured what out?" I really hadn't figured everything out. I simply had some nagging suspicions. I needed more time to piece the puzzle together. And I really needed more time to stall and come up with a plan to save my life . . . and Chad's.

"I didn't kill him, you know."

"I know you didn't, Bob. He ate one of your neighbor's cookies, not realizing that she used peanuts in them. When he went into anaphylactic shock, you panicked."

Sweat poured down the man's forehead. He said nothing, so I continued, testing out my theory.

"You couldn't call the police. If you did, they would find out that you've been stealing people's identities. You're the tie with all the ID theft I've heard about lately. You worked on Darnell's computer and accessed information about his entire fan club by hacking into his server. I didn't take you for a killer, but desperate times must call for desperate measures."

"I had no idea the man was allergic to peanuts!"

"How did he find out about you, Bob? How did Darnell know you'd stolen his identity?"

He wiped his brow with his free hand. "Oh no, you don't. This isn't an episode of *Scooby-Doo*. I'm one bad guy who's not going to answer all of your questions while you stall for time."

I held my hands—or I should say hand since my injured shoulder didn't allow for much raising—in the air. Not so much in surrender though. More to say calm down, relax. Don't shoot.

"I'm assuming that Darnell put two and two together. You worked on his computers, and members of his fan club were being hit with ID theft. So he tracked you down. You asked him to meet you over here to discuss things. What was your plan after that? If you didn't plan to kill him, what did you plan to do?"

Sweat had once beaded on Bob's face—now it melted like a doughnut under heat.

"I was going to pay him off." He let go of the gun with one hand and wiped his sleeve over his forehead. "ID theft is the perfect crime. It's nearly impossible to track down people involved with it. But Darnell started to blackmail me. I had to keep stealing money in order to pay him. I was going to offer him five hundred thousand dollars to be quiet forever."

And Darnell was going to take that money and run, telling people he'd taken a gig in Vegas. "Killing him was the only answer," I muttered.

"No! I didn't kill him. He ate that cookie. I didn't know." He pointed the gun at me again. "That's when I called you both. I couldn't forget about his body. I needed someone to discover it."

The man continued talking. The more he talked, the longer I lived, so I wanted to keep him going. "And you shot him later, after putting some thought into it, to make his death look like a drug deal gone bad, right? What I don't understand is why you killed the mold remediation man."

"He came inside my house to use the bathroom—without asking. He knew that Elvis had died here. He even asked me about it earlier. When he saw a package that had just been delivered with Darnell's name on it, I knew he'd figured things out. It was never supposed to get out of hand like this." His gaze darkened. "And now I'll have two more murders to add to my rap sheet."

"Man, you don't have to kill us. We won't tell anyone." Chad tried to negotiate. The amateur. Didn't he know that never worked?

But it did seem like a good option when your life was on the line.

"Really, we won't tell a soul," I echoed.

Doughboy chuckled. He pointed the gun again. "Get under the house. Both of you."

I remembered the surroundings beneath the house. The smell of decay. The cobwebs. The snakes. I shuddered.

"Now!"

I started toward the crawl space. "What are you going to do to us?"

"You're going to work under the house. But unfortunately, another tragic accident is going to occur. The gas line is going to break."

"You don't think the police will be suspicious that two more people have died under your house?" I tried reason. Reason had to work, didn't it?

"I've saved enough money to start a new life under a new name. I'm getting out of this business and skipping the country."

"You'll never be able to get away from what you've done, you know. Even if you manage to escape Virginia, you'll never escape your conscience."

Bob's face became redder by the second. "Get under the house. Now!"

"You won't get away with this." I had to try and keep talking. Try to buy a few more minutes of life. Plus, I really didn't want to go under that house. I'd almost rather die by gun than by gas fumes.

"Now!" His voice rose.

I'd made him angry. Angry people did stupid things. Like pulling triggers. At least under the house, I might be able to escape.

I stared at the computer guru one more minute. Could I take him down? Chad and I together could surely overpower him.

But not his gun. That small little Glock could stop my heart in one second flat.

"I'm going."

Chad and I exchanged glances. I couldn't read the emotion in his eyes. He seemed rather at ease. Of course, Chad always seemed at ease. Maybe he knew something I didn't.

I stared at the opening to the crawl space. The door—probably pulled off by Chad earlier—was gone. Various pieces of equipment lay scattered on the grass.

Bob pointed the gun at Chad. "You get in first. Try anything funny, and the girl dies."

"I'm going." Chad glanced at me before getting on his hands and knees, lowering himself to his belly, and then army crawling forward, inch by inch. When his feet disappeared, I felt my stomach churn with nausea.

My turn now.

I got on my hand and knees. Stretched until my stomach hit the prickly grass. Used my elbow to pull myself into the darkness. My injured arm ached with all the jostling and movement.

"Move faster!" Bob yelled.

If you hadn't shot me in the arm, maybe I could.

I saw Chad beyond the darkness as splashes of sunlight filtered inside. Seeing him somehow comforted me. At least I wouldn't die alone.

I shook the thought out of my head.

I wouldn't die. I was smart. Chad was smart. We'd figure a way out of this. This house would not be our grave.

My elbow hit the mushy ground under the house. Flashbacks of finding Elvis stormed into my head. I could smell his rot again. See his lifeless body. Hear the insects feeding on him.

Creepy crawlies flickered up my spine. Bile rose in my throat. Scenarios crashed into my mind.

"It's okay, Gabby," Chad whispered.

"Have fun with the snakes," Doughboy said. I looked back and saw his sorry excuse for a face leering into the crawl space. He actually smiled.

I wanted to claw his face off.

Before I had a chance to, darkness closed in.

CHAPTER 45

"STAY CALM, Gabby." Chad's voice sounded miles away.

"Stay calm? We're going to die under here. How can I stay calm? If the gas doesn't kill me, a snake will."

"We'll get out."

Steady your breathing, Gabby. It's going to be okay. Chad's right. We'll get out of here.

I reached forward. "Where are you?"

"I'm right here." He grabbed my hand. My heartbeat slowed some.

I remembered the crawl-space door, a shoddy wood compilation. How hard could it be to kick it off? Probably just a nudge would do it. "We can get that cover off, right?"

"He got a new one that locks." Chad's voice sounded grim.

"Still, there's got to be a way." Think, Gabby. Think. "We can scream."

"He has a generator on outside. The noise will drown out our cries."

"You're not making me feel better." I couldn't give in to defeat. "We need to think quickly. When he releases that gas . . ."

"I'm trying to think quickly!"

Chad's near panic made me forget about my own . . . for a second, at least. "How about the little vents along the sides of the house? Can we knock one of those out?"

"Maybe." Chad let go of my hand, and I heard him moving.

"What are you doing?" I heard my pitch go high.

"I left a flashlight in here somewhere."

A flashlight! Then we could see any snakes. "Great."

"Finding it is another story."

My muscles froze. I should try to help, but I couldn't move. I imagined the cobwebs I might encounter, that would drape over my skin, sending spiders scurrying through my hair. I imagined reaching forward and grabbing another snake. This time, the creature would be alive. Its fangs would dig into my skin. Venom would stop my heart.

And Chad wouldn't even be able to find my lifeless body because of the utter blackness around us.

"Gabby?"

"Yeah?"

"Keep talking to me."

"Okay." Yet I could think of nothing to say. I tried. I really did. But chatting about my favorite songs just didn't seem appropriate at the moment. "All I can think about is music."

"What songs are you thinking about?"

"'The Great Gig in the Sky' by Pink Floyd."

"Think of another song."

"'See That My Grave Is Kept Clean.'"

"Huh?"

"By Blind Lemon Jefferson. A blues singer—"

"And guitarist from Texas. Van Morrison referred to him on his album *Beautiful Vision*. Said he was one of the most influential blues singers ever."

I was seriously impressed. And temporarily distracted.

"Okay, the music thing isn't working." Chad moved around in the distance. "Are you going to let me teach you to surf this summer?"

"You're still going to be around?"

"Of course, I'll be around. We're going to be partners, remember? I can't leave my partner."

"But what about your plans?"

"Plans change. So about my question. You want to learn to surf?"

I remembered my father trying to teach me as a child. If I learned to surf, would that help me to understand my father more? Or would I only come to dislike the man more?

"I'll think about it."

"Fair enough. There's nothing like riding a wave, Gabby. I'm telling you, nothing in the world like it. It gives you such a rush—"

"Did you find the flashlight yet?"

"I thought it was over here somewhere." I could hear Chad moving. "Here it is!"

Relief washed through me. Everything would be better with some light.

"What?" Chad sounded frustrated.

"What? What's happening?"

"This was just working a minute ago."

"Don't tell me." I would have let my head drop to the ground, only the mushy ground was the last thing I wanted my face to touch.

"The flashlight won't turn on."

Another sound distracted me. Coming from the area around the crawl-space opening. I could hear something rubbing against the metal.

I knew what was happening.

Doughboy was about to gas us.

And I couldn't do anything about it.

CHAPTER 46

AT LEAST I'd die peacefully.

Rumor has it that death by gas is painless. You go to sleep. You never wake up.

There were worse ways to die.

Only, I didn't want to die. It was like Mrs. Mystery said—I had undiscovered potential.

Mrs. Mystery!

In excitement, I jerked my head up and promptly hit a beam. I moaned and rubbed my scalp.

"You okay?" Chad asked.

"Yeah, just great."

What was my neighbor doing? Was she still in the van? Would she realize something was wrong and get help?

Or worse, would Doughboy find her on the street and kill her also?

Please, Lord, protect the woman. She doesn't deserve to die like this. Me, on the other hand, I probably deserve a lot of things. Riley said you're not a God who dishes out punishment based on who deserves it. I hope he's right.

While I'm praying, if you could nudge Mrs. Mystery that maybe she needs to find a phone and call the police, that would be great.

Suddenly, it smelled like someone had left a gas stove on.

"Gabby?"

I swallowed the lump in my throat. "Yes, Chad?"

"Are you okay?"

"As okay as I can be considering I'm paralyzed with fear and starting to feel like a turkey sitting in the oven at Thanksgiving."

"Good to know."

"Isn't it?"

"We can still get out of here, Gabby Girl."

It sounded a bit like Supergirl, didn't it? I pictured myself in a crime-scene cleaning uniform with a big G across the front. Maybe that should be my new company logo.

Maybe the gas was already starting to affect me.

The G could stand for Gas.

I could see the headlines. "Gabby Girl Gagged by Gas." Try saying that five times fast.

"I'm going to try and push this hose back out," Chad said.

"Good idea."

I heard him moving. Thought about the plastic beneath us. The gas streaming inside. The closed quarters.

"Stop!" I screamed.

Silence hovered. "Why?"

"We're sliding around on a mixture of plastic moisture barrier and dirt. It's dry and cold outside. We could form static electricity, which would cause a spark, which could cause this whole place to explode."

Silence again. This time filled with apprehension. Heaviness settled on the air.

"We can't just sit here and die," Chad finally said.

"I think I'm going to throw up, Chad."

"Stay with me, Gabby!"

The gas was getting to me. I knew it was. I'd had prior experience while locked in the trunk of a car that sat running in a garage.

At least Chad would be here with me when I died. That was a nice thing about having a partner— A partner! I'd never answered him.

"Let's do it," I said.

"Do what? Am I missing something?"

Nausea rose in my gut. My head twirled. My thoughts collided.

I had to keep talking. "If we get out of here, let's go into business to-gether, you and me."

"Really? You won't regret it."

No, if I died, of course I wouldn't regret the decision. It was an easy choice to make here on death's door.

I couldn't pass out. I couldn't succumb to death.

"Gabby?"

"I'm here."

"Gabby?" Chad's voice sounded awfully high-pitched and squeaky.

"Chad?"

"That wasn't me." That sounded like Chad. The other voice sounded like . . .

Mrs. Mystery!

"In here!" I wanted to crawl toward her voice, but I stopped myself. I had to remain calm. It helped that the gas was making me lethargic. If you would consider that helping. "We're under the house."

"The door is locked." I heard Mrs. Mystery rattle it.

"Can you pull the hose out?" Chad asked.

"This one?"

"The one going into the crawl space." I could hear the weariness in Chad's voice. The fumes were getting to him too.

"Let me see if I can pull it out. It doesn't look very complicated, though it is attached to this big old tank of something. I have a feeling it isn't helium."

Brilliant deduction, Sherlock. "Hurry. Please."

"Okay, I've got it."

We needed fresh air and fast. But if the crawl space was locked . . .

Was this all for naught?

"Don't worry, I called Riley."

Riley? Why would she call Riley? I mean, sure, he'd gotten me out of some scrapes before. But how about the police?

"Mrs. Morgan, you could be in danger. You should go back to the van and lock the doors."

"Don't worry. I did some reverse feng shui of the internal sort on your villain. He'll be out for a while."

I heard metal against metal. I paused, waiting for the gassy air to explode.

Then the crawl-space door opened. Fresh air flooded in.

"I'm going to crawl out, Gabby. Then I'll give you the respirator, okay?" I heard Chad but barely. Stars and stripes exploded in my head. And I'm not talking about the patriotic type.

I held my breath. Waited for a spark. Braced for an explosion.

Please, God, no.

Chad's feet disappeared outside. Then a tank appeared. I quickly put the mask on and greedily gulped in the oxygen.

CHAPTER 47

"GOBBLE, GOBBLE, gobble, gobble." Chad could imitate a turkey about as well as Sierra could do bird calls.

"Would you stop saying that?" Sierra paused from peeling potatoes for long enough to shoot eye daggers at Chad. "That bird used to be alive. It deserves more respect than your leering eyes are giving it."

Sierra looked with compassion at the turkey I basted in my apartment kitchen. For a moment, guilt pounded at my temples. Then I remembered how yummy sliced turkey smothered with gravy tasted, and my guilt disappeared.

For our Thanksgiving feast, Sierra had brought her own turkey tofu. Enough to feed a houseful, which was too bad since she'd be the only one eating it.

I angled my body to block both Sierra and Chad from seeing the bird, and I basted it again. Only one more hour in the oven, and it would be ready to eat.

"Are you finished peeling the potatoes?" I asked both of them.

"Peeling away, my dear." Chad grinned and held up a particularly long potato skin ribbon. He'd been trying all day to get one long enough to use as a turkey belt. And yes, a turkey belt is just what it sounds like: an accessory to go around Dinner, my affectionate name for the turkey we would later devour.

I didn't mention that detail to Sierra.

I saw my best friend eye the turkey again and knew I had to move to Plan B: get Sierra out of the kitchen before she called her coworkers over for a protest. A rap sounded at the door.

Perfect! "Sierra, can you answer that?"

She scowled at Chad. "Just don't let him gobble anymore while I'm gone."

"Chad, stop gobbling."

He made a turkey wattle with his hands and gobbled silently behind my friend's back.

I elbowed him as I heard Sierra welcome Parker and Charlie. I got Chad to put the turkey back in the oven for me—my injured shoulder was still in a sling from my run-in with a bullet a week and a half ago. Parker entered the kitchen and kissed my cheek. The greeting seemed like something sophisticated people did. Nothing about me remotely resembled Park Avenue. Why had I ever thought Parker and I went together as a couple?

"Hey, Parker." I soaked in the bandage still around his shoulder. "How are you feeling?"

"Getting back up to speed."

"Good to hear." I smiled behind him at the other redhead. "Hi, Charlie."

"I brought my specialty." She pushed a glass bowl into my hands.

"A tossed salad?"

"What can I say? I'm not much of a cook."

We laughed.

Riley arrived next with Amy. I wondered about their relationship. Amy wasn't the type I saw Riley with. I mean, sure, she was pretty and nice. But she wasn't supermodel pretty. Nor was she rich or particularly cultured. Just down-home kind of welcoming. Maybe I'd been too quick to judge Riley.

I glanced at the two talking. Maybe I just didn't want to see anything developing between them. Even if I'd sworn off dating, that didn't mean my feelings were nonexistent.

I'd gotten to know Amy a little better this past Sunday at church. Yes, I'd finally gone. And you know what? The service hadn't been that bad. In fact, I told Riley I'd go back this Sunday.

"You can place your 'Turkey Day Item Display' on the table." I pointed to the living room, where I'd cleared out most of the furniture and pushed the couch against the wall. Then I'd connected my dinette to a card table and another folding table and placed a white sheet over all of them. That was our dinner table.

The centerpiece? Everyone's "Turkey Day Item Display." Yes, I thought of that term all by myself. The display was an item that represented what you were grateful for.

Mine? A college textbook.

I made sure the page it opened to didn't contain any crime-scene photos, though. In two weeks, I'd be taking my final exams. If things worked out the way I wanted, next year at this time, I'd get getting ready to graduate.

I couldn't wait to see what my friends had brought.

"Uh, Gabby. You might want to come in here." Chad's voice seemed abnormally loud coming from the kitchen.

"Coming." I placed the salad on the table and followed the smell of . . . smoke . . . into the kitchen.

"I think your turkey is on fire."

"On fire?" I glanced at the oven and saw orange flames dancing inside. "How could Dinner catch on fire? We just put him back in there!"

I opened the door, and flames shot out. Riley appeared with a fire extinguisher. Suddenly, my bird really was dead. And covered with white foam, which made Dinner look more like Dessert.

I took my "Kiss the Cook" apron off and threw my uninjured hand in the air. "I was doing so well. I don't understand."

Riley touched the bird with an oven mitt. "It looks like something was stuck to the bottom of the pan."

I straightened. "What?"

"Some type of list."

My list of reasons not to date that I'd written last night! I kept my mouth shut. "Really?"

Riley pointed to a puddle on the counter. "It looks like the pan was set on some grease. So when you put it into the hot oven . . ."

"It caught fire."

Sierra held up her molded tofu turkey. "Never fear."

I groaned. "Oh, but I do."

Chad picked up the phone. "I know just what to do, Gabby."

I paused, waiting to hear his brilliant plan.

"Chang? I'd like to order some takeout. Let's start with chicken chow mein..."

＊ ＊

Finally, all the guests arrived and food decorated the uneven table. One thing was for sure: no one would ever forget this menu. Tofu turkey, chicken chow mien, mashed potatoes, a tossed salad, leftover green bean casserole from Bill McCormick, and an ice-cream cake that read "Happy Birthday!" from Amy. She'd found it on sale at the grocery store.

So what if this wasn't the picture-perfect Thanksgiving I'd imagined? Today would be a success whether or not things worked in my favor. After all, I was alive, and Bob Bowling was in jail, awaiting trial for murder, attempted murder, theft, attempted arson . . . the list was long.

Thank goodness all of that was behind me.

As we all dug into the food, I stared at the memorabilia on the table, anxious to see what my friends had brought.

I rose. "If I can have your attention." I tried banging on my plastic cup with a fork, but it just didn't have the right effect.

Chad snickered. "Good one, Gabby."

I ignored him and continued with the eloquent speech I'd planned. "I just want to say thank you for coming over today. Each of you is very special to me, and without you, my world would be lonely and boring."

"Uh . . . I hate to say it Gabby, but without us, your world would be nonexistent," Parker said. He looked around the table. "Who here has saved Gabby's life at one time or another?"

Riley, Parker, Sierra, Chad, and Mrs. Mystery all raised their hands.

I cleared my throat, undeterred. "I just wanted to thank you all for being my friends, in the good times and bad. You all mean the world to me. It's much easier going through life knowing I have people like you to fall back on."

My cheeks flushed at the admission. "So, with all of that sappiness out of the way and without further ado, would everyone share what you brought over on this lovely Thanksgiving afternoon? And I'm warning you: if no one wants to talk, I'm going to have to begin a rousing rendition of 'Turkey in the Straw.' I'm sure no one really wants to hear that."

"Poor turkey," Sierra muttered.

I ignored her and started with my textbook.

Sierra went next. She brought a newspaper article detailing her account of crab liberation. She grinned with pride when telling the story, while Parker and Charlie scowled. Her court date was in two weeks. We'd all see if she was still grinning then.

Parker said he brought Charlie. Charlie blushed, and I felt like puking over how happy they were. But it was a good kind of puking. Like a they're-so-happy-they-make-me-sick kind of puke.

Charlie brought a piece of mail with her new address. "This move here was probably the best thing I've ever done." Another smile exchanged between her and Parker.

The phone rang as we were going through the items. I snatched up the receiver, hoping someone wasn't calling about a crime scene. Not today. Today I wanted to honor my friends, the people who made my life a little less lonely and a whole lot more fun.

"Is this Gabby St. Claire?"

"Speaking." I held my breath, waiting to hear tears or mourning. Waiting to get the job request.

"This is Richard Spruce's son."

I sucked in a quick breath. "Hi."

"Thanks for the packet you sent me. I almost didn't go through it, but my wife wanted me to. I found the letters that I never opened."

I leaned on the kitchen counter, immediately setting my hand into the pool of grease left there by who knows what. "So you realize that your father actually did care about you." I grabbed a dish towel and rubbed my fingers in it.

"Thanks to you, yes."

I smiled. "You're welcome."

"I'm sorry I didn't make it to his wake."

"I'm just glad you called today."

I hung up, beaming.

Bill McCormick brought an award he'd received for his talk show.

Mrs. Mystery brought a copy of her latest book. What do you know? I did recognize her pen name.

Amy held up a dog bone. I guess she was really thankful for her new Lhasa apso.

Chad brought a Trauma Care business card that listed both of our names. I glanced at him and blushed when he smiled at me.

Riley brought a picture of the two of us together. I looked at him and blushed again.

Yes indeed, I did have a lot to be thankful for.

About the Author

CHRISTY BARRITT is an author, freelance writer, and speaker who lives in Virginia. She's married to her Prince Charming, a man who thinks she's hilarious—but only when she's not trying to be. Christy's a self-proclaimed klutz, an avid music lover who's known for spontaneously bursting into song, and a road-trip aficionado. She's won only one contest in her life— and her prize was kissing a pig. Needless to say, she doesn't enter contests anymore. Her current claim to fame is showing off her mother, who looks just like Barbara Bush.

When she's not working or spending time with her family, she enjoys singing, playing the guitar, and exploring small, unsuspecting towns where people have no idea how accident prone she is.

E-mail Christy at: cebarritt@kregel.com.

Don't Miss Gabby St. Claire's First Mystery

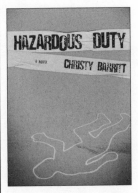

Buying a gun to kill your wife: $3,000

Hiring Trauma Care to clean afterward: $1,500

Having that same cleaner uncover evidence that frames you: priceless

Hazardous Duty introduces Gabby St. Claire, Christy Barritt's feisty crime-scene cleaner. When Gabby finds a piece of evidence overlooked by the police on a seemingly routine cleaning job, she realizes that the wrong man is in jail. Unfortunately for Gabby, her evidence—the murder weapon itself—belongs to senatorial candidate Michael Cunningham, a man with a reputation at stake and the connections to protect it. With the help of her neighbor, the intriguing and attractively single Riley Thomas, Gabby decides to play detective to set an innocent man free.

"*Hazardous Duty* is a delightful read from beginning to end. The story's fresh, engaging heroine with an unusual occupation hooked me, and I couldn't put it down. I highly recommend *Hazardous Duty*."

—Colleen Coble
Author of *Fire Dancer*